Totally Bound Publishing books by Claudia Ambrose

Falling Leaves
Build You Up

I0673780

Falling Leaves

BUILD YOU UP

CLAUDIA AMBROSE

Build You Up
ISBN # 978-1-80250-748-5
©Copyright Claudia Ambrose 2024
Cover Art by Kelly Martin ©Copyright September 2024
Interior text design by Claire Siemaszkiewicz
Totally Bound Publishing

BUILD YOU UP

Dedication

To Jeremy, for believing even when I didn't.

Acknowledgements

I started this book in 2020. Words were hard to come by, back then. Listening to Taylor Swift's song *Betty*, an idea came to me of high school sweethearts getting a second shot at love. The story came together quickly. Now, I'd love to say the rest came easily. After spending years on submission with this and another project, I'd pretty much given up hope again when I received the offer to publish *Build You Up*. This little book is special to me, as well as the people who've supported me during this (very long) journey.

Firstly: to my family: my husband Jeremy, for his love and support as I chased after this dream. It took a lot longer than planned, but I wouldn't be here without your support. My parents, for encouraging a life-long love of reading, which turned into a desire to write my own stories. My in-laws for being wonderfully supportive. To my nephew Cooper: you're my favorite little bookworm.

This book would've stayed a draft on my computer if not for my agent, Jana. Thank you for finding the perfect home for Falling Leaves. To Anna Olson, for seeing something special in the world I created, and Rebecca Scott for her editorial expertise.

Barb Curtis is the oldest writing friend I have. Thanks for always being there and for writing the perfect blurbs for this book. Cass Scotka for listening to my whining and for your insight into the publishing process. A huge thank you to the Romance Friends for their support over the years: Nikki Hodum, Julie Cassidy, Dallas Rose, Mallory Marlowe, Maria Millage, Jamie, Amber Roberts & Dani Frank.

Lastly, to the reader holding this book in their hands: thank you for taking a chance on my work. I hope you love Falling Leaves as much as I do.

Chapter One

Her dad was a dead man.

"You tricked me. You said the job was out of town." Sabrina glanced first at him then at the midnight black Victorian manor home in front of her.

He pulled his coffee from the truck's center console. "Pardon me for not wanting to lose out on a six-figure job just because you hold some stupid grudge against the Blake boy."

It was more than a grudge, and he knew it.

"He's not really a boy anymore, is he?" Knowledge she was far too familiar with. Which was why whenever Brandon crossed her path, she ran away like her ass was on fire.

He slurped his coffee. "Nope, but your beef is as big as ever."

Some rivalries were eternal. The Bears and the Packers. Hatfields and the McCoys. Sabrina Ellis and Brandon Blake. Starting off as rivals in the classroom, after years of teasing, the rivalry had turned romantic for the last year of high school.

Before it had all gone wrong.

The wipers swished across the windshield, obscuring the view of The Peculiar Pumpkin, the B&B the Blake family had owned for decades.

Emphasis on the past tense. Brandon wanted to hire Ellis & Daughter to renovate the Pumpkin before he sold it. Then he'd hightail it out of town again. This time, there would be nothing to bring him back.

Which was a good thing, obviously. Even though it meant his mom was gone. A founding member of the Coffee and Knitting Society — A.K.A. the biddies — Maggie Blake had been a well-loved fixture in town for decades, until her long battle with cancer had ended a week and a half ago.

"It's not a blood feud or anything. I just think he's a know-it-all." *A handsome one. Why couldn't he have gotten ugly since he left town?* The opposite was true, somehow.

Her father cut the engine. "Probably because you also tend to think you know it all, darlin'."

"I'm going to pretend I didn't hear that."

Sabrina grabbed her coffee cup and laptop bag. Hood pulled up against the rain, she pushed the truck door open.

She gazed up at the dark old Victorian before making a run for the porch. She counted no less than four loose boards. Black paint peeled up here and there, revealing rotten wood underneath.

Pumpkins of various shapes took up residence below the railing. Fake plastic flowers in shades of orange, yellow and brown were woven into a garland around the front porch. It gave a little bit of hominess. But this inn would need more than a few decorations to return it to its former glory.

Sabrina tried the front door while her father lingered nearby, his eyes on a gutter hanging off the roof. "Come on, Dad. I don't want to be late."

Because Brandon Blake was the type to count every second.

Her father rubbed at his knee as he alighted the last step. Arthritis. Of course, the rain made his aches and pains worse.

Sabrina hadn't been to the Pumpkin since Brandon returned. The place gave her the creeps, with its year-round spooky aesthetic. Dark wallpaper with glossy skulls hidden amongst the flowers, but paired with grinning pumpkins to let you know that nothing here was *too* threatening.

"Pick a theme already," she muttered under her breath.

Someone cleared their throat from behind her. Sabrina knew without turning that it was Brandon. That man should really wear a bell. She'd seen glances of him since he'd returned to town. But this was their first time face to face in three years and seven days. Give or take. It'd been far longer since they'd exchanged more than three syllables.

She whirled around so fast that he took a step back to avoid getting smacked with her ponytail.

"Brandon." She allowed herself to take a brief look at him. Still handsomely bookish after all these years. Although now, everything about him was expensive. The tortoiseshell glasses, well-fitted dark pin-striped suit, and silver cufflinks. A shadow of a beard had grown in, although with his ruddy blonde hair, it was hard to make out in the dim entryway light. He smelled fantastic — like the lobby of a high-end hotel. Fitting, given his profession.

As much as she hated to admit it, she felt something other than hatred when she looked at him.

"Sabrina. Funny running into you for the first time since I've been back. It's only been, what, five months now?"

She chose to ignore the fact that he'd caught onto how she'd been avoiding him. "I'm just here to help my dad go over the presentation. He's not so great with technology." She hefted the laptop bag over her shoulder. She would *not* admit that her dad had had to trick her into stepping foot inside the Pumpkin.

"I have everything set up in the conference room, if you'd like to follow me." He nudged his glasses up his nose. He still seemed to stare down at her from atop them.

Smug bastard. He didn't bother to wait before he started down the hall. When his back was turned, Sabrina rolled her eyes at her father. He shook his head.

The warning was clear enough. Although there weren't any competitors of their quality for nearly sixty miles any direction, Brandon was the type of petty to hire another company for the hell of it.

The slow time of year was right around the corner. This job could keep them busy for part of it. It'd been a rocky year for Ellis & Daughter. They needed this job. Especially as her dad had been more vocal lately with his worries about the business, combined with worries about his health. He wouldn't have lied to her to get her in the door, otherwise.

Brandon pushed open the conference room door. It appeared as if 1992 had been laid to rest. The table and chairs had seen better days, along with curtains in a color scheme reminiscent of Taco Bell's golden age.

"You can set up your computer there." He gestured to the end of the table. "I have to check on the guests for breakfast. I'll be back in a few minutes."

He closed the door behind him. Sabrina exhaled before jerking open her laptop.

"Well, since you gave me fake information for this report, I'm glad Brandon gave us a few minutes to change things up."

Thank God.

"All the specs I gave you were right. All you have to do is a find and replace for the name."

She jabbed a key to wake it from sleep. "What do you know about find and replace?"

He grunted as he eased himself into a chair. "I know more than you think I do, darlin'."

Sabrina brought up the report and did as her father instructed.

"I don't know if he's going to want to pay what it costs to get this place ready for the highest bidder. He might be better off to just sell the business as is." Sabrina scanned the report to make sure everything looked right.

"He'll pay. He wants to be sure this place shines before he puts it on the market. Wants to get the most for his money, after all. Maggie wasn't so keen to change anything, you know."

The door opened and Brandon stepped inside.

"We're about ready."

He held the door open, and a member of staff followed him in. They placed a tray of the inn's famous pumpkin rolls in the center of the table.

Sabrina's gaze shifted. The pumpkin rolls were a thing of legend. Not that she'd admit to having one since Brandon returned to town. Rather than risk a run-in with him, Sabrina would send her roommate and best friend Eleanor on a covert mission.

As if the plate wasn't bad enough, his smirk was devilish — showing off the dimple in his right cheek.

"Your favorite, Sabby dear." He gestured toward the rolls.

The door closed, leaving them in privacy.

Oh, hell to the no. "Call me that again and you'll see what I prefer to pumpkin rolls." Her childhood nickname had almost gone the way of the dodo until Brandon had formed a summoning circle for it to return. Suddenly, she was Sabby to half the town again.

"Now, come on. We're here for professional reasons. If you can't get past your childhood squabbles, perhaps Brandon should go with another contractor." Her father leaned forward, wearing a stern expression. "I may be able to pull some favors, if push comes to shove."

Sabrina grabbed a pumpkin roll with one hand and a napkin with the other. "The job will take twice as long, and the quality of work will be poorer for it. But it's your choice."

She hoped her false bravado did a good enough job convincing Brandon that he needed them more than Ellis & Daughter needed him. Because the opposite was very much true.

Brandon held up his hands. "I meant no harm. Let's get started, shall we?"

It'd probably been wrong of him to goad her. After all, she seemed to hate him far more than he hated her.

Which was to say not at all. Sure, they'd squabbled when they were kids. Each of them scrabbling over the same academic prizes. The smartest two kids in Falling Leaves, Virginia, had always butted heads. He'd admit that he'd been a smug little shit, thinking Falling Leaves was beneath him, after he'd moved to the town in the second grade when his parents had come to take over the Pumpkin from his grandparents. That opinion hadn't changed much.

Sure, he was a little offended that she treated him no better than a plague rat. He'd hoped they could move on. Reality was a shade more complicated than that. Some things time didn't wash away.

He stole glances at her while she went through the presentation.

Somehow, she'd become more beautiful. Her blonde hair was tugged into a high ponytail. She wore minimal makeup. He could tell, because she still had the scar she'd gotten jumping off the monkey bars in fifth grade.

Normally, she spooked when she saw him. Like he was the ghost of Old Levi, famous for haunting downtown.

If he planned on staying in town, maybe he'd have talked things out with her. But he wasn't, so there was little point. Besides, teasing her was far too fun. Seeing the fire rise in her eyes and spread across her cheeks gave a man ideas. The kind best not considered during work hours.

While she rattled off figures for the project, his gaze never left her. She stayed focused on the presentation. She pushed her long ponytail over one shoulder, revealing the Ellis & Daughter logo on her fitted button-up denim shirt.

A female contractor was just as qualified as a man. Sabrina had built her first treehouse at twelve years old. Besides, the Ellises had been good friends of his parents, despite his history with Sabrina. The work would be done on time, at a good price. Period.

He would've left town right after the funeral if it hadn't been for this last promise to his mother. So, he'd do right by her — sell the inn to the best buyer and move on, for good. She'd known as well as him that most buyers wouldn't want the hassle of running the inn. They'd gut it and make it a home, destroying decades of Blake family history. Running the Pumpkin had never been his dream — he had bigger ideas in that regard — but he had to do right by his family legacy.

And that meant shining the old girl up and hoping for the best.

Brandon peered at the timeline Sabrina had come up with. It was workable, and with the main goals he'd laid out to Glen addressed. Brandon had assumed he'd be the point of contact — not his infuriating only daughter.

Sabrina came to the end of the presentation and closed her laptop.

"Did you have any questions?"

Brandon thumbed through the paperwork. "Not that I can tell, as of right now. You've both done an excellent job of outlining the project and costs."

Sabrina's only response was to take a hearty bite of pumpkin roll.

Glen coughed into his elbow. "Well, there is one thing I'd like to discuss, if it's all right."

Brandon pushed the papers away. "Of course."

"I know when we originally spoke, I said I'd be managing this project. Well, something's come up and I'm not sure that will be possible."

Sabrina swiped at her mouth with a napkin. "What do you mean?"

Whatever it was, it must be a doozy if Glen was springing it on both of them with no notice.

Glen heaved a sigh. "I need to get surgery. The doc says my knees are hanging on by a thread. I'll be going under the knife next week."

Sabrina's face broke into surprise. She'd looked at him like that once. Although then, she'd been more heartbroken than surprised. He pushed the memory away.

"Why are you telling me this now?" Sabrina asked.

Glen shrugged. "I knew if I told you, you'd say no to this job because of, well, you know." He gestured vaguely in Brandon's direction.

Ah, so she really did loathe him still. Which meant that this could be fun, working together. A second chance, if not at romance, to make amends.

Sabrina's head pivoted toward Brandon as though a puppeteer was pulling her strings. He'd hoped reaching out to Glen would be an olive branch. Now he wasn't so sure. They'd have to muddle through the past — dredging up all kinds of negative memories — if they wanted to move on.

The room was quiet, save subtle creaking of the pipes as a toilet flushed somewhere upstairs. Sabrina reached for another pumpkin roll.

"I'll be off my feet for a few weeks, but I'll be able to look things over after that. But I trust Sabrina. She's managed many a job."

"None this big," Sabrina said between bites. "When's the surgery, anyway?"

"Day after tomorrow."

Sabrina dropped the remaining pumpkin roll on the plate and wiped her mouth.

Brandon grinned. This development was the first good news he'd gotten in months. Having Sabrina around would be fun. If for no other reason than turning getting on her nerves into a high art.

"I believe that Sabrina and I can put our differences aside and work together."

"It won't be for the whole job, just while I'm recovering. Sabrina will oversee the first part of the interior work. Then after that, I should be able to get around okay enough to help her oversee things." He paused. "From my wheelchair or walker, if I have to."

Sabrina flashed a worried glance at her father.

None of this was a problem for Brandon. But admitting that would be akin to confessing his feelings for Sabrina. He wasn't ready to do that.

"We can make it work, right, Sabby?" He grinned as wide as he could manage.

She regarded him with all the warmth of an iceberg. "Sure, *Brando*."

Glen chuckled to himself. "Excellent. So, work will begin on Friday? How about we start with signing contacts, then?"

Before Brandon could respond, Glen's phone trilled out a guitar rhythm. He excused himself and stepped out into the hall.

"You seem a little too chipper about this," Sabrina said.

"What's not to be chipper about? I'm making my mother's dying wish a reality."

"Before you sell for big bucks and get out of town," Sabrina fired back. "Back to DC, right?"

He wasn't sold on returning to his old life. What was the point of it all, just to slide back into what was comfortable?

Brandon ignored the dig and began to gather the papers. "I've never been a fan of the small-town life."

That earned a scoff from Sabrina. "I've only heard you say that, what, a million times by now?"

Brandon closed the folder. "Look, it's obvious we're never going to be friends, but can we put the pettiness aside for the sake of the project? I know you loved my mom too. You should understand why I'm doing this. If the Pumpkin isn't going to stay in the family, she wants it to go to buyers who will carry on the legacy. Or at the very least, keep the house up."

When she only glared at him, he continued, "The B&B industry isn't exactly full of buyers."

He'd been putting feelers out for nearly a year now. There'd only been two nibbles worth anything.

He hoped to make enough to pay off the mortgage, any remaining business debts and have a sliver left over. The cost of renovations should increase his profit. At worst, he'd simply make his money back. But his conscience would be clear. And maybe make his long-wanted dream of running a mountain lodge a reality. Not that he'd tell Sabrina anything about that. It didn't fit in with the idea she had of him—a big city hotelier.

She held his gaze for a heart-wrenching moment before she spoke.

"I can if you can." She paused. "As long as I get one pumpkin roll per day."

He hid a grin at her request. It was so like her to tack on an addendum to an agreement. He leaned across the table and dropped his elbow down halfway between them. "Deal."

He extended his pinky—like they were kids again, making deals for pudding cups at recess.

She hesitated before looping her pinky around his. A jolt went through his body at the brief press of her skin against his. As soon as it came, it vanished.

Sabrina pulled her hand away and stood. "I'm going to get the rest of the paperwork from the car. I think Dad left it there."

She left, reappearing in front of the window as she darted out in the rain to the truck. Brandon smiled and sipped his coffee.

Perhaps this renovation wouldn't be all misery and sawdust, after all.

Chapter Two

"You have to speak at some point, Sabrina." The Ellis & Daughter pick-up truck rolled to a stop-sign outside of downtown.

"I don't know, you can get a lot across with hand gestures." She cursed under her breath. She hadn't meant to say that out loud.

"I think that's the shortest amount of time you've stayed quiet since you learned to talk."

"Ha, ha."

Dad turned the truck onto Silver Spring Street. The three-stoplight main drag went through the whole of downtown. The far reaches of town were still a little rough around the edges. Luckily, that paired well with the designation of Falling Leaves being the most haunted town in the Commonwealth.

Or so the town's tourist literature claimed, at least.

The heart of downtown was as charming as any picture book. Garlands of orange, black and white looped around every light post. All the shop windows they passed were decorated for Halloween. Given the town's name, autumn had become the biggest tourism season. Because of the rain, the Blue Ridge mountains were like a half-obscured watercolor painting backdrop.

Her father's voice cut into her reverie. "Like I said, you wouldn't have agreed otherwise. Besides, you two are nearly thirty. It's time to let it go. Especially as it's what his mama would've wanted."

Some part of her had ached to comfort Brandon when she'd seen him at his mother's funeral. Even though that was the last thing either of them wanted.

Still, seeing him had dredged up all kinds of memories that she'd buried at the bottom of her mind.

"Easier said than done." When he grumbled, she added, "I'll be professional, I can promise you that. Besides, we declared a truce once you left the room." She reached for her coffee cup and pulled a long sip.

"But you can't make me like Brandon Blake. Once an ex, always an ex."

"As long as you agreed to be professional, that's all that matters."

"I'll treat him like any other client. I promise. Especially since you won't be there as a buffer."

Her mind was as mixed up as a bowl of alphabet soup. How awful was it that Brandon Blake had made her forget the reason her father wouldn't be on the job in the first place?

Her father was having major surgery, for Pete's sake.

He pulled the truck in front of Missing Screw Hardware. Run by Dad's twin brother Gordon, Ellis & Daughter kept a small office upstairs. It was either that or be at home, where Mom would be in their hair twenty-four-seven.

"I'm going to get sample books for the design meeting with Brandon tomorrow. Then I'll start contracting our usual subcontractors."

He grunted. "Good. I trust you, Sabrina."

Dad was the type to speak plainly.

"Thanks." She paused. "I wish you would've told me about the surgery. But I'll help however I can. After all, we need to keep the business running, right?" She tried to keep the worry out of her voice. They needed this job—now more than ever, since her father would be out of commission for weeks, if not months.

His smile was subtle. "I'm more concerned with you keeping the Pumpkin project moving. Your mother will help with the rest."

Sabrina ran from the rain to the refuge of the red-and-white striped awning that spanned across the front of the hardware store. She waited for her father to ease his way across the parking lot. It probably was a good thing he was finally getting surgery.

They shook off like dogs before opening the front door.

The tinkling of the bells above the door alerted Gordon to their arrival.

"How did it go?"

She set her bag down onto the battered hardwood floors and unzipped her coat. "Did you know about this little bit of espionage?"

Uncle Gordon went full Santa with his laugh. Though her father and Gordon were identical, he was the scruffy twin, with shaggy hair and a long beard when her father kept his hair crew-cut short and his face clean shaven.

"He only told me and your mother."

"Well, I know now." She grabbed her bag. "I'll be upstairs. Don't disturb me unless the building is on fire."

She alighted the rickety metal stairs to the second floor.

"Remind me how you're single with that winning personality of yours, Sabrina?" Dennis called from the back of the store. She saw only the top of his ginger head as he stacked paint cans.

"Hmm, and you're on, what, baby momma number two now, Denny?"

A freckled middle finger found its way above the shelves. "I should've known better. You don't just dish it out, you fling it."

At only six months apart, Denny was more like Sabrina's younger brother than a cousin. They'd been jabbing at each other since the sandbox.

She took the rest of the stairs two by two and pushed open the door to the office. It was a tight, unorganized space. Boxes keeled over onto themselves, obscuring the lone window at the back of the office. It was dark and depressing. Hardly the type of place they'd bring clients.

Her father's desk was a pit. Hers was neat as a pin. She fumbled for the chain on the desk lamp and set down her bag. With it bucketing it down outside, it was a perfect day to work in the office. Despite her mixed feelings for Brandon, it was exciting to manage this project on her own.

Maybe this would be the project to get them featured on a blog, or local magazine. It would help expand their business beyond Falling Leaves and the surrounding area. It got old redoing kitchens from the nineties to the same bland aesthetic.

No matter how snarky Brandon may be, she needed to plaster on a smile and get the job done.

She powered on her laptop as a phone call came through on the land line. She cleared her throat before picking up the handset.

"Ellis & Daughter, this is Sabrina, how can—"

"Cut the shit, it's me," Eleanor said. Her best friend, roommate and Falling Leaves' police chief wasn't known for beating around the bush. "How did the meeting go with Falling Leaves' resident super villain?"

Sabrina's mouth dropped open. "How the hell do you know about that already? I didn't know who the client was until we pulled up to the Pumpkin."

"You know how the biddies are. Gossip spreads like wildfire throughout town. So, out with it."

Sabrina could only sigh. "Short version or long?"

Eleanor chuckled. "Long, duh."

Sabrina cradled the phone between her cheek and shoulder while she filled Eleanor in on the meeting. Her calling Brandon a super villain was tongue-in-cheek. She hadn't lived here during the worst of Sabrina's rivalry and relationship with Brandon, so she'd never really understood it. The traitor was known to say she liked Brandon "well enough," and that he wasn't bad looking if you overlooked the glasses.

Which would lead to Sabrina somehow defending Brandon by telling Eleanor that men with glasses could be sexy. Which would lead to Eleanor asking if Sabrina had the hots for Brandon, after all. Which would usually lead to Sabrina storming out of the room.

She didn't have time to give Eleanor every detail, but she knew the rest would come out over dinner.

"So, it's just gonna be you and Brandon, huh? That sounds mighty interesting."

"If by interesting, you mean infuriating, sure. He's the client. And you know how badly we need this job."

Eleanor chuckled. "Oh, don't act like it'll be some great agony. He's a good-looking fella. One you have a mysterious history with, to boot."

It wasn't that mysterious. Their rivalry had remained until they'd hit high school. Then it had turned into a relationship that had ended badly. They'd had countless good times, too. Although with how he'd left town after his dad died, those were easy enough to forget.

"I just want to get through this job. Hopefully, it'll mean bigger things for Ellis & Daughter. The sooner Brandon leaves town for good, the better."

A drawn-out sigh crackled across the line. "If you say so. I'm making pot roast for dinner. See you later." Eleanor ended the call.

She slammed the receiver down and began scanning in signed copies of the contracts to the database.

This could end up working out. By the end of it, a jewel of Falling Leaves would be restored. Sabrina was bursting with design ideas.

That Brandon would probably nix. She exhaled and swapped out a page on the scanner for another.

"So, be open to interpretation."

Because after all, a truce had been declared. Only time would tell how long it would last.

* * * *

"You're going through with it after all, huh?"

Babs appeared in Brandon's doorway. With her cat-eyed glasses and constant wardrobe of black on black, she resembled the witch role she played so well every Halloween.

She'd been his mother's best friend and manager at the Pumpkin for nearly twenty years, which meant that she felt more than entitled to break off a large chunk of her mind and give it to Brandon. Whether he wanted it or not.

"It's what Mom wanted. You know this as well as I do."

She pulled a pencil out of her wiry silver bun and scratched at her temple with it. "Interesting choice, hiring Ellis & Daughter."

Brandon tapped on his computer keyboard to wake it from sleep. "Don't make this something it's not."

When Babs continued to peer at him from over the top of her glasses, he added, "Mom wanted me to contact them first. She stayed friends with the Ellises, even if I didn't."

"Hmm, true. Maggie always adored Sabrina. There are other firms nearby, though."

He pulled up the hotel reservation program on his computer.

"I'd prefer you stop beating around the bush and hack at it directly, with a butcher knife, preferably."

That got her to smile. "My point is that you and Sabrina Ellis are oil and water. I don't want to have to be putting out fires while I'm also looking for a new place to work."

Brandon kept his eyes on the screen as he scanned the weekend's bookings. Down fifteen percent from this time last year. Only part of that downturn could be attributed to his mother's illness. Recent reviews of the Pumpkin talked about how the inn's rough around the edges feel went further than just the décor.

"I've told you a million times that odds are any new owner will keep on the staff. It's just easier for them to transition that way. But if they didn't, you could move to Florida and live with Jenny and your grandkids. Or where is Elliott living these days?"

"Pfft, too much sun and fun down there for me. I prefer things gloomy. And we both know Elliott doesn't want his mother barging into his bachelor lifestyle."

"Falling Leaves wouldn't be the same without you, anyway." Not that the town was particularly gloomy. Although, the further you strayed from the town's main drag the rougher things looked. Some of the storefronts were empty. The town's resident metaphysical shop, The Weird Sisters, was the only thriving business in that part of town.

But you weren't likely to run into any poltergeist here. There was Old Levi, but no one Brandon would trust of having sound mind had ever had an encounter with the so-called specter.

She harrumphed again. "Flattery will get you everywhere, young man. When you have a second, come down to the café. Adalyn's trying out a new recipe and she wants your opinion." She started to leave, then ducked her head in. "While you're still here, anyway."

Brandon rolled his eyes. Babs should know he was immune to her barbs by now. Besides, construction would likely take the rest of the year. He'd be staying put for at least that long. He owed it to his mother to make sure the inn sold to the right people.

He hadn't worked out exactly what he'd do after it sold. He'd taken a leave of absence from his job back in DC. Assistant General Manager at Hotel Blaque was a cushy, comfortable job. He could perform the daily functions in his sleep.

That said, he'd always had a dream of running his own lodge, high in the mountains. That seemed like a dream that would always be out of reach. It was safer when someone else was signing your paychecks. Besides, a mountain lodge was totally out of his comfort zone. He was an Ivy League-educated hospitality graduate. He was used to working in the finest hotels, not cozy mountain retreats.

Perhaps that's why the dream called to him the way it did. It was the opposite of his life up until recently.

He closed out of the reservation system and left his office. He was hungry anyway, and Adalyn was the best baker in southwest Virginia.

He paused in the lobby to adjust an errant pumpkin on the front desk. It'd been hand lettered by a local artist with a cheery *Welcome!*

He'd tried to add these little touches around the inn to take away from the curling wallpaper, threadbare carpet and other less-than-charming details.

He caught up to Babs in the lobby, chatting with a couple from Memphis.

"You must go on the ghost tour. Now that it's October, we have them every Friday and Saturday night. The first one happens to be tonight!"

The guests let out an appreciative *ahh.*

Babs grinned. "Brandon here leads the ones on Friday. I can get you booked in for tonight, if you'd like."

He might not believe in ghosts but having a B&B in the most haunted town in Virginia meant pretending.

"We leave shortly after sundown," Brandon said. "Be sure not to miss it!"

The young couple laughed. Brandon kept a smile plastered on his face until he rounded the corner. He opened the door leading to the narrow corridor that connected the inn to the café.

"There you are!" Adalyn waved to him from the doorway of The Frosted Squash, the upscale café arm of the B&B. This was the prettiest spot on the property thanks to his mother, who had overseen the renovation two years ago, before she'd gotten sick.

The old wooden floors had been shined up new. Harlequin wallpaper in shades of purple and green lined the walls. Low hanging Edison bulbs hung over the display case, well stocked with wares, and a small selection of gifts and other trinkets for sale. This addition was the reason they'd taken out a second mortgage on the inn, but it was worth it, as it brought in a lot of income. Especially their Sunday brunches.

"Babs said you had a new recipe for me to try out." He shifted his wrist to catch the time. "Sweet or savory?"

"Both." Adalyn gestured for him to sit at the bar that overlooked the small kitchen space.

A moment later she returned with a bowl of puréed tomato soup, one of her signature corn muffins and a slice of pumpkin pie.

"Not another one." He gestured to the pie.

"What? I've got to get the recipe just right."

His mother had died without giving any of them her signature pumpkin pie recipe. Adalyn was spending her days trying to recreate it before they were deluged with Thanksgiving pie orders.

"I'm going to look through her things again this afternoon to see if I can find it," Brandon said. "You know how she loved a mystery. It's here somewhere."

"Let me know if you do, because I don't feel this is any closer."

Adalyn left him to eat. Momentarily alone with his thoughts, memories of his mother, lying in her bed as life slipped away from her, clouded his mind.

She wouldn't want him to wallow. No matter what his staff or the town may think, fixing up the Pumpkin was his way of honoring his mother.

Even if it forced him to face his past. Like how Sabrina's face had crumbled when he'd sprung on her that he was leaving right after graduation. It had meant skipping out on the magical summer she'd planned for the two of them. He'd taken that from her. But he'd had his reasons for leaving then, just as he did now.

Chapter Three

The weather had cleared by the time Sabrina headed home. A little bit of summer still lingered in the air, although you'd never know it in Falling Leaves.

Pumpkins were stacked up six deep on nearly every porch she passed.

A group of children in costume rushed past her— likely on their way to rehearsal for the Halloween pageant. It was still a way out, but Sabrina knew from experience that the rehearsals went on for weeks before the big day.

She laughed as the little ghosts and ghouls weaved around her before they took off around the corner.

A memory of her and Brandon floated to the forefront of her mind. The two of them in costume— monsters, instead of ghosts—arguing over the proper spelling of onomatopoeia.

She turned from Silver Spring onto Jackson Street. She let her mind drift as she took in houses in desperate need of TLC. There was a reason the houses on this block were referred to as the Tattered Ladies. Some had

Claudia Ambrose

been passed down through the generations. For many, it was a chore to keep up with a house where something was always going wrong. In hundred and fifty-year-old houses, those problems could get expensive, fast.

Sabrina squinted up at the houses lining Jackson Street. The house she shared with Eleanor had once been among them, until her father had bought it for her as a college graduation gift nearly eight years ago.

Now, Emerald House was the prettiest house on the block. The deep green paint glinted in the late afternoon sunlight.

The house had been awfully empty until Eleanor and her son Dutch had moved in the year before, at Sabrina's instance.

Sabrina was grateful for the company, as a nearly four thousand square foot house had been a bit much for her and her two cats.

She paused to check the mail and rifled through it as she stepped onto the porch. Dutch and three of his friends from the high school basketball team sat on the rocking chairs on the front porch.

"Hey, Aunt Sabrina. Heard you're fixing up the Pumpkin," Dutch said.

Sabrina looked up. "How'd you hear that?"

"The Wi-Fi went down at school," Dutch's best friend Jamar said. "Town gossip was all we had to get us through lunch. Well, that and deciding what our group costume is going to be this year."

Sabrina had to laugh, that the teens were bored enough to care about local gossip.

"Hmm, I think the costume took more precedence, huh?"

"Yeah—we're gonna do a collaboration of the best horror movie killers. But anyhow, my mom said you and Brandon have hated each other forever," Dutch said. "No wonder everyone's talking about it."

"Hate's a bit of a strong word," Sabrina demurred.

Eleanor flung open the heavy wooden and leaded glass door as though it were nothing.

"Whoever's eating, get your tails inside now." She pivoted toward Sabrina. "That includes you."

Caught up in the rush of boys through the door, Sabrina was halfway through to the kitchen before she could drop her bag and belongings.

The boys were already lined up at the make-shift buffet on the kitchen island, piling their plates high with pot roast and salad.

"You fed the cats?" Sabrina asked.

"Obviously, or they'd be begging. Get you a plate before the boys eat everything."

With a nearly fifteen-year age gap between them, it was easy for her to consider Sabrina another kid to boss around. Especially as like her son, Eleanor was well over six feet tall. Sabrina was no slouch at five nine, but she tended to feel like a shrimp in a house full of sharks.

After she'd piled her plate, the boys retreated to the screened porch at the rear of the house. Eleanor and Sabrina sat down at the oversized dining table.

Down the center was a smattering of ceramic pumpkins and candles. She'd hardly decorated the house for Halloween—save a few pumpkins on the porch and an old wreath. She didn't exactly have a ton of cash for extra expenses this year.

"Well? Am I going to need to dispatch an officer to look in on you two when construction starts?"

Sabrina pulled apart a hunk of buttery garlic bread. "We've declared a truce."

Her phone chimed with a new text. She craned her neck over to get a look. "That's him now, see?"

Eleanor tapped on the screen before it could go dark.

"'That tile isn't what I had in mind. Here's more of what I'm after.'" Eleanor arched a brow. "There's a link to some hoity-toity website."

Sabrina shoved the garlic bread into her mouth and angrily chomped on it.

He had a right to want things just so, but why did he care, especially if he was just going to up and sell the place? It didn't make sense. Still, they had a long few months ahead of them.

"What the client wants, he'll get," Sabrina managed once she'd finished chewing.

"At six dollars a square foot, he damn well should." Eleanor pushed Sabrina's phone across the table. "FYI, everyone knows you're working together. Be prepared for questions."

"Tell me about it. Dutch and the boys were grilling me before I got inside."

Eleanor blew on her pot roast. "Y'know, maybe there's something stirring under that mutual dislike."

"Something other than two decades worth of spite? We can both cling onto a grudge like it's a lifeline."

"You know, when Eddie and I met, we hated each other on site. He was the typical sexist cop, thinking women had no place in the force."

"You quickly proved him wrong. Then you fell in love and followed him to Falling Leaves for a job. Haven't they made a movie about your love story yet?"

As soon as the words left her mouth, Sabrina regretted them. This was an old joke between them. One she'd made countless times before cancer had taken Eddie.

Sabrina reached over the table to grab her friend's hand. "I'm sorry. Sometimes I forget he's gone. The joke's turned sour."

Eleanor gave Sabrina's hand a half-hearted squeeze. "It's been over a year. I can laugh about it, a little." She cleared her throat. "Anyway, you should think about it. Brandon is a good-looking guy."

She coughed as the image of him took over her mind. He obviously lifted the odd weight in his spare time, because his physique wasn't exactly hard to look at. A far change from the scrawny little boy who'd used to bully her.

She should be thinking about how he was a pain in the ass. Not how his dress slacks framed his actual rear end so nicely.

"With a stick the size of Kentucky wedged up his rear end." Sabrina paused. "No, Kentucky is too small. More like Texas."

Eleanor harumphed. "He seems nice enough to me."

"You haven't known him long enough to see his true colors." Sabrina knew she sounded defensive. Like she was trying to convince herself as much as Eleanor.

Eleanor stabbed a wedge of lettuce. "You're really gonna have to tell me that story if you want me to go all-in on hating him."

It'd been years, but the memory was too tender to linger on for long. She found herself spilling the story to Eleanor.

She'd thought leaving for college would be a stopgap in their relationship. Sure, she was at Virginia Tech, and he'd gone to Cornell. But they could've made it work. Then Brandon's father had died suddenly, three weeks before prom.

Brandon had broken up with her — via text message, no less — and had promptly left town. A devastating loss made all the worse by how she'd been by his side during the sudden loss of his father. They'd grieved together. Then, only weeks later, he'd barely been able to give her the courtesy of a goodbye before he'd fled town.

She exhaled. "I know it sounds stupid to still hold a grudge. But he broke my heart. I know it's not the same, but his dad meant a lot to me too."

In all these years since, no one had come along to mend it. Sure, she'd dated some. But there'd never been fireworks, like there'd been with Brandon. Which made the wound cut all that much deeper.

"Sounds like he hurt you. And you won't give him a chance to do it again."

Sabrina stabbed her fork through a lettuce spear. "That's one way of putting it. Anyway, tell me about work. Any bear sightings today?"

While Eleanor launched into a story about the family of black bears that had been seen on the outskirts of town, Sabrina tried to put Brandon out of her mind.

As if the devil could read her mind, another text chimed on her phone. There would be no escaping him while the work was going on.

But those hurtful memories would have to stay buried for now.

* * * *

"How many have we got?"

Brandon peered into the dining room, where guests were having dinner. As soon as the sun dipped in the sky, the ghost tour would begin.

Babs pulled her readers down from the top of her head to peer at her tablet. "Five guests, and a few locals, eager to get in on the first ghost tour of the year."

Brandon pulled up his phone and ran through the new bits he'd added to the ghost tour. He didn't know why he was nervous, as he must've run these tours countless times before he'd left Falling Leaves.

This was his first time running the tour since he'd returned in late winter. He'd put it off long enough. Guests came from out of town for the Halloween experience.

"I hope the locals aren't just eager to see me fail."

"No, they're probably eager to ask you about Sabrina. Because that news has made the gossip circuit by now." Babs grinned.

Brandon kept his gaze on his phone. Reason number one on a growing list of why he hated this stupid town. Nothing ever happened, so every mole hill was Mount Everest.

"There's nothing to tell. We're working together. That's it."

Babs tucked her glasses back onto her head. "Sure."

Brandon shoved his phone into his jacket pocket. "Don't you start, too. You're supposed to be my ally, especially now that Mom's gone."

If his mother was here, she probably would've agreed with Babs that he needed to lighten up. It was probably low of Brandon to appeal to Babs' sense of grief, but he was desperate to steer the conversation away from Sabrina.

Although dwelling on the recent memory of his mother's death wasn't exactly his happy place, either. Even when death was inevitable, it didn't make the loss of a loved one any easier.

"Oh, fine. I'll run interference and repeat your party line. There, happy?"

Brandon nodded. "Yes. I'm going to grab a quick bite to eat, then I'll meet the guests out on the porch."

He ducked into the kitchen and snatched a sandwich out of the fridge before sneaking out onto the back patio. The air had a chill to it, so he was alone as he scarfed down dinner.

Even though things with Sabrina hadn't gone as smoothly as he'd hoped, he was glad that construction was moving forward. Now he'd have to get serious about passing the torch to the Pumpkin's next owners.

So far, there were only two somewhat serious buyers in the mix. The Westmore Group was owned by a married couple, Gabriel and Merit Westmore, who ran a small group of boutique inns and hotels around the world. They could show the type of care that the Pumpkin needed to really thrive.

The other potential buyer wasn't interested in the business at all. They'd take the house and turn it back into a private residence for their large family. Not ideal, but they loved the house and would do right by it.

Not that he'd heard much from either buyer lately. He needed to drop them both a line and let them know about the renovations.

Brandon sat in quiet reflection at the pond until his phone chimed with an alarm.

It was time for the ghost tour.

Chapter Four

Despite her best intentions, Sabrina couldn't stop thinking about Brandon. She puttered around the house, fixing the odd item on her to-do list until Eleanor emerged from her bedroom, telling her she was going to bed and to quit with the banging.

She attempted to read a book. Normally, it took little effort for her to fall into a novel, especially one in her favorite genre, fantasy. She read the same sentence over four times before she rose to her feet.

The far wall of her bedroom was a wall of built-in bookshelves, painted dark green, inlaid with gold trim. She'd peppered in miniature book nooks and hidden doors into the bookcase. Though she was nearly thirty, she still liked to imagine that there was a little mystery behind them.

She moved aside one of the books and pried open the tiniest door with her thumb and index finger. She hesitated before reaching in.

Inside lay the gold locket Brandon had given Sabrina for her seventeenth birthday. She'd stowed the trinket away years ago. Even looking at it had stirred up all sorts of negative feelings.

Now, she took out the locket and opened the photo compartment. Inside was a photo of Brandon and Sabrina at the fourth-grade spelling bee. Brandon had won, Sabrina had taken second prize. They'd been rivals then, before that arguing had started to have a flirtatious bend to it, right around the time they entered middle school.

She sighed and shoved the locket back into the hidden door then picked up her book.

She'd managed no more than a page when her two cats—Sarah and Jareth—wouldn't stop attacking her hands as she turned the pages.

Unable to stand it any longer, she put on a coat. She might as well get a jump on pulling different samples for the design meeting in the morning. It might take longer since Brandon wasn't exactly a fan of her design style.

Well, they'd just have to meet in the middle. While he didn't exactly have a beer budget, it wasn't the biggest she'd worked with either.

She paused under a streetlight on the corner of Jackson and Silver Spring Street. There was a fair amount of activity. Groups of diners sat on the outside patio at Luci's—the fanciest restaurant in Falling Leaves.

The Peculiar Pumpkin was aglow, shining a light on the shabbiness. Several of the upstairs windows on the side of the house were boarded up—likely to keep the draft out of disused rooms. Brandon's mom had played up the spooky appeal of the place.

Out-of-towners bought it but locals knew the Pumpkin was far from its glory days, although a few strings of pumpkin lights added along the porch was a nice holiday touch.

As she passed by, the front door opened and several people scattered onto the steps. Bringing up the rear was Brandon, dressed in full ghost tour regalia. She exhaled, not quite recovered from finding that old locket and the memories it'd dredged up.

The outfit wasn't unsimilar from when he'd started giving tours as a teenager, but with an updated twist. A tatty top hat and a cape with gold brocade around the edges. And flickering lanterns for everyone to carry. Sabrina had accompanied him many times on the ghost tour, sometimes even popping up to scare the guests.

"Why hello there, Sabrina!" Babs Dodge waved from the front porch.

Sabrina had a soft spot for Babs. Not only because she'd been one of her prime sources of pumpkin rolls since Brandon had returned to town earlier this year.

"Hey, Babs." Sabrina kept it moving as she waved.

"Where are you off to? You should join us on the first ghost tour of the season!"

"That's not necessary. She's heard the ghost tour countless times before." There was a desperate tinge to Brandon's voice.

"It's changed a lot since then! Come on, Sabrina. Tag along. To keep me company, if nothing else. All our guests are taking the tour."

"And a few locals, don't forget about us!" Inez Munoz called.

From beneath the unshapely brim of the top hat, Brandon regarded her with pleading eyes. Her presence was *not* wanted.

She should give him a break. After all, rumors were flying since the news had spread that they were working together.

But his last text about tile *had* been unnecessarily snarky. Just because he was the client, didn't mean he could walk all over her.

"Sure, I'll come. I wasn't doing anything anyway."

She half-expected Brandon to argue, but he never would in front of guests. He'd save his snark for when they were alone.

He'd have plenty of opportunity over the coming months.

He thrust out a lantern to her. "Come on, then."

She grabbed the lantern from him, the artificial light swaying over her feet in the process.

"Give me just a second and we'll get started, everyone," Brandon called.

Sabrina stood over to one side. It took Inez all of thirty seconds to sidle up next to her.

"Attending your boyfriend's inaugural ghost tour, huh? What a good girlfriend you are."

"And what a good *chismosa* you are." Sabrina narrowed her eyes at the older woman.

Inez's mouth opened and closed like an out of water fish. "I hate that you speak Spanish," she murmured in English.

Inez's role in the biddies meant that every rumor in town went through her. She was likely the reason the rumor about Sabrina and Brandon had gotten so blown out of proportion. That said, she was a powerful ally to have. She could turn the tide of gossip away from the rumor, too.

"Stop trying to weave away from the point. You're here to support Brandon. That's nice of you."

Sabrina rolled her eyes. "I'm going to start calling you *Tía Chismosa* from now on."

That earned Sabrina a not-so gentle bump of the hip. "I can't help that news gets passed along in my establishment."

Inez ran The Over Easy Café. Everyone in town was in there at some point or another during the week.

"I'd believe that, but you just referred to Brandon as my boyfriend, when in reality, he's my client. I'm here to support him in that manner, and that manner only." She leaned down to whisper in the older woman's ear. "So, ensure *that's* the rumor spread around with *huevos rancheros* in the morning, please? I know how much you hate when lies and gossip get twisted up."

Inez might have been a gossip, but she prided herself on not spreading malicious rumors.

Inez shook her head. "All right. I'll admit I hadn't heard any of this news about the two of you from the horse's mouth. I'll do my best to correct the course of news in the morning."

Sabrina gave a curt nod. "Good. I'll be by at six a.m. for my eggs."

"All right, everyone, follow me."

The group turned in unison as Brandon hopped down the last two steps from the porch to the sidewalk, cape billowing behind him.

A pair of young female guests whispered to each other. "Is he included with the price of room and board?"

They both giggled and elbowed each other.

Sabrina had to admit, the Victorian garb did suit him. Under the cape he wore tight-fitting trousers, a white button-up shirt and a vest, topped off with a cravat. Riding boots capped off the look. The beard gave him a proper Victorian aura.

"Hmm, you're looking for an awful long time for him to be just a client," Inez mused.

Sabrina ignored her, but that never stopped Inez.

"Brandon is a good-looking young fellow. I'm surprised he's not dating anyone in town. I wonder if he's got some girl stowed away in DC."

Ah. He probably did. Some snooty woman who would never deign to leave the confines of the capital. With a carefully curated life, just waiting for Brandon to return to his appointed place in it.

In his spotless condo, without even a speck of dust for company.

Sabrina held her lantern up to the older woman's face. "I think you're getting older and don't see as well as you once did. Maybe it's time to book an appointment to see Doc Murphy."

That earned her a half-hearted jab in the side. "Keep it up and I'll be out of *huevos rancheros* in the morning."

"If everyone could be quiet?" Brandon shot a pointed glance at Sabrina.

That earned him a chuckle from Inez and a hearty eye roll from Sabrina.

He cleared his throat. "Thank you for coming this evening for the inaugural ghost tour of the season. As many of you know, Falling Leaves has a history filled with specters and things that go bump in the night. Starting here, at The Peculiar Pumpkin."

He shifted toward the inn, which on cue lit up dark red, smoke billowing out from the back of the porch. Babs was inside, flipping switches, and the low-level special effects wowed the guests.

"The Peculiar Pumpkin has been in and out of the Blake family since it was built, nearly one-hundred and sixty-years ago. That's a well-known fact, published in any guidebook. But what you might not know is that within the first year of the opening of the inn, a murder took place."

The lights illuminating the house shifted from red to white—the cue for Brandon to begin the story of the first murder in Falling Leaves history.

"Now we call him Old Levi, but in his day, he went by the nickname 'Devil'. Devilishly handsome, he had a habit of sleeping with other men's wives. This would be his undoing, as it was only a matter of time until he was taken down by the jealous husband of a lover."

A lover who happened to be Brandon's who knows how many times great-aunt. It was a sordid tale, although one she'd heard countless times before.

"On an early autumn evening, not so different from this one—" A scream cut through the night.

The guests looked around. Sabrina nudged Inez. "Who did he get to scream? That's a nice addition to the tour."

The whites of Inez's eyes were visible in the quickly falling darkness. "That's not part of the tour."

Brandon swallowed the lump in his throat. Should he stay in character? Send one of his members of staff to search to see if anyone needed help? If he had to add another item to his list of why he hated Falling Leaves, it was that he *hated* Halloween and all things scary. Not that he believed in ghosts. No sir, not him.

During October, it wasn't uncommon to see people in costume at random times. The metaphysical shop—

once the scourge of the town—brought oddly dressed people in from all over the state.

Still, Halloween was his least favorite holiday. If it wasn't for his mother, he would've scrapped the ghost tour altogether. He'd been missing her since he'd donned the costume. He couldn't help but think what she'd be making of this impromptu addition to the tour.

He wiped at his brow. He'd rehearsed this damn ghost tour down to the minute. A distraction—and on the first night, to boot—was not what he needed.

Especially with Sabrina watching.

"Well?" Mr. Paulson, an accountant from Pittsburgh, prompted. "Are we going to investigate?"

Brandon measured his next step. Why not go for it? At best, it could add a little spice to the tour. At worst, the tour would have to be halted as they tended to someone injured.

"The screaming usually starts later in the tour," Brandon quipped.

That earned him a laugh. His courage came back to him, and he gestured to the crowd.

"Follow me."

He paused at the creaky old wrought-iron gate. The latch caught, so it took a moment before it eased open. In that time, another high-pitched scream shook his nerves.

"I think I hear footsteps," Sabrina said.

She ran off in the direction the screams had come from. Of course she did. He didn't know whether to be grateful for her playing along or hate her for continuing to disrupt the tour.

"This is quite a show," Mr. Paulson murmured to his wife. "Do you think everyone has their part to play?"

Brandon didn't have the heart to tell him this wasn't part of the show.

"Over here!" Sabrina called.

Brandon held up his lamp. "Follow me, everyone. Quick as you can."

The assembled crowd took the instructions literally and nipped at his heels as they ran around to the back of the house.

Once there, he found Sabrina crouched on the side of the pond, a dense fog surrounding her.

If this was Babs' idea of a prank, she was going to get one mother of a chewing out, come morning.

"Well? What is it?" Inez scurried to the front of the crowd.

Sabrina rose to her full height. Brandon had forgotten how tall she was—especially in high-heeled boots. They rarely saw eye to eye on anything, but as he approached her, he realized he only had a couple of inches on her.

"I found this, and some muddy footprints."

Pinched between her fingertips was an old-fashioned linen handkerchief.

He pinched the note between his index finger and thumb. Written in a messy, red ink was a chilling message.

We know what you have planned. You're being watched.

Chapter Five

Rousing Eleanor out of bed to report…whatever had happened…was not the best way to end the night. Once the assembled guests realized that it hadn't been part of an act, they'd quickly dispersed.

All except Inez, of course.

"What do you reckon it means?" Inez peered over at Eleanor.

She slid the handkerchief into an evidence bag. "I don't know. But I mean to find out." Eleanor was in full cop mode.

This was the most action Falling Leaves had seen since someone had kept breaking into garages and moving things around, stealing nothing except residents' sanity.

"Do you have any skeletons rattling around in your closet, Brando?" Sabrina asked.

She regretted the jab as soon as she looked over at Brandon. He'd removed the top hat, gloves and cape. He sat on a bench, his elbows on his knees. His skin was paler than usual, which was saying a lot, since he got his fair looks from his mother, who'd had strong Danish roots.

"Oh, I forgot. You're not actually a fan of things that go bump in the night."

He ran his hands through his dark blond hair and raised his gaze. "Now you remember, *Sabby*. Funny how this little unscheduled spook happened after you dropped by the tour."

"Are you accusing me? Seriously? I wouldn't stoop that low."

A subtle shrug told her all she needed to know.

Sabrina huffed out an angry breath. "So much for a truce, you pumpkin-roll-hoarding weirdo."

That got a dry laugh out of Brandon.

"Hey now," Eleanor said. "I can tell you Sabrina had nothing to do with it." She leaned down to take an imprint of the muddy print. "Mainly because she takes too much pride in her handwriting to ever scrawl something so terribly."

Sabrina rolled her eyes. "Jeez, thanks. Don't use facts. Like how you're dealing with some kind of stalker makes my life difficult, too. Since I'll be here every day for the near future?"

Brandon stood. Sabrina's stare drifted southward — to the visible rippling of muscles underneath that tight white shirt. She forced her gaze onto the muddy ground.

Lord almighty, this sudden attraction to Brandon meant one thing. She needed to find a man, stat. Pickings were slim around Falling Leaves, making that task a tall order. God forbid she ask her mother or the biddies to intervene — she'd be on blind dates with every man with a pulse between here and the state line.

"I'm sorry, Sabrina. I'm rattled. The last thing I need is some kind of supernatural drama when we're starting work on the Pumpkin."

"Who said anything about the source being supernatural?" Eleanor said. "You sure you don't have any enemies in town, Brandon?"

"Other than Sabrina?" He gestured at her with his top hat.

"Har-de-har," Sabrina said. "I'm going to head home, if you don't need me for anything else."

"Fleeing the scene of the crime?" Inez asked.

"Unless I've been stowing away an evil twin all this time, it would've been impossible for me to throw my voice, leave a handkerchief and look"—she bent down—"those footprints are way smaller than my size tens."

Inez chuckled. "I was kidding, lovely. I'll see you in the morning."

"I'll see you at home," Eleanor added.

"Don't fill up on *huevos rancheros*. I'll have pumpkin rolls at our meeting tomorrow." Brandon's smile seemed genuine.

Which meant perhaps he was serious about their truce, after all. In the morning, she'd have to endeavor to keep things professional.

Because there would be no escaping him, not until he left town again. This time, for good.

"No promises," she said. But—*crap*—that wasn't very truce-worthy. "See you then. Try not to dump on my design choices, okay?" *Whoops. Okay, neither was that.*

She turned away before he could answer.

"I promise nothing!" he called after her.

She waved dismissively and kept walking, not stopping until she was home. The image of him half-in his Victorian garb still hadn't left her by the time she'd shed her coat and shoes and made her way up the stairs.

Funny how the handkerchief threat hadn't crossed her mind once on the walk home.

"You all right, Aunt Sabrina?" Dutch poked his head out of his bedroom door.

"Yep, just muttering to myself like any completely sane person does." She reached up to fist bump his outstretched hand. "You'd better be in bed before your mom gets home. You know she'll check."

"One more game." He held his finger up to his lips and closed the door.

She was the cool aunt, so she'd keep his secret. As long as he kept his promise, and she didn't hear him shouting at the TV in an hour's time.

She walked to the end of the hall and flicked on the light. Sarah and Jareth were curled up at the end of her bed. They didn't stir as she approached.

She hoped a good night's sleep would rattle those idiotic thoughts about Brandon Blake from her mind, once and for all.

* * * *

Brandon pushed aside the velvet curtains in his bedroom and peered out at the crime scene, if you could call it that. He'd half-expected Eleanor to tape off the area with police tape, but she'd merely taken the evidence and instructed him to keep the front doors locked at the inn until morning.

He was the most spooked by the scene by far. Growing up in a creepy mansion could do that to you. Not that he believed in ghosts. But snooping small-town residents could be just as creepy.

When he'd returned to the Pumpkin, the guests who'd attended the tour had been assembled in front of the fireplace, sharing stories over hot cocoa and Adalyn's ginger snaps.

He'd managed to escape up to his room without being observed, which was a feat in and of itself, considering the creaky old stairs.

He set aside the top hat, gloves and cape and sat on the edge of the bed to unlace his boots.

His phone rang while he was tugging off his left boot. He looked over and sighed when he saw Cassandra's name on the display.

He wasn't in the mood to talk with his ex today but he knew well enough that if Cassandra had something to say, she wouldn't stop badgering him until she got through to him.

He grabbed his phone. "Hello?"

"Oh! I'm surprised you're awake this late. I thought everyone in that sleepy town went to bed at sundown."

If Brandon disliked Falling Leaves, Cassandra flat-out despised it. He'd brought her only once, to meet his mother. That had been enough for her. She was the type of woman who craved concrete and skyscrapers.

"Did you call just to insult me and my hometown or did this call have a purpose?"

The click of her tongue against her teeth was evidence of her displeasure. "Grumpy, grumpy. You need to get back to the city. That place is changing you."

He tugged off his other boot and stood it up against the left. "I have a busy day to prepare for."

Her sigh crackled across the line. "My call did have a purpose, you big grump. I wanted to know how much longer you're going to be in that hovel, because an interesting job opportunity passed by my desk today. One that had your name *all* over it."

Cassandra was an executive level recruiter specializing in the hospitality industry. It was how they'd met, five years previous. She'd scouted him for the Assistant General Manager job at Hotel Blaque. That nice, comfortable job he hadn't missed one iota since returning to Falling Leaves.

No, that wasn't true. He missed the normalcy of his life there. Especially with the night's theatrics, he couldn't wait to get back.

He tossed his glasses onto the bed and rubbed at the skin between his eyes.

"I'll be here at least through the new year." He pulled the phone away from his ear, his finger hovering over the disconnect button. Surely the job would start well before then. Besides, the last time he'd talked to his boss at Hotel Blaque, he still had a job.

"Hmm, that might end up working out, after all. This job won't start until after then, give or take. Because of the visa requirements."

Brandon grunted. She would bread-crumb out information for the next hour unless he cut her off now.

"Cassandra. I beg of you. Arrive at the point."

"Oh, fine. The job is a step down in terms of your current position. That said, I think you won't see an issue with it."

She paused again. Brandon groaned. "Cassie, I swear to God."

Her laugh crackled across the line. "It's night manager at the Hotel Fleur in Paris."

He exhaled and let the news settle for a moment.

It'd always been a dream to work in Europe, especially Paris. It was the last place he'd traveled with both parents before his father had died.

Yet as much as he longed for a change in his life, he wasn't sure this was the right one.

"I'll take your silence as contemplation and send you over the details. If you're interested, get back to me."

He exhaled. It was nice of Cassandra to loop him in on this opportunity. She'd never come out and say it, but he knew it was her trying to make amends for the implosion of their relationship.

"I appreciate you keeping me in mind. Thanks."

Why not. It wasn't as though he had any viable ways to make that bigger dream come true right now. It wasn't like mountain lodges simply fell out of the sky.

The tip-tap of her acrylic nails was all he heard before she replied. "There. Sent. Do you need me to look over your resume before you send it?"

"Maybe. Thanks again."

"Anything to get you out of that backwater town. Toodles."

She disconnected the call. Before he tossed his phone aside, an alert came in for Cassandra's email.

While he prepared for bed, he looked over the job requirements. They wanted someone highly educated—preferably with a degree in hospitality. He was a graduate of Cornell's School of Hotel Administration, so he fit that qualifier. Full professional fluency in French. Second box checked. He went down the rest of the list. He fit nearly every qualifier.

Which was why Cassandra had sent the job along. Because he was a good fit, and she'd get her commission for filling the role. Not because she cared about him. He reminded himself about her narcissistic tendencies.

He replied to her email saying he'd get back to her by the start of the week with a decision.

Her reply was immediate.

Good – because they're going to be in town interviewing next week! Don't miss out on this.

He'd been stuck in a rut since returning to town. This could be a good opportunity for him.

With change on his mind, he fired off emails to the two parties interested in purchasing the Pumpkin. It couldn't hurt to keep them in the loop about starting renovations.

He turned his phone on night mode and turned off the light as he climbed into bed.

With the events of the last hour, he had a lot to think about. But somehow his stupid brain just repeated the day's interactions with Sabrina on a loop until sleep finally took him.

Chapter Six

Sabrina groaned as she approached The Over Easy Café. Through a window painted with an autumnal scene, she could make out the biddies seated at a circular booth. Officially known as The Coffee and Knitting Society, no one called them that. Falling Leaves technically had a mayor, but it was the biddies who truly ran things.

She'd slept terribly and was in no mood to put on false smile when dealing with her mom and her friends.

Sabrina had been a daddy's girl since birth. A disappointment to her mother, who had finally gotten the daughter of her dreams after two boys. She had the little doll to dress up, take to tea, and enter in Falling Leaves' annual Miss Autumn pageant.

Too bad that Sabrina rarely wore makeup and while she did paint her nails on occasion, that was as far as her interest went.

Lainey Ellis was at the salon weekly, getting some service done. Not that Sabrina begrudged her that — it just wasn't her thing.

"There's my girl!" Her mother stood and waved at Sabrina. "Inez said you were coming, so we saved you a seat."

Sabrina cut a glance across the cozy — if crowded — cafe at the exposed kitchen where Inez was busy cranking out orders.

"Come on now." Lainey grabbed for her daughter's elbow. "She's already working on your *huevos rancheros.*"

Seeing no escape, Sabrina allowed her mother to guide her to the table.

She squeezed in beside Babs and Tiffany Gonzalez, assistant to Mayor Ford.

"So, how's things going at the Pumpkin? We heard all about what happened last night at the ghost tour," her mother said.

"Nothing happened. It was a stupid prank."

Bobby, their waiter, swooped in to fill her empty coffee cup and drop off a packet of sugar and cream.

"That's not what I heard," Tiffany said. "The mayor is taking it all quite seriously."

"Well, that's a good thing, in case it wasn't just a prank." Sabrina slapped her sugar packets against the side of the table before ripping them open and pouring them into her coffee.

Lainey shook her head. "Your nails are a total mess. You should come with me to the salon tomorrow."

"Why? They'll just get chipped by Monday."

"They have these new gel manicures that last for weeks," Babs cut in. "No saying you can't be feminine in your line of work, sweetie."

"I am feminine. Y'all just need to expand your definition." Sabrina picked up her cup. She took a long sip to keep more words from spilling out of her mouth.

Lainey exhaled a put-upon sigh. "You're never going to land a husband looking like you tumbled off a jobsite."

To that, Sabrina let out a most un-ladylike snort. "Mom, I get asked out by men of all colors of the rainbow and every socio-economic status. Catching a man has never been the problem."

Sure, she didn't date much. But she had offers. She turned most down, especially those from those guys who thought her a novelty — a female general contractor.

Besides, most of them didn't live in town. She would never leave Falling Leaves. She'd worked for nearly a decade to turn her house into a home. She'd rather die than live in some cookie-cutter suburban nightmare.

"It must be keeping one then," Babs said.

Sabrina sat there, too stunned to speak.

"Oh hush," Tinesha Jameson said. "Look, here comes our food. Maybe y'all need to eat instead of piling on poor Sabrina." Tinesha gave Sabrina's hand a squeeze.

Tinesha was Eleanor's mother-in-law and Dutch's grandmother. She was the one person in the biddies Sabrina could always count on to have her back.

Lainey whipped her napkin from the table onto her lap. "I'm just saying, I'd love to see you married. Some grandkids would be nice."

"You already have grandkids. Four of 'em." Her oldest brother, Sebastian, had been married for over a decade, her next oldest brother Caleb, eight. They had four kids between them. Too bad they lived in San Francisco and Charlotte, respectively.

"That I see twice a year, if I'm lucky." Her pout intensified. "But your brothers said they'll come in for a visit after your father's surgery, so I suppose that's something."

Sabrina already knew this, as she'd been the one to text her brothers to let them know — they'd been even more out of the loop than her.

"Mom, please let it drop. I want to eat my breakfast in peace. I have enough irritation on my plate dealing with Brandon Blake for the next few months."

Babs let out a chuckle. "I don't know about that. You two sure have a spark."

"Always have," Lainey added. "Too bad they never used that spark to start a fire."

Sabrina turned her attention to her eggs. "I'm two seconds away from putting in headphones and listening to a podcast if you don't stop badgering me."

Tinesha huffed out a sigh. "Let's talk about the cider festival and leave poor Sabrina alone."

Soon enough, the conversation shifted to the following weekend's festival, and she was let off the hook.

For now, anyway.

* * * *

"Since when do you care about which pumpkin roll is the prettiest? You normally shove them down your gob without looking." Adalyn peered over the display case at Brandon.

"That's not true."

Adalyn tucked a lock of long hair behind her ear. "Could it be that Sabrina is finally fetching her own pumpkin rolls? Instead of resorting to espionage to obtain them?"

It was news to him that Sabrina had been sneaking pumpkin rolls since his return to town. Proof of just how much she wanted to avoid him. He hoped they could leave the past in its place.

"Why is everyone so obsessed with this? I just wanted the prettiest roll in the front. Not everything has a deeper meaning."

Adalyn bent over and reached for one of The Frosted Squash's signature orange ceramic plates.

"Maybe it does. You want to make a good impression. There's nothing nefarious about that."

"Yes, because today marks the official start of construction." He cleared his throat. "Obviously."

"Mmkay." She placed four rolls on the plate and passed it over to him. "Good luck with your new partnership, boss man."

She turned to tend to a customer before he could reply. Brandon made his way back to the conference room.

As he passed through the lobby, he had to stop twice — first to give advice on how to get to the highway to a guest who was checking out, then to pass on a message to the front desk that a room needed fresh towels.

By the time he reached the conference room, Sabrina was already there, setting up her laptop. She wore the standard uniform of an Ellis & Daughter button-down and khaki pants.

Well-fitting khaki pants that clung to her ample backside. Not that he should be noticing things like that. He cleared his throat.

"Here I thought I was early."

Sabrina glanced up at him. "I'm always early for everything. I detest tardiness."

He set the plate down on the center of the table. "That's something we can both agree on."

"Maybe there can be peace in Falling Leaves, after all." She stood and reached for her bag. "Any updates on the handkerchief bandit? Eleanor had already left for work by the time I got up."

"You know as much as I do. Hopefully we'll find out it was just a stupid prank. It's not like anyone has anything better to do in this town."

Sabrina grunted at that. "Of course, you'd think that."

"Look, I'm not worried about it. It's not that big of a deal. Remember the pranks that happened when we were in high school? Your cousin Dennis and his friend Rory were behind them."

"Dennis has matured past those pranks. Well, barely."

She began pulling sample books out of her bag and laid them in a tidy line down the conference room table. "Is anyone else joining us for this meeting? It's common to include managers and other members of staff in the construction meetings. Once work begins, I like to have a brief meeting every Monday. Just so everyone's on the same page."

His eyes were drawn to one of the sample books — more to the hideous wallpaper sample on top. He hoped it wasn't a reflection of what was inside the book. "That's a great idea. I think this one can be just the two of us, though."

The words hung in the air. *Just the two of us?* Jesus, could he have phrased that better? He didn't want to give her any indication that he was interested in anything besides a professional relationship.

Especially as he'd dreamed of Paris all night long. Sabrina wasn't the short-term type, a truth he knew all too well.

If Sabrina felt any awkwardness from the statement, it didn't show.

"Sounds good. So, let's tackle the design choices for the lobby and main stairwell, since that's our first area of construction. I'm assuming you want this work done the quickest, I pulled from my samples of materials I can pick up for same-day delivery from my suppliers."

She nudged the books across the table. With a sigh, he began to rifle through them.

She snatched a pumpkin roll off the plate and took a bite. "You have the world's best poker face. I can't tell what you're thinking."

He paused at a tasteful dark brocade carpet sample. It was dark gray with a subtle gray pattern. "I like this one. No sense in looking at anything else." He shoved the carpet book across the table and reached for another one. "Obviously we'll need the front desk repaired, as it's seen better days. Do you have ideas for who to hire? I know a few good furniture restorers. Comes in handy in my line of work," he said.

"I haven't given it a good once-over yet, but unless it looks worse than it appears, I'll probably handle it. It just needs some wood filler and a fresh coat of stain from the look of it. If it needs any millwork, I can handle simple stuff, or contract it out."

He arched a brow. "I didn't know you were a woodworker, in addition to a general contractor."

"I'm my father's daughter." Her smile was impish. She was so damned cute. He had to stop thinking of her that way.

He flipped open a book of wallpaper and paint samples. "I'd hate to get rid of the custom wallpaper in its entirety. I think we may have an odd roll of it in the attic or somewhere."

"We could re-do the lobby bathroom with it. That way it's not so…overwhelming."

"Fantastic idea." He tapped a grayish-green paint sample. "I think we paint the stairwell. That way it won't clash with the carpet."

He flicked the paint chip between his fingers. She reached for it. "I'll get a few similar colors from the hardware store today and paint some test swatches."

He got to the end of the sample book and exhaled. The final wallpaper sample was black with elegant gold, white, gray and aubergine flowers.

"For the wall behind reception," they said at the same time.

Brandon looked up and found Sabrina staring at him. She managed a dry laugh. He didn't want to be a dour bastard, so he cracked a smile.

"Perhaps our design ideas aren't so different after all."

"Famous last words. I think that covers the bulk of the main design choices for the lobby and stairwell. Trim and paint colors staying the same?"

They went over the remaining niggling details. Brandon appreciated that Sabrina was thorough. She understood it was vital that the job be completed on time. Until this work was completed, they'd had to reduce rates and would have to bring guests in through the side.

"No more than ten days to get everything done once I confirm my supply list and get my punch list together. My sub-contractors will be here first thing tomorrow. I only ask that the space is cleared out."

"We'll start this afternoon."

She reached for another pumpkin roll at the same time he did. She jolted her hand backward.

"Sorry, I was just taking this one for Dad. I'm sure he'll need it after his doctor's appointment."

"He'll be back on his feet before you know it," Brandon said.

"From your lips to God's ears."

She began to gather her things. "I'll let you know if I have any trouble sourcing the supplies. Text me if you need anything. Otherwise, I'll see you in the morning."

She left without giving him a chance to say goodbye.

Chapter Seven

Before going on a supply run, Sabrina stopped off at her parents' house to fill her father in on the meeting. It'd be a good way to take his mind off surgery the following day.

She parked behind her dad's truck and looked at the house. Her mother had gone all out with decorating. There wasn't an inch of the porch that didn't have a pumpkin or decoration shoved onto it. Including the large BOO, Y'ALL! on the front porch.

She opened the door, sending the dogs running toward her. Petty and Earnhardt, her parents' ancient hounds, were always underfoot.

"Get out from under Dad, you silly old dogs." She rubbed their heads.

"Your mother is threatening to send them to the garage if they don't behave after I've had surgery."

To that, Petty let out a baleful bark.

"Oh, stop." Sabrina rubbed his chin. The dog gave her hand a quick lick before trotting off toward the kitchen.

"You two managed to agree on design choices without killing one another? Well, shoot. That means I owe your mother a twenty."

Her mother poked her head in from the kitchen. "I keep telling you, there's something there! You're a lot alike."

Sabrina groaned. "I thought differences were what made a relationship. Look at you and Dad."

It was true that her parents were as opposite as night and day. They used to be known around town as the beauty queen and the handyman. But they'd made it work for nearly forty years.

"True, but only because your dad is so laid back about things. You two are both type-A. You'd bring out the best in each other." Her mother came behind her and smoothed down a bump in Sabrina's ponytail. "And you'd give me the cutest grandkids ever. Blonde-haired babies? *Swoon.*"

"Mom, stop." Sabrina swatted her mother's hand away like it was an errant fly. "Even if I *did* like Brandon, don't forget this construction is to make the Pumpkin as appealing as possible for potential buyers so he can put Falling Leaves in his rear view forever, never to return."

"Oh, I think there's more to it than that."

This was her mother's attempt to goad her into a gossip session. Sabrina wasn't having it.

"I've gotta hit the road if I want to get to Roanoke and back before dark." She made her way into the kitchen to grab a to-go cup of one of the apple cider blends her mother was trying out for the upcoming cider festival.

As she filled her cup, she glanced over to a pile of papers on the counter. Her gaze was immediately drawn to the logo for the annual Falling Leaves Ms. Autumn pageant.

With a groan, she placed the to-go lid on the cup. "Mom, I know you did not apply for me to be a contestant for the pageant without my permission. Please tell me you didn't?"

Sabrina wasn't sure why she'd asked, as she had the entrance form in front of her — her mother's excellent attempt at her forged signature at the bottom.

Her mother went into full pout mode. It worked well enough on her dad and brothers, but it only made Sabrina angrier.

"It would mean so much to me — "

"To dress me like a turkey and parade me in front of town? Hell, no." She slapped the form down on the coffee table.

"Now, Sabrina, your mother gets ahead of herself sometimes, but what's the harm? It's one weekend of rehearsals, the pageant, and the parade. It'll take no more than a few hours of your time." Her father managed a slight shrug. It was like her parents had rehearsed this. She loved her father, but he could be a terrible enabler for her mother's schemes.

"A few hours I don't have if we want to get the Pumpkin done in time."

"Well, funny you mention that." Lainey said. "As Brandon is on the committee this year, too. You know his mama always loved the pageant. She had to live vicariously since she didn't have a daughter."

The implication that Lainey had *also* had to live vicariously, despite birthing a daughter hung heavy in the air.

"It's not that big of a deal, darlin'. I already have your dress picked out. I'll make your appointments for hair and makeup. You just have to learn a little dance routine and a speech. I'll help you with that."

"I'm too busy for the town's annual dog and pony show. It's a good thing you didn't turn in the application. I'm not doing it. And that's final."

Lainey's years in pageants meant she could turn on the tears on a dime. "Oh, fine. I'll be on the sidelines, just like I am every year. Last year, at least you had a decent excuse. You and your father were out of town on a job."

"I may be in town, but I'm still working on a job," Sabrina shot back.

Lainey turned and reached for a conveniently placed handkerchief. "Fine, fine. Break your mother's heart." She gently dabbed at her eyes to keep from smudging her mascara.

Sometimes Sabrina wondered how she'd spawned from a woman so very different from herself.

"Oh, Mom. Stop crying."

Lainey waved her off and made for the kitchen.

"It'll be easier if you just let your mama have this one," her father said. "She doesn't ask for much."

As much as Sabrina hated to admit it, he was right. She hadn't asked about the pageant in years. She'd stood by as everyone else had entered their daughters. She hadn't forced Sabrina to be anyone other than herself.

Sure, she'd made the odd comment about Sabrina being a tomboy. But her mother had been the one to buy Sabrina her first pair of work overalls.

Sabrina tapped her boot against the hardwood. "Fine. But you'd better not ask for so much as a coffee run out of me until the end of the year, both of you. I'm tired of your secretive ways."

Lainey turned, her face lit up like the sun. She clutched her hands to her chest. "I promise." She raced over to embrace her daughter.

Sabrina had never been the touchy-feely type. Another way that she sometimes felt like she'd failed her mom, who very much showed her love in hugs and kisses.

"I'll see y'all later." She paused to give her father a kiss. "I'll check in tomorrow after your surgery to be sure you're doing okay."

"Don't go worrying on my account," he mumbled. Her father was never one for a fuss.

"Yes, we're all worried. Especially since you dropped the news on us so suddenly." She squeezed his hand and turned toward the door.

"Saturday night at town hall," her mother called. "It's the first meeting for the pageant."

Sabrina rolled her eyes, grateful her back was to her mother. "Fine, I'll see you there."

She ran down the front steps of her parents' home to her truck. Once the door was shut behind her, she pulled down the mirror and inspected herself.

Not a bad specimen, sure. But Falling Leaves had no shortage of pretty girls. She doubted she'd even come close to placing in the competition. But everyone in town knew and liked her, for the most part, so she'd get a few pity votes.

She flipped up the mirror and pushed the ignition-start on her truck. She couldn't even use this stupid pageant to take her mind off her annoying attraction to Brandon because he'd be there too, micromanaging every detail the way his mother used to.

She put the truck in drive and let her mind wander as she drove out of town and onto the highway. As much as she loved Falling Leaves, the town could feel stiflingly small sometimes. Especially when she was on the day's menu of gossip du jour.

An afternoon in the big city was just what she needed.

* * * *

You've got guests at the front desk.

Brandon sighed at the message from Babs. He replied, requesting more details. She left him on read.

She had a habit of doing that. When pushed, she'd claim ignorance to technology. Brandon knew the truth — she enjoyed him running around like a headless chicken.

Funny behavior from someone who didn't want him to sell the Pumpkin.

He'd hoped the visitor would be Eleanor, or one of the two other members of the police force, with an update on the previous night's incident.

He left his office and walked down the hallway to the lobby. On the way, he started to picture the changes he and Sabrina had laid out. It would be beautiful.

For the next owners, of course.

He peeked around the corner, finding one pair of potential owners in front of him.

Neither the Westmores nor Halford had replied to his email, so it was quite a surprise to see the couple of boutique hotels in his lobby. A southern Alabama girl and a posh Englishman—they had the winning touch. They owned a stable of twenty hotels spanning the globe.

They sat together on one of the tatty velvet couches in the lobby, their heads inclined.

Gabriel laid his hand on Merit's pregnant stomach. It'd only been a matter of weeks since Brandon had last spoken to them on video chat, but she appeared much further along now.

The couple were one of the annoyingly in love sort. It was one of the reasons they sometimes grated on his nerves. Well, that and now their tendency to pop in without calling.

He cut Babs an irritated glance for not telling him who his guests were before he composed himself. She took that opportunity to take her leave.

"Hey there, Brandon!" Merit stood. "We were just on our way from DC to our home in Nashville. I was checking my email, saw the update you'd sent. Gabe said we should take a detour to check in on y'all!"

Gabriel stood and offered his hand. "I wanted to call, but Merit insisted on the surprise. You wouldn't happen to have a room for us, would you?"

Normally they'd never have a spare room in the height of tourist season. But with renovations starting soon, they had space.

"I realized we'd never stayed the night here. And we should remedy that if we're considering purchasing."

He'd asked Gabriel and Merit if they would consider purchasing as-is but they'd declined. They didn't have the time to oversee a renovation before the baby came, in addition to their existing properties. Besides, they'd reasoned, didn't he want to get the best possible price for the inn?

They had a point. But he didn't think this visit was as simple as them dropping by because he'd emailed them. This visit was akin to a test.

Whatever that might entail.

If the Pumpkin didn't pass muster, he'd have only one other interested buyer. He had to impress them if he wanted to get out of Falling Leaves anytime soon.

Especially as that possible position in Paris was alluring. *Ish*. He still hadn't shaken his dream of starting a mountain lodge, although he hadn't quite worked up the nerve to search for a property just yet. It scared him, the idea of owning his own business. He'd seen how the Pumpkin had run his mother ragged until she'd died. He wasn't sure that he wanted the same fate.

"Absolutely, we have a room for you two." He walked over to the front desk. "Your timing is great, as we're going to be starting construction on the lobby and front areas of the hotel tomorrow."

"Well, isn't that just wonderful," Merit said. "I knew we were right to come."

"Javier, can you reserve the Jacobean suite for the Westmores?"

The clerk began tapping away on his computer. "I'll see right to it."

"If you can excuse me for just a moment," Brandon said.

"Oh, take your time," Merit said.

He walked at a measured pace until he rounded the corner, then he broke out into a run. He didn't stop until he reached Babs' office.

"The Westmores are here. We need to alert the staff that everything needs to be tip-top for the duration of their stay."

Babs' reading glasses slid from the top of her head to sit haphazardly on her face.

She started to speak, then stopped. "Of course."

Brandon whipped off his glasses and rubbed at a spot on the lens. "That was rather agreeable of you. I figured you'd try to sabotage me or something."

She stood. "You have enough to worry about, with that hullabaloo last night. I'll check in with Eleanor to see if there are any updates. Do you think you'll be up for doing a ghost tour while the Westmores are here?"

He'd rather impale his eyeball with a salad fork than run another ghost tour after the previous night's shenanigans.

"Are you sure you don't want to run it? After all, it is your specialty."

Babs had run the tour from the time he'd left for college, save the odd weekends he was home.

"You should be making an impression on these people, not me."

She had a point. He wouldn't put it past her to stir up shenanigans.

"You're right. I'll give them a private tour if they're interested. Mrs. Westmore is about seven months pregnant, so she might not be up for the full tour."

Babs nodded curtly. "Okay. I'll take care of it." She brushed past him on the way out the door.

"Thanks for being so agreeable, Babs."

She shrugged. "Don't thank me for doing my job while I still have it."

He took the back stairs two-by-two to reach the Jacobean suite to be sure everything was in order.

On his way back downstairs, his phone chimed with a new email. The other buyer, Halford, had replied to Brandon's update with a brief message.

You can take us out of the running. Just signed on for an off-grid property in rural West Virginia. Best of luck to you!

Not that he'd particularly wanted to sell to Halford, but it had been nice having a back-up plan in his pocket. Now, he only had one interested party on the line.

This visit had to go well. His future depended on it.

Chapter Eight

Sabrina's afternoon slid from bad to worse. She pulled up in front of the Pumpkin, not quite prepared to be the bearer of bad news.

Or in this case, middling to bad news, depending on what mood Brandon was in. Her supplier had sold the last of the carpet they'd chosen for the entryway and stairs.

The only options immediately available were...not to Sabrina's taste, so she could imagine what Brandon would think of them.

Luckily, she was an enterprising sort. She'd reached out to other contacts and come up with what she hoped would be suitable replacements. Unfortunately, as she put out one fire, another one lit up.

The wallpaper they'd chosen was also out of stock. This foul-up made her feel like a fool—especially on the first job she was running solo.

She gathered up the new samples. Hopefully, Brandon would be in a decent mood.

She walked into the Pumpkin. The ancient bell above the door chimed as she stepped into the entryway.

Javier waved to her from his post. "If you're looking for boss man, he's currently running through the place like someone lit his pants on fire."

She walked through the lobby toward the front desk. "What's going on?"

Javier shifted to Spanish—which meant he must have serious dirt. Sabrina understood Spanish better than she spoke it but had been somewhat fluent since high school.

"Potential buyers just checked into the Jacobean suite. He's in a panic."

Oh.

"Where's the last place he was spotted?" she asked in English.

"Upstairs, dealing with some emergency." He mimed air quotes.

She headed up the creaky stairs to the second level of the Pumpkin. Edison lamps gave a slightly spooky look to the darkly painted corridor. It was one thing to have a theme, but quite another to have lighting so dim guests had to risk injury to return to their rooms.

After finding no trace of him on the second floor, she scurried up the stairs to the third. There, she found the man in question in a whisper-argument with Babs.

"And I'm telling you Randy *can* be roused out of the house after six p.m. Especially if we're paying emergency rates."

She snuck up behind Brandon. "What are we arguing about?"

Brandon jumped back and stumbled into the wall.

Babs snorted. "You should know better than to sneak up on him, Sabrina. He's as jumpy as a long-tailed cat in a room full of rocking chairs."

Brandon adjusted his glasses before running a hand through his blond hair. "I am not." He rounded on Sabrina. "What are you doing here, anyway? I thought you were getting supplies."

"Ah, well there's been a slight snag. Hence my presence."

He let out a sigh that could've given Lainey Ellis a run for her money. He turned to Babs. "Call Randy, will you, please?"

Randy was the town's resident woodworker, as well as her father's best friend, aside from Uncle Gordon. She'd learned everything she knew about woodworking by standing at his elbow from the time she could see over a table saw.

"Randy is probably sitting in my dad's man cave, two beers in. Is there anything I can help with? Seeing as I'm a woodworker, too?"

For a moment, it looked like Brandon might argue with her. Instead, he pointed to the Jacobean suite door. "There's a rocking chair in there, missing a spindle. We weren't aware that a spindle was loose until a pregnant woman sat down in it, looking to ease her feet." He nodded to the chair, wedged into the corner of the hallway.

"Oh, that's easy-peasy. And Randy would've charged you after-hours rates for a five-minute fix. Help me carry it out to the workshop."

He didn't argue, instead he picked up the chair and followed her.

"What happened with the samples you were supposed to bring me from Roanoke?"

"We need to make some adjustments. If you want to get the work done in time, that is."

Again, with the sighing. They came to the second-floor landing, and she turned to face him. He did look rather handsome, harassed and strong-arming a hundred-year-old rocking chair as though it was nothing.

"Even if I keep in touch with my suppliers, items go in and out of stock. They don't keep me abreast of everything."

He managed a shrug. "We'll figure it out. I have bigger things on my mind right now, anyway."

They didn't speak again until they were in the workshop at the rear of the Pumpkin's property.

"Do you know what tools you need?"

Sabrina flicked on the light. "I don't need any tools." She walked over to a row of drawers on the back of the wall and rifled around until she found what she was looking for.

She palmed the small bottle and turned to Brandon. "Put the chair on the work bench, please."

He did, without argument. She looked over the spindle to be sure the wood hadn't cracked anywhere. Then she looked at the chair, to see if she'd have to remove the top position to get the spindle back in.

"What are you doing?"

She angled the spindle in and smiled when, after a moment, it slipped perfectly into place.

"It just needs a little wood filler to hold it in place." She uncapped the container and took a gob of filler with her index finger. She filled in the space and inspected it again. "Do you have another chair you could swap in the meantime?"

"Wait, so I can't put it right back in the room? None of the other chairs I have match." He leaned back and clapped his hand to his forehead. Sabrina caught herself staring at the subtle bob of his Adam's apple as he sighed.

Knock it off, brain. He is an uptight asshole!

She cleared her throat. "She wants a rocking chair to take a load off. I don't think she'll care that it matches."

He turned to her. "Okay, then let this dry. We'll swap out the chair. We'll touch up the paint tomorrow. Then it'll be returned to their room. If they don't want to buy the inn because of one chair, they were just looking for an excuse not to. Problem solved, right?"

"One of many." Sabrina sighed. "Come on, let me help you with the chair. Then you can help me by picking out samples, since I'll have to drive into Roanoke again tomorrow to pick up everything that's still missing."

"Fair bargain."

Brandon insisted on going to three different rooms to find the best of the tatty looking rocking chairs. Then she helped him carry it back to the Jacobean suite.

They ran into Babs heading down the stairs, on their way up. "The Westmores have gone to dinner, so your timing is perfect. I was about to see to their turn-down service myself."

"Thank you, Babs." Brandon angled the chair, so it hit the railing, scuffing the black paint in the process.

Thank God the whole place was getting a paint job.

"Ugh, let me help, you stubborn goat."

She took the back end of the chair, and they carried it up the rest of the stairs. After he fumbled with the ancient keys to open the door, they carried it over to the window.

Brandon left her there for a moment to hunt for a blanket to throw over the arm of the chair.

Seeing as this was the best suite at The Peculiar Pumpkin, it was one of the few rooms that didn't need any touching up. Brandon's attention to detail could be seen—down to the tasteful, subtle Halloween decorations—like the cluster of white and gold pumpkins nestled in the fireplace.

"There. It looks good as new." He looked around the room. "Thankfully, they know the inn is going to be renovated, as it's clearly seen better days."

"It's not that bad. Come on, let's make some decisions so I can get home, okay?"

Brandon nodded. "Okay."

Sabrina turned to the door. She noticed one of the pumpkins in the fireplace had gone askew. She leaned forward to adjust it.

After making sure it was just so, she somehow caught her foot in the crevice where the tile met with the ancient carpet. Her ankle gave out from under her, and she tumbled toward the floor, obscenities flying out of her mouth as her arms windmilled.

Her head landed on the floor—only an inch from the marble fireplace. All her breath left in a *whoosh*.

"Are you okay?" Brandon hustled over to her.

She wanted to crawl into a hole and die. The last thing she wanted was his attention.

She opened her eyes, finding him leaning over her. Her heart ratcheted up like a table saw cutting at three-thousand rpm. Why did she have to work here? If they didn't need the job so badly, she'd find some excuse to quit. Having Brandon hovering over her like this had her mind digging ditches deep into the gutter.

Sabrina cradled her head. "Been better, honestly. But I think I'll live after an aspirin or two. That's what I get for letting your perfectionist tendencies rub off on me." She gestured to the pumpkins, somehow still perfectly in place.

He nudged his glasses up and leaned further forward. "You didn't need to do that. I'm sorry if my anxiety was rubbing off on you." He snaked an arm around her shoulder, bringing her closer. Now they were eye to eye. "How many fingers do you see?"

"I didn't hit my head that hard." Sabrina leaned up onto her elbow. "But since you're asking, three."

Brandon gently touched the back of her head. Her face brushed against his shoulder as he held her close. She inhaled a sharp breath. This was beyond inappropriate. But she didn't. Instead, she allowed Brandon to hold her.

He was just doing the honorable thing. There was no romance here.

She tilted her head to find his gaze steady on her.

"Are you sure you're okay?" He brushed her hair from her forehead.

She huffed out a breath. "Why are you being so nice all of a sudden?"

His hand came around to cradle the back of her head. "Do you think I'm that callous? That I wouldn't care if my contractor knocked herself out?"

Of course, that's all she was. She'd been stupid to think otherwise. Especially given their history. She tried to push him off, but he held fast. "Of course. Your contractor. Let me go, Brandon."

"I don't want you to hurt yourself, Sabby. And you will if you rush to your feet."

"Call me that again and you'll be the one in pain, Brando." They were so close together now. Since construction started, they'd always maintained a respectable distance. This closeness was…bordering on intimate.

His hand slid from the back of her neck to her shoulder. Of all the sensations happening in her body after banging her head, why did her brain laser-focus in on the feeling of his large hand bracing her?

He held her as though she was the most important thing in the world. Not just his contractor—and as an afterthought, his very distant ex. It was probably ancient history for him. So why did the wound seem to be splitting open again?

"I think I'm okay now, seriously. Let me up." She exhaled a breath—an effort to settle her rattled nerves.

He held her gaze. They were so close she could make out the speckles of gold in his brown eyes. "You seem eager to be away from me." His voice was scarcely above a whisper.

Sabrina exhaled. "Why aren't you just as eager?" Her gaze stayed steady on his face.

Before Brandon could answer, someone else spoke. "Oh my, did I interrupt something?"

The slow southern drawl alerted Brandon to Merit Jenkins-Westmore's presence. She stood in the doorway. Far enough away that it was unlikely she could overhear them, given the size of the suite.

Still, Brandon didn't want to take any chances.

"Oh, I was just helping Sabrina to her feet. She had a bit of a disaster trying to right an errant pumpkin."

Gabriel Westmore appeared behind his wife, wearing a wide-eyed expression. "We'll get our things and get out of your way."

"N-no," Brandon started to stutter. "Sabrina is my contractor. She was helping me fix the rocking chair for you before the pumpkin disaster."

"Looks like something more than contracting going on up here that has nothing to do with pumpkins," Merit said. She reached forward to grab a sweater off the edge of the bed. "I'm sure we'll have a lot to talk about at the ghost tour. See you soon!"

The door closed quietly behind them.

"Fuuuck," Brandon muttered under his breath.

Sabrina snorted. "I don't think I've heard you curse since high school."

"Proof you've tried to avoid me. I've been known to curse a blue streak or two." He extended a hand to her. She took it and he brought her easily to her feet. "How did I not hear them coming? The room keys make a racket turning in the locks."

"Woah there, lil' doggy," Sabrina said. "Now I'm really lightheaded. I wasn't expecting the elevator treatment. Especially given that you didn't seem so eager to release me just a moment ago."

He was in no position to address that statement, so he guided her to the chaise by the window. "I'm sorry. Take a seat."

She sat down, with him following. "Here, while the blood returns to the rest of my body, look over these samples."

He took the folder of samples and opened it, not seeing anything but a blur. Was there any way this day could get any worse? No, he shouldn't even think it. Fate had a funny sense of humor lately.

"Now they're going to think something is going on with us. Can you come to the ghost tour? To tell them that you're just the contractor?"

"Why would I need to come to the ghost tour? I could tell them over dinner." She paused. "Well, as soon as the room stops spinning."

"Take a breath," he instructed her. "I'd rather you not do it at dinner, with the way gossip spreads around town. The ghost tour will just be for them."

She was just as keen as him to avoid gossip, especially this early into their working relationship. "Oh fine, I'll go, even if I think you're being dramatic. As long as you don't make my life miserable and put off deciding on these new design choices."

He snapped to attention. In less than two minutes, he'd settled on one main choice for the carpet, and an alternate he preferred, in case they could rush order it to arrive before they needed it. The wallpaper was also an easy choice.

A well-needed distraction from his little interaction with Sabrina. What had gotten into him? If he'd promptly helped her to her feet, there would have been no misunderstanding with the Westmores.

"Wow, I should do favors for you more often. You're never this agreeable."

"I'm not agreeable, just tired. And hungry. Come on, let's get something to eat before the ghost tour. If the room's stopped spinning, that is."

She rose to stand, covered one eye, then began to hop around the room.

"Everything's right as rain, bosserino."

He chuckled to himself. "Keep that energy for when you're talking to the Westmores."

"Sure thing, Brando the boss man. I'll be sure to inform them that there is absolutely no one in the commonwealth of Virginia I'd rather be in any kind of relationship than you."

She left before he could respond. Was he imagining it, or did she sound a little offended at his perceived disinterest? Given how she'd seemed so eager to get away from him, he wasn't sure.

That was a thought for another time. First order of business — dinner. The second was convincing the Westmores what they'd seen was as G-rated as a children's film.

Chapter Nine

"Are you sure she hasn't changed her mind?" Sabrina peered out into the café's dining room. Merit Jenkins held court like her presence had always been a fixture.

"Does she look tired to you?"

"No, she looks like she's just getting started."

Brandon let go of the door into the dining room and it swung shut. He opened the hall and pulled out the garment bag that contained the ghost tour orator costume.

"Hopefully her energy will start to wane after dinner. Then you'll explain that what the Westmores thought they saw is *not* what they saw. All it takes is a simple explanation. Then they'll be on their way back to Nashville in the morning. Then they'll forget all about it by the time they come back in the new year to hopefully buy the inn."

Sabrina watched as he rifled through the closet, annoyed with herself yet again for finding him attractive even when performing the most menial of tasks. The light caught the copper strands in his beard, making him look like one of the mages in her favorite books.

She exhaled. She hated herself for allowing him to get to her.

"Is this worth getting stressed about? I mean, it's just a misunderstanding."

He reached up onto a high shelf to pull down the tatty top hat. "A misunderstanding with the best prospect I have for buying the inn." He paused. "Especially considering the only other interested party just bowed out."

"That's breaking news," Sabrina quipped.

He let out one mother of a sigh. "I need this to go well. For Mom. You'd do it for her, right? So, the Pumpkin's legacy will live on?"

Obviously, it was all about the sale of the inn.

"What if they change their mind? Will you stay until another buyer can be found?"

His face clouded over like a storm coming in over the mountains. "I suppose I'd have no choice. Who knows how long that could take? It's not like you can pluck buyers from the ground like a pumpkin. I'd much rather return to the life I had before Mom got sick."

"Back to DC, then? And that snooty hotel off K Street?"

He pulled the cape out of the bag and ran his fingers over the fine silk. "Maybe, maybe not. I'm considering my options. Especially with my parents gone, there's really nothing tying me to this area any longer."

She wasn't sure why, but that singular word — *nothing* – hit like a bullet to the chest.

"You all right?" He took a step closer.

Her expression must've betrayed her. Although she wasn't sure what she even had to be upset about. It was a good thing that Brandon was leaving. They were chalk and cheese. Even if they now got along better now than they had in years, they'd still be a combination that never quite paired together.

Yet her stupid teenage heart liked to squeak out reminders of what things had been like when they'd dated. Especially after their dalliance in the Westmores' suite. Why couldn't he leave well enough alone?

"I'm fine. I was just thinking about…carpet."

He leveled her a glance before swooping the cape around his broad shoulders. He brought his hands up to his clavicle to tie the ribbons securing the cape into a neat bow.

"Tell me they don't have either of our other choices, and I think I'll throw myself under a bus."

"I haven't gotten a response from my supplier yet. Although it would be kind of entertaining to see you follow through with a dramatic scenario like that."

He rolled his eyes. "Ha, ha."

"Ah, there are our little lovebirds!"

Merit's voice couldn't have been louder if she had a megaphone. Sabrina cringed.

Before either of them could respond, she clapped her hands together. "I was getting all the scoop from some locals who were dining near us. How romantic is it? The innkeeper and general contractor working together. Both off and on the clock, hmm?"

Brandon and Sabrina exchanged a look that screamed *oh, shit.*

"Oh, that's just old gossip. People in this town love to talk," Sabrina said.

Merit batted her eyelashes. "I'm from a small town myself. One you've probably never heard of. Jefferson Forge, Alabama. I know what it's like to have everyone all up in your business."

Maybe there wouldn't be a need for a drawn-out speech, explaining that this was all a misunderstanding.

"Besides, I have a soft spot for couples working together. Gabriel and I formed our business together before we were married, too. So I know a little something about keeping secrets." Neither of them could manage a word before Merit leaned forward and took them both by the shoulder. "I won't feed the gossip grist mill. Especially with a potential deal on the line, right? Especially from one business owning couple to another, am I right?" She chuckled to herself. "Oops. I didn't mean to say that part. Don't tell Gabriel I said anything."

She mimed zipping her lips closed and tossing away the key.

"But—" Brandon started. "We would never do something so inappropriate. Especially not in a guest's room."

"I didn't assume *that* was what you were doing. I just remember the thrill of sneaking off with Gabe. Back before anyone knew what was happening."

"That was *definitely* — " Brandon interjected.

Merit closed her eyes and exhaled. "Ooof, that baby sure is doing a dance in my belly tonight."

"But—" Brandon flustered over his words. "I don't think you understand."

Gabriel came out of the dining room, a lantern in each of his hands.

"Babs gave me these for the tour." He turned to Sabrina. "Will you be coming along with us then, Sabrina?"

His accent was super posh. Or at least she thought it was. The only thing she knew about England was gleaned from the period dramas she binged-watched with her mother.

Sabrina cut a glance at Brandon, inviting him to take the out before she answered. If they really wanted to squash this rumor with the Westmores, this was the moment to do it.

Unfortunately for her, it appeared that the stress of the day had worn on Brandon. A fine sheen of sweat coated his face, and his eyes were locked in a thousand-yard stare.

He was her client. And she'd do whatever it took to keep the client happy. Even if it meant pretending to be his girlfriend for a night. Now she worried what could happen—that the lie would stretch too far to bring it back.

What harm could it do? They'd dated for over a year. It wasn't as though she was unfamiliar with treating him with some modicum of affection.

"I'll tag along to help Brandon. Do you have a second cape somewhere, Brando?" She looped an arm around his waist.

At his touch, his gaze snapped into focus. "What?"

"A cape. I'll help give the tour. The bits I know, anyway. Or I can improvise, if needed."

She'd known Brandon long enough to gauge the *WTF* expression he aimed her way. She could almost hear him, telepathically, in her mind.

We're supposed to be convincing them we're not *together, you idiot!*

Instead, he coughed. "I don't think we do."

"Oh well," Merit said. "I'm sure the tour will be just delightful. We'll meet y'all on the porch when you're ready." Merit took Gabriel's hand and the two of them walked through the lobby.

"What the hell, Sabrina?" Brandon rounded on her.

"I tried to give you an out! But you were spaced out."

His expression softened. "I'm sorry. This whole thing is becoming messier by the minute." He wiped his brow with the back of his hand.

"Look, it's one night. They've convinced themselves we're together. Based on what they saw, further fed by the town's gossip mill. The more we deny it, the worse it looks." She exhaled.

"Besides, it's just the two of them on the tour. Hopefully no one else will be the wiser. They'll be gone in the morning. And when they come back to buy the inn—and they will, I can tell they're charmed—we'll have conveniently broken up. Easy-peasy."

"My glasses are fogging up. I've got to stop sweating." He whipped them off and wiped at them with the cape. He turned to her.

"You're right. With everything on my plate, this isn't a hill worth dying on. After all, we don't have to go overboard or anything. Just pretend we like each other. Merit seemed keen on the couple partnership idea."

A burst of laughter escaped Sabrina before she could stop it. "I mean, I don't actively hate you anymore, but okay."

He slid his glasses back onto his face. "You know what I meant." He leaned forward. "Like *that*."

Pretending to like Brandon wouldn't be a problem. Stopping herself from liking him for real was the real problem. No matter the heartache, some part of her would always care for her former rival turned first love.

But it was only for one night.

"It's one night, that could lead to what you want, right?"

He kept his gaze locked on hers for a heartbeat before he stepped back.

"Right. I'm glad we could agree on this. Let's get a move on. We wouldn't want to keep them waiting."

* * * *

Gabriel and Merit were the best kind of tour guests. They laughed at all the corny jokes and lapped up the town's — only somewhat fabricated — history.

Sabrina added dramatic effect to the stories, appearing behind one of the gravestones in the cemetery at the far side of the Pumpkin's property for a silly spook with her lantern held under her chin when she made an attempt at a ghastly wail.

Brandon jumped — as she'd likely expected him to.

"Sorry, he's a bit of a fraidy cat," Sabrina said. She came around him and leaned up to give him a kiss on the cheek.

Brandon let out a grunt that turned into a cough. Why was she hamming up her role? It was as if she was trying to mess with him just for the hell of it.

Merit gave a satisfied chuckle. "See, I told you, Gabe. These two remind me of us, back when we were in Jefferson Forge."

Brandon blubbered until Sabrina gave his back a pat — likely a reminder that it was easier to lie.

Her kiss was a benign gesture — so why did it make him feel all kinds of alive?

Gabriel gave his wife's shoulder a squeeze. "So, the inn comes equipped with its own graveyard? The new owners would have to care for it, as well?"

Brandon adjusted his cape. "Yes. It's the Blake family graveyard, so some of the other Blakes in town pop in once or twice a month to tidy up the graves. Especially before holidays. But nobody new has been buried here in over eighty years."

His mom hadn't wanted to be buried. Half of her ashes were waiting for him to scatter them in Shenandoah National Park, on his way back to DC. The other half had already been spread in the Pumpkin's rose garden, where they'd long ago scattered Dad's ashes.

He cleared his throat. "It's not something you'd have to worry about if you purchased the inn. Especially if you kept the staff."

"We would," Gabriel said. He and Merit exchanged a glance. "If we purchased the inn, of course."

Brandon turned away and tried not to smile. The Pumpkin would be in good hands with the Westmores. He'd have kept his promise to his mom, while finally being able to get back to his own life.

Or perhaps a new one. He'd been pondering that Paris job offer more than he should. Although Cassandra hadn't been in touch with any further details. Maybe it was time to muster the nerve to search for a mountain lodge property.

"Shouldn't we press on, darling?" Sabrina appeared at his side. She slipped an arm through his. She'd taken the playing up their fake relationship seriously. He took the invitation to slide his arm around her waist. It'd been years since they'd been this close.

Yet, she still made his breath come in stutters and starts.

A thought that quickly passed when she jabbed her thumb into the crook of his arm. They'd paused too long. It was time to get back to the tour.

"Come, follow me, past the cemetery. There's a footbridge. I've heard a rumor there's a troll who lives under it." He turned and led them toward the bridge. Sabrina fell into step next to him, her arm tightly tucked against his body.

"Which type of troll?" Gabriel asked. "The ghastly kind that demands payment for passage or the type to comment 'you look fat in that jumper' under your social media posts?"

All of them laughed again except for Merit, who had fallen a few steps behind.

An odd expression had taken over her face.

"Are you okay, Merit?" Sabrina asked.

"Something isn't right."

Sabrina swept away from Brandon and ran over to Merit. "With the baby?"

Merit managed a weak nod of her head. "I feel a contraction, I think? I don't know, I've never done this before." She bent over and huffed out a hell of a breath. "I should've paid more attention in those birthing classes."

Gabriel swooped around and embraced his wife. She leaned against him.

"I think we should go to the hospital. Just to be sure. It's probably nothing, but…"

"But nothing. We should go. Especially since it's not exactly straight down the road," Gabriel said.

"Do you need any help?" Brandon called out after them.

His inquiry went ignored as they shuffled off. For the second night in a row, the ghost tour ended abruptly.

Chapter Ten

"What's the latest?" Sabrina shoved a pumpkin roll into her mouth.

They had twenty minutes before her crew showed up to begin the first day of work on the interior. She wanted the gossip to keep her mind off her dad's surgery. Even though her mother had assured her the surgeon had done thousands of knee replacements, Sabrina was worried.

She felt like a shitty daughter for not being there, but her father wouldn't hear of it. He was right, since it wasn't like they could afford to hire another contractor to fill in for her.

Brandon sighed and grabbed a roll of his own. "Gabriel called early this morning. He was foggy on the details—rightfully so—but Merit had to have an emergency C-section. The baby is okay, but she's going to be in the NICU for a while. I believe Merit was about seven months pregnant, so the baby is early. They're in Roanoke right now."

Sabrina dropped into her chair. She couldn't imagine giving birth unexpectedly, especially away from home. "But the baby will be okay? And Merit?"

Brandon licked frosting from his fingertips. And as much as Sabrina cared about mother and child, for that moment her mind was one hundred percent elsewhere.

That elsewhere being the gutter. His gaze slid over to hers and she looked away. *Busted.*

He coughed. "Anyway, mother and baby are both okay. Merit is recovering from surgery. The baby's name is Lakyn."

"That's a pretty name." Sabrina paused to chew on the pumpkin roll. "Well, then I guess they'll be heading back to Nashville as soon as Merit recovers, and the baby is well enough to travel. I hope this doesn't upset their plans to potentially purchase the inn."

Their dating charade had ended before it'd even begun. A shame, since it'd been kind of fun.

Brandon dropped into his seat. "I hadn't even thought about that. I hope it doesn't change anything. I mean, this visit was unscheduled, anyway. They weren't planning on visiting until the new year. By then, the baby should be out of the hospital—"

Sabrina swallowed her final bite. "I didn't mean to upset you. It probably won't change anything. They weren't going to buy it until after the work was done. That'll be next year. By then their baby should be thriving. Don't fret, okay? We won't have to pretend anymore. The rumors will die down."

She considered reaching across the table to give his hand a reassuring squeeze. Then she remembered there was no one there to convince that they were anything but client and contractor.

"*Hola, jefa.*" Carlos, her second in command, appeared in the doorway. "Wanna go over the plan for the day?"

Brandon looked over his shoulder. Carlos was the reigning Mr. Autumn—three years running. He was one of the best-looking men in town, and those who didn't think she was dating Brandon thought she was with Carlos. Townsfolk liked to craft their own narratives to fit with the reality they wanted.

"Give me two minutes and I'll meet you in the lobby."

Carlos flashed that pageant smile and retreated.

Her stomach dropped. "Oh, shit, that reminds me. My mom entered me into the Miss Autumn pageant. I figured I should probably tell you, since that's your thing."

He wiped at his mouth with a napkin. "It was my mom's thing. It's just one item to check off of the long list I'm doing to honor her memory before I leave."

"Last item on her bucket list?" She held his gaze.

"No, more like a way to ensure she doesn't haunt my ass. C'mon, let's get started."

* * * *

It took the better part of the morning to clear out the lobby and main areas of the entrance to the Pumpkin. They'd set up a separate front desk area, to the left of the stairs so that guests could check in and make their way to the room, without having to enter the construction site. Babs had insisted on over-decorating the areas that were accessible to the guests. It looked like Tim Burton had barfed all over the lobby.

Not that she'd tell Babs that. She'd likely get a goblin figurine to the side of her head if she tried.

In the meantime, Sabrina received confirmation that her father had come through surgery just fine. He'd be spending the night in the hospital for observation, but then he'd be able to come home.

It was much needed good news. Especially since Brandon was in a nit-picky mood and she was about to flick him between the eyes.

He'd hovered over them, only helping occasionally while they cleared out the lobby.

A reminder that regardless of that handsome outer shell, he was as fussy as the biddies at a Black Friday sale. She tried not to let it get to her, but if she heard him say "pivot" one more time as furniture was being moved around, she'd find a dictionary to wallop him with.

"I think that's lunch," Carlos said. He came up behind her, and whispered in Spanish, "I think lunch is preferable to homicide."

Sabrina laughed, which made the crease between Brandon's brows deepen yet again.

"Are you two talking about me?"

"That would be rude of us, wouldn't it?" Sabrina said. "Sometimes it's easier for Carlos to talk to me in Spanish, right? I mean, especially with these complex construction terms."

That earned an eager nod from her second in command. Even though they both knew Carlos had a fabulous command of the English language — far better than her Spanish — Brandon didn't.

"Yeah, right," Brandon said. "Whatever, I see how you two are."

Ooh, is that a hint of jealousy in Brandon's voice?

"Tell the guys to be back in an hour. We'll go over the plan for the lobby then."

Carlos nodded then left. Sabrina turned to Brandon. "You know I speak Spanish. I wasn't lying when I said sometimes it's easier for me to speak to the crew in their native language."

"You're right. I think I'm just hangry." He gestured to the dining room. "Want to share a bite? Chef Adalyn's broccoli cheddar soup is the lunch special today."

As long as they kept things professional, she didn't see a problem with sharing a meal with her client.

On the way to lunch, they talked about her father's surgery.

"I give him until Monday until he tries to finagle his way over here," Brandon said.

"Hopefully not. I just want him to recover and take his physical therapy seriously."

Knowing her father, it would be a challenge. He never wanted to make a fuss. In turn that made him kind of a pain in the ass when he was forced to do something outside of his comfort zone.

Brandon held the door open for her as they entered the café. They were seated in the corner booth of the dining room, closest to the window facing the street. Brandon gazed out of the window as she looked over the menu.

"Do you know the menu by heart?" She peered at him over the top of it.

"I already told you, I want the special. Half sandwich is a turkey and Brie on sourdough. It can't be beaten."

Sabrina set her menu down. "I'll take your word for it, then."

He turned from the window to face her. "Thanks again for going through with that little...charade last night. We should be able to go back to normal now that the Westmores are leaving."

Any warmth that had been building between them snuffed out like a Jack-o-lantern at the end of the night.

She swallowed down the lump in her throat. "That's not past tense. Have they checked out yet?"

"No. Gabriel mentioned swinging by later today, so I'm sure he'll do it then."

The waitress came by to take their orders. Sabrina pulled out her phone and went through her emails. He did the same.

She wasn't sure how long they'd been sitting there when a posh, British accent roused her from responding to an email.

"Ah, that's how I know it's the real thing." Gabriel leaned over their table and lowered his voice to a conspiratorial whisper. "You're sitting there ignoring each other until the food comes."

If only what Gabriel was saying was true, Sabrina would've laughed. She put on a fake smile. "You speak like a man who knows what he's talking about."

Brandon sputtered and clicked his phone closed. "You're back earlier than expected. I can fetch one of the porters to get your things." He slid out of the booth and gripped Gabriel's hand. "Congratulations on the birth of your daughter."

"Yes, congratulations," Sabrina added.

Gabriel pulled up a chair and sat at the edge of the table.

"Thank you. Although hold off on fetching the porter, if you please. There's something I was hoping I could talk to you about."

Several minutes passed before Brandon could press Gabriel for details. Their drinks and soups arrived, prompting Gabriel to realize he hadn't eaten anything all day, so he placed a lunch order as well, as well as a to-go order for Merit.

Brandon cleared his throat. "What did you want to talk to me about?"

"Ah, that." Gabriel unfurled his napkin and draped it across his lap. "It appears that we'll be in town for a while. Lakyn's lungs aren't as developed as they need to be for us to travel with her back to Nashville. We'd have to get an ambulance and a NICU nurse to tag along. It would be a whole thing." He shook his head. "American healthcare being what it is, we're better off staying put for now."

"Do you need me to find you a place near the hospital in Roanoke? I can call in some favors. I have friends who work in all the hotels there."

"We've got that covered on our end. We found a hotel near the hospital for us and Merit's mother. She's on her way up from Alabama."

"Dear lord, then what is it, man? You're doling out information like you want to torture Brandon," Sabrina reached over to playfully jab Gabriel.

Brandon blanched at her boldness. Thankfully, Gabriel laughed. "Sorry, I don't mean to. The cogs aren't quite working yet. It's been a long morning."

"I understand. I'm just asking on Brandon's behalf." Sabrina smiled at Brandon. He managed a meager smile in return.

He should be grateful she'd fallen so easily into her role as supportive girlfriend.

A dimple deepened on Gabriel's cheek. "Of course." He turned to Brandon.

"I was hoping we could book two rooms for my family. They're scrambling to find flights now, since the baby wasn't due until December."

"We'll help out anyway we can. But why not have them stay in Roanoke? We're nearly forty minutes south."

Gabriel leaned forward. "Because my parents, God bless them, are well meaning but a bit on the smothery side. Having them a bit out of town will be good for all of us."

"Even with the construction going on? As you can see, work's underway," Sabrina said.

Gabriel waved his hand. "Mum and Dad could sleep through the apocalypse. My older sister Bea is the same. They should be fine. I'll warn them ahead of time, as well."

Before Brandon could reply, Gabriel's phone began to trill. He fished it out of his jacket pocket. "That'll be the wife. I'll be right back."

He stood from the table and was no more than five feet away before Sabrina reached over to jab Brandon's arm.

"Does this mean we're gonna have to keep up the charade?"

Shit. He hadn't let himself dwell on their little performance the previous night. Because if he did, he'd grow attached to the idea of them being something. No matter how much he might've liked their closeness, he had to keep a barrier between them.

Because he was leaving. And he'd already broken her heart once.

They had to keep their relationship professional. That's why he'd been stand-offish with her this morning. He'd had no other choice.

But now, if the Westmores were staying around, they couldn't exactly say it was all a lie. The last thing he wanted was for the only potential buyers of the Pumpkin to doubt his honor.

"Um, I guess so? I mean, if that's okay with you. I won't blame you for bailing."

Sabrina sat back in the booth and began eating. Her silence could mean anything.

He took it to mean annoyance. "Look, we'll figure this out. It won't be forever, okay?"

"Everything all right?" Gabriel slid back into his seat.

"Yes, of course," Brandon answered before Sabrina had a chance to.

"Well, the wife wants me back at the hospital as soon as possible, so is it possible to take my lunch to go?"

"Say no more." Brandon waved down the waitress as Gabriel and Sabrina started speaking.

"Which hospital are you at? Community?" Sabrina asked.

"Yes, why?"

"My father is there. He had knee replacement surgery there this morning. I was going to visit him tonight. We could bring you food or stop by if she's up for it. No worries if she's not."

"Oh, that would be nice."

Brandon cut a glance to Sabrina. Would this mean they'd have to make an appearance at the hospital together?

"That settles it, then. I" — she turned to Brandon — "I mean *we'll* stop by to visit this evening."

Brandon nodded. "Yes, of course."

This fake dating scheme was quickly getting out of hand. He should put a stop to it, but part of him didn't want to.

"Anyhow, I think my parents will be happier here than in the city. They live in Cheshire, in England. They like small towns versus big cities," Gabriel said.

"Roanoke isn't London, my friend."

I guess it's not. But I'm sure you and my sister will get on like a house on fire. You both have a rapier wit."

Sabrina chuckled. "I don't know what that means, but I'll take the compliment."

Brandon listened with a rising sense of dread. Playing boyfriend for one night was one thing, stretching this scenario out for weeks was another. Hopefully, for everyone involved, baby Lakyn would be able to be moved home to Nashville sooner rather than later. Keeping up this charade for weeks would do him no good. Not when he was almost free of Falling Leaves forever.

"How long do you think you'll be in Virginia?" Brandon asked.

"Hopefully no more than a week or two at most. But it'll depend on how Lakyn does."

"Well, your family will love Falling Leaves. Everyone will just love their English accents," Sabrina said.

"I'll leave them in your capable hands. And don't worry"—he dropped his voice—"they have a keen understanding of village gossip. I'll tell them about the delicate nature of your relationship."

Their waitress returned with Gabriel's to-go order and soon left.

"So much for a one-night thing," Sabrina said. She quickly blanched — likely realizing the double entendre the same time Brandon did — and ducked her head.

An image of the two of them came to the front of his mind before it dissipated like a pebble skittering across water.

"It'll only be for when the Westmores are around. Hopefully their little one will recover quicker than anticipated and they'll be gone before you know it, with only good things to say to Gabriel and Merit. It'll be a family memory for them. One that might encourage the sale of the inn."

Sabrina reached for her drink. "Gee, don't talk as though pretending we're a thing is akin to a trip to the gulag. I mean, I am helping you out here. I could tell the Westmores the truth. That would really land you in a pickle, huh? Especially with no other interested parties on the line?" She leaned forward.

His eyes widened. Could she be that petty? "You wouldn't."

"You don't know the current version of me well enough to say that. Besides, it wouldn't look good of you to start nosing around for other buyers either. Right? Especially when they seemed so charmed."

She had a point. It was best to keep the Westmores as his main prospect for now. If the sale fell through — well, it couldn't. They were the perfect buyers.

His cheeks flushed. "I didn't mean it like that. This was the last thing I was expecting, is all. I'm grateful for your help. And you're right, it doesn't exactly make sense to make inquiries into other buyers while they're in town."

She finished drinking. "It seems when the two of us get together, the unexpected will always find a way. Quicker you get used to that, the better."

He had no response for that, so he merely picked up his spoon and tried to force down lunch.

* * * *

"I know you don't like hospitals."

Brandon swallowed down his anxious feeling. "That's not true. I don't like *this* hospital. You know why."

At seventeen, Sabrina had been by his side when he'd gotten the devastating news that his father had died. It'd been a terrible shock. He still had nightmares about being in the waiting room while the doctor approached, in slow-motion. His mother had died at hospice. As awful as her death was, he'd known it was coming—unlike his father. It'd been sudden and gutting.

"Well, you've been in and out of hospitals with your mom before she died. This is no different, right?"

He unbuckled his seatbelt. "Can we get it over with? I don't want to think about my parents right now."

"Um, sure. We can move onto another awkward situation if you want. Like how I'd rather you not come up to visit my dad?" She reached around to grab her purse from behind her seat. Her shirt stretched tight across her chest, revealing the swell of her breasts. Brandon jerked his head away.

Hell, why did his brain have to go there *now*? He coughed and tried to think about tile patterns to keep from remembering what was under Sabrina's shirt.

Before he could respond to that request, a knock on the driver's side window had them both bolting upright.

Lainey Ellis waved and motioned for her to unroll the window.

"Ah, shit," Sabrina muttered under her breath. "Hi, Mom. We were just on our way up."

"*We?*" She stretched the word out to several syllables. "This is an interesting development."

Brandon ducked his head against his shoulder.

"Brandon is here to visit business associates who just had a baby. I offered to give him a ride."

Lainey pursed her lips, trying to hide a smile. "That makes sense. Now, come on up. Your daddy wanted fried chicken for dinner. I bought enough for everyone. Help me get it out of the car."

* * * *

An hour later, Lainey finally released them to visit the Westmores. Thankfully, Glen had kept the conversation steered toward the job at the Pumpkin. Sabrina was relieved to not address the elephant in the room.

Even if Lainey beamed at him as if he was an angel descended straight from heaven. This had really gone too far now to turn back.

Soon enough, they'd have to tell the Ellises the truth. Unlike the last time he'd left town, he would stick around to be sure Sabrina didn't bear the brunt on her own. Especially as he was the one who'd dragged her into this.

Brandon excused himself after eating to nip to the gift shop to get the Westmores a gift. When he returned to the room, Sabrina met him in the doorway.

"Thanks for leaving me alone with them. Mom wants to plan our wedding. With the colors blush and bashful, like I'm Shelby in *Steel Magnolias*."

Brandon chuckled. "You can't show up without a gift to meet a new baby."

"Likely story." She closed her father's hospital door behind her. "I already said goodbye for you. Come on, let's get this over with."

His mood was a storm cloud the whole way up to the labor and delivery floor. When they checked in with the nurses, they were informed that the Westmores were in the NICU visiting their daughter. Visiting hours were almost over, so they left the gift in their room with a note. Brandon had been sure to sign Sabrina's name on the card, so the Westmores knew they'd both been there.

"I guess we lucked out," Brandon said. "No more pretending. For tonight, anyhow."

Sabrina stabbed the down elevator button. "What, that I like you?"

The elevator arrived. He filed inside after her. "I just meant it's been a long day. We can go home now." He paused. "Are you pretending to like me?"

She shot an exasperated glance at him over her shoulder. "The whole fake dating thing was meant to be one night. It's quickly getting out of hand. Especially now that my parents are involved."

He nervously tapped through apps on his phone for something to do. "To be fair, it's not like this is out of nowhere. We did date for a year, Sabrina. I was part of the family."

"Sure. Until you left. Funny that we're having this conversation here of all places, huh?"

She didn't need to expand on that thought. Brandon felt like shit for abandoning Sabrina so soon after the death of his father. Clearly, the wound had never quite healed over for her. It had just been easier to leave before the summer. They'd had a whole summer planned out, but he hadn't been able to do it. He'd left a note for his mother, texted Sabrina, and left the day after high school graduation.

Sabrina didn't speak much until they arrived at her truck. When he tried to broach the subject of their dating scheme, she held up a hand.

"My head is full to bursting. Can we talk about whatever it is later?"

The streetlight cast a glow across her face, keeping her half in shadow. Again, he was struck by how beautiful she was.

But this was not the time for that kind of declaration. With the mood she was in, she'd leave him hoofing it all the way back to Falling Leaves. Or at least a mile or two before guilt had her turning around to retrieve him.

"Deal." He pulled his headphones out of his pocket. "I want to listen to my podcast. I'll leave you be."

After inserting his headphones, Sabrina put the truck in drive. As much as she said she didn't want to talk about what they were doing, he caught her looking at him more than once.

Perhaps there was something still there, after all.

Chapter Eleven

"Wait a minute, you're *what?*" Eleanor kicked Sabrina's bedroom door closed, drowning out the hooting and hollering of Dutch and his friends as they played on his gaming console.

"Don't make me say it again. It's like something out of a poorly crafted spy novel," Sabrina said.

Eleanor sat on the bed next to Sabrina. "You're not doing craftwork. You're pretending to date a man that you claim to hate." She waggled her eyebrows and jabbed Sabrina lightly in the ribs. "Emphasis on the word *claim* there, friend."

Sabrina huffed out a breath. "Okay, maybe that's true. But now my parents are full of ideas after that hospital visit." Sabrina scooted away from her. As if moving away from her best friend would keep her from sniffing out the truth eventually. "Any updates on the threatening handkerchief?"

"No. We do have patrol keeping an eye on the Pumpkin. To help ease Brandon's nerves more than anything. I suspect it's nothing but a prank. I've told Brandon as much and given him the information of a local security company to beef security there."

"Hopefully it was just bored teens or something. Lord knows we have an influx of them in town."

Brandon and her brothers had all rattled against the confines of small town life. Sabrina had always favored the slow pace.

Eleanor murmured in a way that told Sabrina she wasn't considering the identity of the prankster. She was about to badger her about Brandon once again.

"So, this fake dating. Will you two be out on the town together? The hospital in Roanoke doesn't count."

Sabrina groaned and stood up. She walked to the window to pet Sarah and Jareth.

The young cats were siblings and had a tight bond. They were snuggled so close together that they appeared like one cat, with two heads.

"The charade was only for the Westmores. But the misunderstanding has gone too far to bring it back now. We thought it would only be for one night. But Brandon really wants them to buy the Pumpkin. They have a stellar reputation. Besides, it's not like he has any other interested parties."

"What of the misunderstanding came from finding you two intertwined on the floor? Is there something else you want to tell me? You just sped past that little bit of information earlier."

"I slipped and fell. He was helping me up when Mrs. Westmore returned for her sweater. He had one hand on my lower back, the other on my face. Our faces were kind of close together too, I guess. It kind of looked like we were kissing." She silently added, *I kind of wish he had.*

"Now this *does* sound like the plot to one of those British mystery shows your mom likes so much," Eleanor said.

"It's the truth." Sabrina patted Sarah's head.

Sarah yawned before nestling her head under her brother's once again.

"Sounds like a likely story." Eleanor came behind her and rubbed behind Jareth's ears.

"Will you let this drop? I'm doing Brandon a favor to save face with the Pumpkin's potential buyers. I could be a bitch and rat him out. But I'm trying to mend fences here. It's not like I have to sleep with him or anything. I'm just trying to keep a client happy."

Even though helping with this ruse meant that there would be nothing left to keep him in town. But maybe then she could finally move on. Let her mother set her up with her dentist, or optician, after all.

Eleanor moved past her to sit in the window seat that overlooked Jackson Street. The Jimenez family across the street were busy decorating their yard for Halloween. Holiday decorating was a bit of a competitive sport in Falling Leaves. The last festival before Halloween involved a tour of all the competitors' homes and a small prize was offered to the best decorated house.

"Funny how your mind went right to that," Eleanor said.

"Ugh, you're like a dog with a bone. Let it drop, woman."

Eleanor threw up her hands. "Fine. But when you two dummies start to realize that this fake relationship is the real deal—you owe me a hundred bucks." She paused. "What did you two talk about on the ride home, anyway? That's a fair amount of time to fill."

"He listened to a podcast. I caught up on an audio book."

Not that she'd paid it much mind, with Brandon distracting her just by existing.

"Hmm, already comfortable with each other, I see."

Sabrina started to protest but Eleanor spoke over her. "Don't argue with me, Sabrina. I know something special when I see it."

Before Sabrina could argue that her friend needed to get her eyes checked, Eleanor quietly slipped out of the door.

Sabrina sighed and ran her hand down her face. Eleanor wasn't completely wrong. Sabrina had enjoyed their little game of pretend last night.

Maybe a little too much. Pretending for an hour or two was one thing. Who knew how long she'd have to keep up the game once the rest of the Westmores arrived. She'd be at the inn all the time with construction underway now.

If there was one thing in their favor — it was that the Westmores understood that their relationship wasn't known to the town. And they'd also had their own secret love affair.

But they would expect the two of them to act like a couple in love. Even if Eleanor was right and there was something between Sabrina and Brandon, what was the point? He would be leaving as soon as the sale of the Pumpkin was final. Sabrina never wanted to leave Falling Leaves, especially not for the big city.

She rubbed Jareth under the chin. "Let's all hope that little baby's lungs develop sooner rather than later."

Because no matter what happened, Brandon would be gone before long.

* * * *

"I know you don't believe in fate, but maybe you should." Cassandra's face flickered on the video call.

"It's not fate, just a coincidence."

"A coincidence that you're headed for DC on the same day that the interviewers for the Paris job will be there? Come on. This is too good."

Perhaps she had a point. He'd hung up from one call from Gabriel—informing him that it would be a disaster if his family drove in America, as they considered anything but the British way of driving the 'wrong way'—when Cassandra had called him about the potential interview.

"I don't have to go pick them up myself. I was considering sending someone for the job."

He had enough to manage at the inn with construction newly underway.

"Hmm, not a good look for your potential buyer's family. You should be there, holding a sign and giving them some of that southern charm right from the get-go. They'll be reporting back to the Westmores, you know that. It's not like you don't have a fancy Ivy League degree and you're not used to dealing with stress. You've been in that hick town for too long."

Brandon rubbed the skin between his eyes. Maybe Cassandra had a point.

"I can see you growing frustrated with me. This is a video call, you know," Cassandra quipped.

He rolled his eyes and set his phone down, so all Cassandra could see was the water-stained ceiling in his office. That earned him a haughty scoff, a sound he'd become too familiar with while they'd dated.

"So, should I tell them you'll be there or not? The Westmores' flight isn't in until six p.m. Your interview would be at noon. Plenty of time to do both."

"But it's tomorrow. I don't have time to prepare. I haven't had time to do any of my usual research—"

"Good," Cassandra said. "They're looking for exactly *you*, Brandon. I don't even know why they're interviewing other candidates. Don't ruin it by overthinking. I'll send you some review questions, and info about your interviewers. We can prep over the phone during the drive."

He picked up the phone again, finding Cassandra's gaze on her computer screen.

"Okay, fine. Confirm the appointment. Happy?"

"You getting that job is what's best for you, Brandon. I'll be happy if you get it."

Brandon snorted. "You'll also get a commission, so I'm sure you're happier for that."

She lowered her glasses to look down at him. "Well, duh. You need to loosen up before tomorrow, Brandon. Go in naturally. They don't want to hear their company practices repeated back to them. Focus on you. And why you're the person for the job."

He wasn't sure that he was, but hey. He'd be in DC anyway, so why not go? If anything, he'd been at Hotel Blaque too long. His interview skills were rusty. This could be good practice.

"All right, I will. Thanks again, Cassie. Or should I say *merci*."

She rolled her eyes before ending the call.

Despite his ex's advice, as soon as her email landed in his inbox, he pored over the information about the meeting and his interviewers. All the information was in French. An extra challenge, as he hadn't said more than *bonjour* in months.

And he didn't exactly have time to practice, with less than twenty-four hours until the interview. He wasn't sure what prompted him, but he opened a search for lodge properties. He left it open to the whole country. He scrolled through the listings. So far, nothing decent east of the Mississippi.

"You look serious." Babs appeared in the doorway. He wouldn't put it past her being in the hallway eavesdropping.

"I want to be sure everything is good to go for the Westmores when they arrive tomorrow."

"How's that little baby doing, then? Any updates?"

"Stable, but she'll be in the NICU for a while, yet." He hadn't asked too many questions. After all, the Westmores were potential buyers, not his buddies.

Babs clicked her tongue against her teeth. "The Coffee and Knitting Society will have to make some cute hats for that sweet little baby."

"You do that." Brandon kept his eyes on his screen, as he mentally started a to-do list for his interview.

"You should take the sedan to pick up the Westmores tomorrow. I'll have Javier drop it off to be detailed."

Brandon spun around in his chair so he was facing Babs. "I never said I was going to pick up the Westmores at the airport."

He kept his eyes focused on her—waiting for her to crack and admit she'd been spying.

Babs merely shrugged. "I assumed you'd want to make a good impression. I'll keep everything under control here. Although there's not that much to do, since we don't have many guests with the construction."

"Work is going ahead on schedule," he said.

At least that's what he'd heard from Sabrina in the brief time they'd spoken this morning. He wasn't avoiding her, exactly. He just didn't want to think too deeply on the fact that the Westmores thought he and Sabrina were a couple. It was a good thing he could throw his nervous energy into this interview.

"I know. This place won't crumble without you for one day. Besides, you've hardly left town since well before your mom died. It'll do you good to get out for a while."

He braced himself for a barb, but none came. She turned and left without another word. He had no more than a minute to marvel on that little miracle before Sabrina appeared in the doorway.

His breath caught at the sight of her. Her hair was pulled up into a high ponytail. A tendril at the front had come free, and little bits of sawdust clung to it. She'd removed her boots and work overalls, and was wearing just a long-sleeved tee and jeans. A sign that the work had been completed for the day.

He angled his watch to face him. Right on schedule, too.

"You need anything before I head out? Mom wants me to play dress-up in pageant gowns tonight." She heaved a sigh and rolled her eyes.

He had that to look forward to—seeing Sabrina in her pageant best.

"Ah, yes. The first meeting on the pageant is on Friday, isn't it?" He flicked forward the pages in his planner.

"Unfortunately. I better get all the good daughter points in the world for this."

He closed his laptop. "Let me walk you out."

She side-stepped out of the doorway, and he followed behind her. He'd hardly left his office all day, so as they pushed through the plastic sheeting, his mouth dropped open at the sight.

"Wow, you have been busy today."

"We don't mess around. Each segment of this project has a deadline, and we aim to hit each one."

Carpet had been torn up in the entryway and stairs. Several floorboards underneath had rotted out and been replaced.

"Oh, I wanted to show you something." She led him to the front entryway and pulled back a board. "Look at this original penny round tile, hiding under the carpet!"

He knelt next to her and ran his fingers over the tile. Black tile boarded the edges, with white and gray tiles making up the rest of the design. He stuck his finger into a divot where a tile was missing.

"Do you think we could match it?"

"Maybe. But even if we couldn't, my tile guy could salvage what he could and make a new design. I think this adds a real charm to the inn."

He rose to standing. "I agree. It must've been covered up years ago, as I don't remember it."

She brushed off her hands on her jeans. "All the more reason to bring it back."

Brandon looked around at the bare walls. Javier stood at the make-shift reception desk, gossiping with Adalyn about something.

"I wanted to ask you one more thing." Sabrina motioned for the door.

They stepped out into a humid early October afternoon. Sabrina rolled up her sleeves before unlocking her truck. She pressed the ignition start and turned on the AC full blast.

Brandon angled his face to get some of the cool air.

"The Westmores are arriving tomorrow? At least that's what Babs told me."

She dabbed at her hairline with the back of her hand. The way her head tilted back and her eyes closed gave Brandon the kind of ideas that were hard to shake out of his head.

He cleared his throat. "Yeah. I'm driving up to Dulles to pick them up. We should be back late."

She opened her eyes. "We'll make sure the lobby is tidied so they have a clear path to their rooms."

"I'd appreciate it, thanks."

She turned to him. There was an awkward pause before she spoke. "Let me know when you need me to keep up my end of the charade. I'm assuming Gabriel and Merit have told them everything?"

He shrugged. "I honestly don't know. I was planning on feeling them out on the drive home."

She nodded. "Hopefully this charade won't be elevated to a spectacle. Let me know what you need from me." She reached for the door handle, and he took a step back as she got in.

"Thanks again for your help." He swallowed. "With everything."

"Of course. See ya tomorrow."

She closed the door and drove out of the Pumpkin's circular drive.

He was grateful she was willing to go along with this fake relationship. She had nothing to gain by helping him. She was only doing this because he was her client.

Nothing more. He'd have to try tattooing that statement to the inside of his eyelids, so he'd see that every time he closed his eyes.

Instead of imagining Sabrina sweaty and breathless for an altogether different reason.

He grunted with disgust at himself and headed back into the Pumpkin. He had enough to keep his mind occupied without thinking about Sabrina.

Chapter Twelve

"If you pull that face one more time, it's gonna freeze that way." Lainey sighed and walked around Sabrina.

Sabrina liked to think she had nerves of steel, seeing as her profession had high stakes. So why did her mother's sigh unnerve her like nothing else?

She stood on a dressmaker's pedestal in the middle of her parents' living room. Like she was a kid again, and her mother was making her dress for church.

Only this time there wasn't time for her to make a dress—well, that wasn't true. Lainey Ellis could make a dress in half a day better than nearly anyone else. But not a *pageant* dress. So, she'd gone up to Roanoke and bought out half the stores there. Like this was Miss America instead of a pageant in a small-to-middling size town in southwest Virginia.

This burnt-orange monstrosity washed out Sabrina's pale skin and made her look like a walking corpse. If she had darker coloring, perhaps it would work better. When she told her mother that, she ignored the jibe.

"I just don't know what I'm gonna do about your bosom." Her mother prodded Sabrina's boob.

"Mom, seriously." She swatted Lainey's hand away. It wasn't like she was self-conscious about her curves. Her mother wasn't even trying to shame her for them. She was just being practical as always. In the pageant world, you couldn't be too 'vulgar' with your necklines. Especially if your bust was on the bigger side.

"She gets her big bust from your side of the family, Glen."

Her father ruffled his newspaper. "Can we stop talking about the bosom size of my daughter and relatives, please?"

Earnhardt howled, as if to emphasize the point. That caused Petty to join in. It took a minute to settle the dogs down once they got started. Sabrina gave them each a rawhide and they settled in on their dog beds.

"Go change," Lainey said.

Sabrina stepped off the pedestal and walked over to her father. "You doing okay, though?"

He managed a gruff nod. "Bored out of my damn gourd, but other than that I'm just peachy."

"I told him to get one of those e-readers. You can make the print as big as you need! But he was being stubborn about it, as usual."

"Paper books suit me just fine." Her father took off his glasses and smiled at her. "I'm glad things are going well with the Pumpkin job site. I was worried about leaving you and Brandon alone. But you two seem to be getting on like a house on fire."

Lainey appeared over Sabrina's shoulder. "If the rumors I'm hearing are true, that young man is going to need to come over here for dinner soon. It's not right if y'all are dating without a formal introduction."

Sabrina reached around to tug at the side-zip of her dress. "You've known him since he was seven years old, Mother." The stubborn zip refused to budge.

"It's been a while since I've known him as my daughter's boyfriend." She chuckled to herself.

Sabrina's heart seized at that imagery. "He's not my boyfriend. Jesus, this town has too much time on its hands. And that includes the two of you. We're working together. That's it."

"Well, you went to great lengths to avoid him for years, darlin'," her father said. "Then you showed up at the hospital together. You can't help people for thinking what they want."

"I can and I will," Sabrina muttered. "Damned busybodies."

"Go change." Lainey swatted her again. "And watch your language."

Sabrina grumbled on her way to the bathroom. She slipped off the dress, making sure the tag was still on before returning it to the hanger.

"Try on that one next! With the appliqués! Third garment bag on the rack," Lainey called from the other side of the door.

With a description like that, Sabrina was expecting a 1980's monstrosity. She braced herself as she pulled down the zipper and tugged the dress free. Despite her not being the girly-girl daughter her mother wanted, Sabrina could still appreciate the finer feminine things in life.

This dress was it. She pulled it out of the garment bag. Mounds of autumn-hued tule sprang free. Along the bodice and bottom of the dress was beautiful lace and sequin appliqués in the same shades of dark orange to deep red. Unlike the previous dress, it suited her pale complexion and blonde hair perfectly.

She never would've chosen this dress for herself—it was way too poofy and ornate—but her mother had a keen eye for these sorts of things. She'd likely already squirreled away a wedding dress for Sabrina somewhere in the attic.

Because they both knew if it were up to Sabrina, she'd elope. But if she did have a big wedding, she would never wear an ugly dress.

"What's taking so long?" Lainey called.

"Coming, Mother." She slipped on the dress, taking care not to crush the tule. She reached behind her to struggle with the zipper. She couldn't make any progress beyond the small of her back.

"I'm stuck."

The door opened and immediately closed again. Lainey exhaled a breath. She brought her hands to her face.

"Oh my, I just knew this was the one."

"It won't be the one if it doesn't zip up."

Her mother leaned over and tugged at the zipper. "Ah, it's just caught. There we go."

The zipper made its way up her back. "Let me look at you."

Sabrina turned toward the mirror. She smiled despite herself.

"I don't see how anyone else could outshine you. You look amazing. Even with sawdust in your hair." Lainey reached up and tugged Sabrina's hair out of the ponytail. "There we go." She pulled her hair forward, so it cascaded down the front of the dress. "You'll need to get your hair and nails done before the pageant."

"If I have time."

Her mother leaned over her shoulder. "We'll make time. Now, come on out and show your dad. And I'll need to make some adjustments to the dress before the pageant, so don't go rushing out the door just yet."

Sabrina sighed and scratched at where the zipper met her skin. "I like the dress, Mom. Thanks."

Lainey caught her gaze in the mirror. "Thank you for doing this for me, sweetie. Your brothers will be here in time for the pageant, and it just means so much to have y'all here together. It's like a dream come true."

"Not for me," her father said. "The only way I can get those boys back to Virginia outside of Christmas is for me to go under the knife." He blinked at Sabrina's reflection. "You look lovely, darlin'. Maybe you can catch yourself a man yet."

"Ugh, stop it. Come on, Mom. Make your measurements and let me leave before I change my mind."

They all knew it was an idle threat, but her mother complied. Even as her mother prodded her with pins and jotted measurements down on a pad, Sabrina's thoughts wandered. She wondered what Brandon would think on pageant night, with her dressed up like a dream.

Then she remembered what happened the last time she'd been dressed up—with Brandon at her side. Her smile faded.

The sooner this charade was over, the better.

* * * *

Ten minutes into the interview, Brandon felt certain he'd landed the role. Even with his out of practice French, Jacques and Penny were obviously impressed by him. So much so that their one-hour interview soon stretched out to two, as they talked about their industry contacts, Brandon's work history and eventually, his plans to sell the Pumpkin.

His brain leapt forward — imagining a charming little apartment in the sixteenth arrondissement near where the Hotel Ford was located.

When he stated that his start date would depend on when the Pumpkin sold, Penny's smile dropped slightly.

"Do you think that will be before the new year? We'd really love to have you in Paris right after Christmas. It'll take time to get you settled before the position begins. The current employee is retiring on the first of January."

Brandon licked his lips and considered the answer. After a slight pause, he could come up with no better answer than, "I'm not sure. I have prospective buyers who are very interested. But the renovation work won't quite be finished by then."

Jacques and Penny exchanged a look. Brandon's cock-sure attitude vanished. Had he been over-confident, thinking this job was in the bag? It wasn't like he had a decent plan B, except for returning to Hotel Blaque. Now, he wasn't even sure that was a sure thing. His boss had been rather curt in his last email, asking when Brandon could be expected back.

"It's not a deal-breaker. The latest we'd be able to push this would be the first week of January. Enrique — the current night manager — will be returning home to New York then."

Under the table, Brandon wiped his sweaty palms on his trousers. "I'll work to ensure that the potential buyers are hooked, then. As a matter of fact, I'm running an errand for them straight after I leave here."

"That personal touch is important," Jacques mused. "What sort of errand are you completing for them?"

"Picking up their family at Dulles. The Westmores are flying in from England to see their new granddaughter."

Penny cocked a brow. "Merit and Gabriel Westmore are your potential buyers? Well, that's interesting. I know they're very hands-on. They wouldn't have visited your property at all unless they were very serious."

He nervously jogged his knee under the table. "Ah, you know them?"

"Of course," Penny said. "I worked with them, years ago, in London." She closed her laptop and stood, taking Brandon by surprise.

"Do what you have to do to make this sale happen, so you can be in Paris no later than the New Year, and you can consider this job yours." She extended her hand.

Brandon stood and fumbled to get his hand out to shake hers. "When would you need to have an answer by? The Westmores have a lot on their plate with their daughter in the NICU. I'm not sure they'll be looking to buy quite that soon."

Jacques rose to standing as well. "We don't have opportunities like this arise very often. You know it can be difficult for Americans to land positions in Europe now."

He nodded. "I understand. I'll keep you in the loop and get back to you as soon as possible."

Jacques gave Brandon's hand a firm shake. "We'll get the employment contract over to Cassandra to look over. But we really will need an answer one way or another no later than Halloween. If you don't think the sale will go through by then, we'll go with our second-choice candidate."

"It's not fair to keep them on the hook forever, you see," Penny added.

"Of course." Brandon's phone beeped. He snuck a look at it.

"It was wonderful to meet you. I hope we'll be seeing you in Paris," Penny said.

"Wow the Westmores so you can work with us in the City of Lights," was the last thing Jacques said before leaving.

Brandon stood alone in the conference room and exhaled. While he would've been happy enough to return to DC, this job was a dream come true. Or at least he thought it was. He'd always wanted to work outside the US. But he was starting to wonder if what he'd always wanted matched up with what he wanted now.

Either way, he needed to get out of Falling Leaves. That meant doing whatever it took to convince the Westmores to buy the Pumpkin before Halloween.

Chapter Thirteen

Sabrina had just put in her night guard and pulled back the covers to settle in with a good book when her phone buzzed. She groaned. It was only nine o'clock, but everyone who mattered knew she went to bed early. Besides, she'd satisfied her daughterly duties and left her parents' house after dinner. Eleanor was working, and she could tell by the chainsaw-like snores filtering through the vents that even Dutch had called it an early night.

She sighed and reached for her phone and found an all-caps message from Brandon. A stickler for etiquette and grammar, this was very out of character.

THE WESTMORES ARE JET LAGGED, DRUNK AND SINGING SHOW TUNES TO BLOW OFF STEAM. THEY'VE LURED THE STAFF INTO THEIR MADNESS. HELP ME.

Sabrina snorted out a laugh. Instead of texting, she phoned him. He picked up on the second ring. Before he could get a chance to speak, she could hear the off-key strains of one of the songs from *Cabaret* in the background.

"Sabrina? Hello?"

She popped out her night guard and set it in the case. "Hey there, Brando. How's it hanging?"

The singing faded slightly as a door closed behind him. "Just peachy keen, Sabby. Hence my SOS text." The last sentence came out in a harassed whisper.

Sabrina lay back against her pillow and rubbed Jareth's head. "You have a degree from an Ivy League school, Brando. You should be able to handle a few drunk Brits. Especially ones that I'm sure are just looking to blow off a little steam after a stressful couple of days."

He sighed. "It's been a hell of a long day, Sabrina. I need reinforcements. Besides, they're asking about you. They were surprised you weren't part of the welcoming committee. I had to make excuses."

"I would've if you'd asked."

Even though she'd much prefer keeping this little fake dating scheme to as few falsehoods as possible, she understood her role. One dutiful girlfriend, on order, for the duration of their stay.

"Please," Brandon said. "I'll double your daily number of pumpkin rolls."

"All right. No need to increase my ration of pumpkin rolls. My mom will be livid if I can't fit into my pageant dress."

"You got the dress already?" His voice dropped an octave, making her heart take a tumble.

It was kind of sexy, as much as she hated to admit it. Like they were sharing a secret. In a way, they were.

She cleared her throat. "I can only stay an hour or so. Unless you want construction to fall behind schedule. This timeline is tight as it is."

His reply was immediate. "No, I definitely don't want that."

"Give me fifteen minutes and I'll be there."

The background chorus started in on another Broadway hit.

"Make it ten and I'll owe you forever."

He ended the call. Sabrina leapt out of bed and pulled her hair down. She tugged on the closest thing she had to fancy in her wardrobe — an oversized shirt dress, tights and boots. After brushing her hair and slapping on some mascara and lip gloss, she hightailed it over to the Pumpkin.

It was easier to walk than drive — especially as all the busybodies would surely remark on her pickup truck being parked in front of the Pumpkin during off hours for the second night in a row.

As she turned onto Silver Spring Street, the Pumpkin came into view. Well, more the flickering gas lamps at the entrance. The inn was hard to spot in the dark, with its all-black paint. She pondered talking to Brandon about changing the paint colors. When the house was originally designed, it'd been painted black, dark purple and green. Another item to add to her ever-growing to-do list.

They'd moved onto Billy Joel by the time she arrived. She peered in, finding a harried Brandon staring back at her through the lobby window. He jabbed at the door with his index finger.

The old front door creaked open as they started in on another song. The Westmores had to be at the parlor, on the other side of the ground floor, yet it sounded as though they were in the room.

Brandon rounded the corner at the chime of the bells on the front door. He stopped in his tracks at the sight of Sabrina. Their eyes met. For a second, Sabrina wondered if he might make a move.

Then, he stomped over to her and took her hand. "Took you long enough."

She threaded her fingers through his. "You should be grateful I'm here at all," she hissed back.

"Oh, is that our Sabrina?" a posh female voice called.

"Maybe you should pretend you like me, Brandon," Sabrina said.

At the sound of approaching footsteps, he tightened his grip on her hand. A gesture that was hardly romantic. She nudged his hand to the side and slipped her fingers through his.

He exhaled a long breath and cut a glance at her. She managed a smile. "You're welcome, Brando."

"Why, hello there!" Despite the peeling paint on the woodwork that stretched across the doorframe and the shabby look of the parlor, Mrs. Westmore appeared as though she stepped out of a fashion magazine.

"Sabrina dear, I'm Jasmine Westmore. Gabriel's mum."

"And mine too," another voice said. "Hi, I'm Beatrice, but never call me that under penalty of death. I'm Bea to everyone." She hiccupped, then burped. "Sorry, we're all a little pissed right now."

"Manners, Beatrice," Jasmine chided her daughter.

"Pissed?" Sabrina ventured.

"She means drunk, my dear." Gabriel's father extended a hand. "I'm George Westmore. Nice to meet you. I've heard so much about you."

"Sorry I wasn't here to greet you," Sabrina said. "I have a busy day of renovations starting early in the morning. I'm afraid I can only stay for one drink."

"How about a drink and a song, then?" Bea said.

Sabrina didn't have much of a choice as Brandon led her into the parlor. "How's baby Lakyn doing?"

Jasmine held a hand to her chest. "We took a video call with Gabriel and Merit from the car. Poor darling is so small, but the prognosis is good. She just may need to stay in the NICU for a few weeks until her lungs are fully formed. She's such a tiny thing." Jasmine wiped a tear from her cheek.

"I can imagine it's been a hard couple of days for you."

"Oh, it was," Beatrice said. "We were expecting to come at Christmas and stay a few weeks. Now everything is up in the air."

They arrived in the parlor, where Babs, Adalyn, Javier and a few of the dining room staff were gathered around the piano.

"Oh, Sabrina's here! I've got just the number for you." Babs began to play the beginning chords of *Tomorrow* from *Annie*. "You have the best pipes of any of us here!"

Because of course Babs had to be here—director of the Falling Leaves community playhouse. Even though it'd been nearly twenty years since Sabrina had played the titular role. The words were still tattooed in her brain.

"Uh, my range isn't quite what it used to be," Sabrina said. "I don't know if I can hit the high notes."

"Don't pressure her, Babs. Maybe we should call it a night. Sabrina needs to be back here in a few hours for work. The Westmores need some rest before they go to the hospital," Brandon said.

Babs sighed and stopped playing. "You probably have a point. But you need to warm up those pipes for the Miss Autumn pageant, Sabrina. I know your mother is gonna want you to sing for the talent portion."

Before she could lament about embarrassing herself in front of the town's populous, Brandon gave her arm a reassuring pat. "I'm sure you'll only embarrass yourself a little. It's not like you'll win."

The Westmores stared at the two of them openly. It didn't take an idiot to realize why. They were supposed to be madly in love. And while *she* knew that he meant she likely didn't have a chance at the title since Angela Jamison had won Miss Autumn three years in a row, the Westmores didn't.

Brandon soon melted under the weight of their stares. "I, uh, only meant that we have a running Miss Autumn who's a bit of a big shot on the state pageant circle. She's hard to beat."

Jasmine Westmore blinked slowly. "Oh, that's much better than insulting your girlfriend in front of a room full of people, hmm?"

Sabrina stifled a laugh. She liked Jasmine.

"Girlfriend?" Babs' mouth dropped open. "Since when are you and Sabrina dating?"

Brandon's face reddened like he'd come down with the hives. A memory of their childhood flashed — of him being anxious at a game of spin the bottle at a party in middle school. He'd broken out in hives then, too.

Like their childhood, when she'd saved him from a punch from the class bully, Sabrina realized she'd have to step in and do something. It was important that the Westmores believed this lie. They'd gone too far to come back now.

"Oh, be nice to the poor guy. He's just had a very long day. We have our own secret language. I knew what he meant." She leaned forward and quickly kissed Brandon. It was no more than a brushing of her lips against his. So why did she feel like she'd stuck her finger in an electric socket? He went rigid, then quickly relaxed. If she didn't know better, she'd swear the rush of hives had decreased from angry red to a more sedate blush pink.

Not that she was spending time looking at his skin. Especially not the bit of russet hair sticking out from the top of his collar.

It wasn't as if this was their first kiss. No, that was half the problem. She was well familiar with the fact that she'd enjoyed kissing Brandon, once upon a time.

Noise erupted in the room. The Westmores let out a collective *aww*, while the staff all began to whisper amongst themselves.

"We'll head up to our rooms now," George said. "Just confirming we'll have a car to take us to the hospital tomorrow morning at ten?"

Brandon cleared his throat. "Of course. You remember how to get to your rooms?"

"Yes, yes. Thank you all for a lovely evening. It really helped take our minds off things," Jasmine said.

Beatrice followed her parents out of the room. As soon as they were out of ear shot, Brandon closed the parlor door.

"Nobody leave."

In the course of roughly two days, one misunderstanding had now spiraled into a lie as large as the room. It was one thing to convince the Westmores that they were dating, it was quite another to have to keep up the charade in front of the staff. He turned around and faced his staff and Sabrina. He had to nip this in the bud, right now. No matter what the Westmores thought, he had enough going on to have to worry about who he had to pretend to be dating Sabrina in front of. He'd never been much of a liar. The longer this went on, the worse it would be. For both him and his skin — he'd need to see the dermatologist if he kept breaking out in hives.

Sabrina's gaze was at her feet. She looked lovely, with her blonde hair cascading across her face. He'd hardly had a moment to register the fact that she'd kissed him. Now, as he took her in, his temper settled.

"What's going on? Are you and Sabrina dating?" Javier asked.

"Again?" Babs asked, just to twist the knife a little to the left.

"Again?" Adalyn repeated. "I thought you two hated each other."

Sabrina raised her head. She pushed her hair back from her face. "We dated. In high school."

"Oh, that actually explains a lot," Adalyn said. "I'm surprised no one mentioned it before."

"Because us old-timers know better. Well, usually," Babs said. "I've had a bit too much to drink and my tongue is freer than usual."

Sabrina wouldn't look at him. It was as if she thought he was going to repeat his biggest regret all over again — failing to realize how important she was.

They may not be dating this time around, but he could still make it up to her.

How, he didn't know. He just knew he couldn't leave here with regret weighing heavy in his heart.

Then maybe those occasional dreams would stop. The one where her tortured expression would repeat on his mind on a loop. Besides, he and Sabrina knew the truth.

He stepped forward and took Sabrina's hand. "All the more reason that we're taking this slow. So, please, keep it under your hat."

"We're in the business of hospitality," Adalyn said. "We're used to minding our own business."

Sabrina surprised him by giving his hand a squeeze. He interlaced his fingers with hers and exhaled a sharp breath.

Babs chuckled as she stood from behind the piano. "I hate to break it to you, kiddo, but that ship has sailed. The whole town knows." She crossed the room and clapped a hand on his shoulder. "At least now you can stop pretending, huh?"

She opened the door and ushered the rest of the staff out, leaving Sabrina and Brandon alone.

"Well, that didn't go as I planned," Brandon said.

"I should've stayed home," Sabrina grumbled. "Now this lie is even more out of hand. It's like trying to herd ten cats into a box."

That decade-old hurt passed across her face.

"Oh, hell," he muttered. He had to make this right. He reached for her hand. "I'm sorry, Sabrina. You know I never wanted this."

Her sorrowful expression deepened. "Tell me about it. You're going to have to get better at pretending. Especially if the Westmores get a hint that you're lying, it won't exactly be a good look for you. They'll doubt your credibility and start to wonder what else you're lying about. You want to keep your best buyer prospect on the hook, right?"

She didn't quite meet his eyes when she spoke. A tell that let him know she wasn't exactly being honest.

"You forget I know you better than you think." He tugged on her hand, and before he even knew what he was doing, she was in his arms.

Chapter Fourteen

"What are you doing?" Sabrina ducked out of the way before he could kiss her. There was no way she'd end up like a broken-hearted seventeen-year-old. No, now she was nearly thirty and knew a hell of a lot better.

"You told me I should try to act like I give a damn. This is me, trying."

She pushed him off her. "I meant when people were around. You don't need to convince me of anything when it's just the two of us. This isn't real, remember?" She turned away from him and shook out her arms. Though being close to him wasn't exactly a new sensation—especially since starting their fake dating escapade—this was different.

This almost felt real. She shot a glance at him over her shoulder. "I should go. Let's just pretend this never happened, okay?"

He started to speak, then stopped himself. Eventually, he crossed the room. "I'm not a kid anymore, Sabrina. I was surprised you still held a grudge when I returned. Remember how mean you were to me?"

"Mean to you? Like when you showed up after being away for nearly three years and wanted to make nice, that summer we were both home from college? Like you didn't vanish without even a goodbye?"

He'd shown up at her parents' house. Her older brothers had told him to shove off without even letting him plead his case.

Her face stormed over. "Besides, if that was true, would I be helping you out? Hell, I would've told my dad that I wasn't willing to work on this job, period. Let alone open my old wounds to pretend to be your girlfriend." She started to speak before she quickly looked away as if there was something she wasn't quite ready to say.

He hissed out a sigh. "I never meant to hurt you. But we both know I'm not meant for this town. I'll never be happy here."

She whipped back to face him, chin jutted up. "I doubt I'd be happy anywhere else. There's no point in rehashing this. It's not like we're dating for real. This is all a lie. Mostly for your benefit, but also mine. Ellis & Daughter need the work."

Brandon reached out to touch her shoulder. "Is the business in trouble?"

She exhaled. "It's slow, this time of year. With Dad on the mend, we can't exactly book a ton of jobs."

She ran her hand over her face. "I'm hoping the renovation will go well. Then I can lure in more clients looking for this kind of renovation work. I want to expand the business beyond Falling Leaves. Starting with having an actual office space. But Dad won't hear about it while we can use a space for free at the hardware store."

"Your dad is being stubborn, then?"

Sabrina groaned. "Dad's in denial. Or maybe he isn't, since he was the one who tricked me into taking this job. This next year is going to mean a change for the business, no matter what."

"All the more reason for you to help me out, huh? So, you can have a glowing client reference and add to your portfolio?"

Why did he have to go there? Bringing everything back to business when she'd opened herself up, just a bit? "Yeah, sure. I'm going to go."

She turned the knob on the door. It opened no more than a crack before his palm pressed it closed again.

"Did you ever think that this might be a way for us to move past this? See what might've been?" He reached forward to touch her cheek. "We both know there's something more between us — that's far beyond pretending to date to protect our interests. Your act wouldn't be so convincing, otherwise." He pushed her hair back from her face. "Not everything has to be forever, you know."

She shifted so she was looking at him directly. "I'm a better actress than you give me credit for." Her gaze stayed steely until he traced his finger from her cheek to behind her ear. Then, her mask slipped out of place.

She sighed and her eyes fluttered shut for a second. "This is just an act. I'm not interested in rehashing the past more than I already have. Especially not for some short-term fling. You should know me better than that. Now if you'll excuse me."

She pulled the door open and brushed past him. She half-expected him to give chase.

Instead, he merely called after her, "You're not as convincing as you think you are, Sabby. See you in the morning."

Her reply came in the form of a middle finger, held aloft.

She hardly registered the walk home. Her traitorous brain repeated every second she'd spent alone with Brandon in the parlor.

It was already a disaster to allow herself to grow close to him. She'd help him out with his little fallacy. Only because the sooner he got out of town—for good, this time—the sooner she could fully move on.

And maybe, one day, find a man who made her feel half as alive as he did.

* * * *

"I hear you're pretty much a shoo-in," Cassandra said.

Brandon lay in bed and took off his glasses. "They liked me well enough. They just want to be sure that the Pumpkin will be sold by the time that they want me in Paris."

"Well? Won't it be? The renovations started this week, right?"

"Yeah. So far, so good. I hope everything will go as planned."

"You and me both. You should tell everyone about your job on the line to be sure they finish in time." Her voice crackled across the line. She'd called him on the way to some posh party in Georgetown. The same sort of party he'd been dragged along to when they'd been dating. Despite spending years surrounded by fancy people, both in his Ivy League university and working in cities like New York and DC after college, he preferred to spend his downtime away from that circle.

Too much keeping up with the Joneses.

"I don't know about that," he said. So far, he'd told no one about his potential job in Paris. Babs might've overheard him talking about it on the phone, but if she had, she'd remained mum. He was a private person. Another trait Cassandra didn't quite understand. She was the woman who'd openly discussed her sex life online.

"Oh, fine. Just make sure the inn sells, Brandon. Because I heard a bit of news that ups the ante a bit."

"Here I thought you were just calling to check in on me after my interview."

She couldn't answer right away, as a car with booming bass drove by. The chatter of passersby blended in with the noise until she returned to the line.

"Yes, that *was* the main reason of my call. But secondarily—when's the last time you checked in with your boss at the Hotel Blaque?"

"I don't know, a few weeks. I've been sending Jamal emails to keep him updated. Although he's been a bit brusque with the responses, if I'm to be honest."

Brandon should be keeping his old job safe and warm. He had a good salary, a nice condo, and a chance for advancement. It was never going to be his dream.

"Well, rumor is that they're putting out feelers to replace you."

Brandon's stomach dropped. Given Cassandra's position as a recruiter in the hospitality industry, she was usually the first to know this sort of gossip.

"I guess it's not that surprising. I've been gone for over six months."

"Perhaps they're just looking around at possible candidates. It wouldn't be a bad thing, for them to be prepared. After all, you could decide to stay in that little hovel."

"Not a hovel, but I'm still not staying," Brandon retorted. Paris wasn't a sure thing. Neither was his mountain lodge dream. Nothing new had popped up in his property search results. Finding a property would be like finding a needle in a needle stack. He should check in with his boss, just in case. The more back-up plans he had, the better.

"Anyway, if I were you, I'd be honest with Jamal about your plans. Paris isn't a sure thing, but you know how small our industry is. Better he hears the news from you."

"Then if Paris falls through, I don't get that job and lose my current one?"

Maybe that wouldn't be a bad thing, his inner dreamer piped up. *You could go after the mountain lodge.*

He shook off that thought.

"Brandon." His name came through as clear as a bell. "I'll help you find a job if it comes to that. Hell, did you forget that you could even start your own hotel if you wanted to? The inn's going to sell for over a million, right?"

He looked at the ceiling. "Yeah, but it's not all profit. There's still a mortgage. I also have student loans." He tapped his finger against his chin. "There's also a condition in the will."

"Go on," Cassandra prompted.

Brandon sighed. "Mom knew me well enough to know that I'd probably just invest the money I earned. So, there's a condition that I won't receive any money from the sale until after the estate is settled. That could take up to a year. I just had my first meeting with the estate attorney last week."

"All the more reason to sell as quickly as you can and get out of dodge. In the meantime, check in with Jamal. Don't burn any bridges, okay?"

Sometimes Cassandra could talk to him in such a condescending manner that it made him want to scream. It was one of the main reasons they'd realized they were far better as friends than lovers.

"Fine, I hear you. Let me know if you hear anything about Paris or my job being replaced."

They ended the call, then Brandon prepared for bed.

As soon as his mind wasn't occupied by work, his thoughts shifted to Sabrina.

She was a horrible place for his thoughts to linger. Babs bringing up his shared history with Sabrina had him remembering a spring evening, over ten years ago now.

The day he'd ended things with a text. Telling Sabrina that he didn't see much of a point in continuing their relationship when he left for Ithaca. A total one-eighty turn from their last conversation.

He took off his glasses and turned on the shower. While he laid out a fresh towel, he considered just how wrong he'd been.

He'd never dated anyone seriously in school. Cassandra had been his one and only serious girlfriend aside from Sabrina. If things hadn't ended before they'd really gotten a chance to begin. After years of circling each other like vultures around a fresh kill, they'd given into temptation the December of senior year.

That year, before the death of his father, had been the happiest of his life.

He stepped under the shower and sighed as the warm water cascaded down his back and shoulders.

Sabrina had thought him cruel to end things out of the blue. Although to him, it hadn't been. His father had passed away less than three months before. Before his death, he'd told Brandon to go for what he wanted, not to stay in Falling Leaves if it wasn't what he'd wanted.

He'd been the one to push him to apply to his dream school. Brandon was still heavily in student loan debt, but he'd never take back his years in Ithaca.

Even though they'd cost him Sabrina.

He swept water out of his face and reached for his shampoo.

As far as Brandon knew, Sabrina had had a string of flings. No real contenders.

Which is why it'd surprised him when she'd treated him like a plague rat when he'd returned to town to help care for his mother. When he'd laid eyes on her for the first time in years his heart had leapt up his throat and nearly out of his mouth. She was more beautiful now than ever.

She had no such feelings about him. Or if she did, she kept them to herself.

He exhaled as he worked shampoo through his hair. He had to make it right with Sabrina. She may never forgive him, but maybe if they talked it out, she could finally understand where he was coming from.

Maybe then, they could both finally move on. Even if their relationship never moved from fake to something real.

Chapter Fifteen

A downside to having an office above a hardware store was the inevitable noise.

Sabrina flung open the door and called down the stairs. "It's a bit early for the herd of elephants to be making their way through, isn't it?"

Her uncle laughed. Her cousin appeared at the bottom of the stairs with a rude hand gesture.

"Didn't I tell you to get some ear plugs if it bothers you so much?" Dennis said. "Perhaps a white noise machine?"

She returned the hand gesture and slammed the door. She'd have to talk to her dad about getting a real office one day. Because as much as the free rent was nice, this wasn't a fitting place to meet clients.

Her backside slammed back into her chair, and her thoughts were already as muddled as a bowl of alphabet soup. Her cell began to ring. She looked over at the display and groaned.

The last thing she needed was a phone call from her older brother to add insult to injury.

Sabrina and Sebastian had never gotten along. Nearly eight years older than her, he'd always seen her as something as a daughter versus a sister. She was far closer with her middle brother, Caleb. He was more like her, where Sebastian was fussy, just like their mother.

She pushed aside her coffee cup and answered the call. "You're up early. It must be, what, three a.m. there?"

"I just got off a phone call with Tokyo. Finance keeps all hours."

"Finance keeps all hours," she mocked her brother. "You've been in California too long. Your job isn't that important. You just move money around."

"As opposed to yours, with a hammer and nails?"

This was how things had always been between them. Jokes that cut like a knife. They usually stopped before one of them got hurt.

Sabrina sipped on her coffee. "Was there a purpose to this call, other than to get on my last remaining nerve? Because that position has been claimed."

By Brandon. Of course. Luckily, he'd be in Roanoke for a good part of the day, making up for the shaky start with the extended Westmore clan by playing driver and tour guide.

"By Brandon Blake, I hear."

She groaned. "Now I get to the real point of your call. You and Mom are in cahoots. You're calling me to bestow Brandon's virtues."

Brandon and Sebastian had a lot in common. They were both seeds planted in the wrong pot. Sebastian had gotten out of Falling Leaves for college, leaving for

UCLA before he was eighteen. He'd rarely set foot here since.

"There you go assuming, little sister. I was clear in my motives. I wanted to talk to you about Dad. I'm worried that he'll be off his feet for longer than he thinks."

Even though the surgery had gone well, it was doubtful he'd be climbing any ladders soon. Especially if he continued to half-ass his physical therapy.

She looked around the office, worry about her future springing anew. Sabrina traced her fingertip along the rim of her coffee cup. "What makes you say that? Did Mom say something?"

"You know how vague she can be. Dad is going to lose his mind if he's off his feet for too long."

"Well, it's more my concern than yours. Seeing as we're business partners."

The birthright Sebastian had tossed away. Not that she would remind him of that now. It was water under the bridge. *Mostly.*

"I'm worried about you too, Sabrina. So, Gretchen and I have decided that we'll be visiting Falling Leaves for an extended stay."

Like she needed her older brother up in her business when half the town already was.

"Define extended."

"We were thinking through the holidays. We're having work done to the house. And this is the last year we'll be able to make a trip like this, with Caden entering school next year."

Sebastian got on her nerves on the best of days, but she loved her sister-in-law and nephews. Caden was four and a half and Graham was nearly two.

"Well, now you're speaking my language. I'll put up with you for the sake of seeing my sister-in-law and nephews."

"Ha, ha," Sebastian deadpanned. "I was hoping you'd say that, since I'd like for us to stay with you."

"We normally stay with Mom and Dad, but with him recovering, I figured it'd be better staying with you. He's going to need to get up and about soon after his surgery and he's not going to want the kids underfoot."

Sabrina began to protest. Sebastian cut her off. "After all, you have that big house."

The second half of that sentence went unsaid, but she could hear his voice in her head, just the same. *And no family to fill it. You're nearly thirty, Sabrina. When will you settle down?*

It wasn't her fault that both of her brothers had met their wives in college and quickly settled down. She'd never been lucky in love.

Instead of getting into an argument she didn't have time for, she merely said, "Eleanor and Dutch live with me."

"You act like I'm not aware that you have a guest suite on the third floor of your house, little sister. Plenty of room for all of us."

She downed the rest of her coffee and set the cup in the sink. "Why are you even calling me if you're inviting yourself?"

"I'm not. I'd hoped that you'd be okay with us staying with you. You're always complaining that the kids are growing up too fast."

She exhaled. Her brother always knew which arrow would land the killing blow. He might work on her last nerve, but she loved those kids. FaceTiming them a few times a month wasn't the same as seeing them.

"Okay, fine. Send me an email clarifying the dates of your stay. I'll have to clear it with Eleanor first, as she pays rent. But I doubt she'll have any issues."

Eleanor would be thrilled to have little ones around, and Dutch was a big goof. Her nephews adored him.

"Excellent. It'll be nice to see everyone again. Especially Brandon. I'd always said he was the one who got away."

"And I've always said you were the biggest pain in the ass on planet Earth. Guess we're both prone to hyperbole. Bye, big brother."

She hung up on him before he could return fire.

As much as she dreaded the thought of having her brother under foot for God knows how long, she had work to do. And she intended on getting as much done as possible while Brandon was out of town.

On her way out of the office, she stopped off to talk to her cousin.

"When are you thinking you'll be taking over the business, then?"

Dennis looked up from counting inventory. "I'd like to take over in the new year. But you know how our dads can be." He paused to jot something down on a clipboard. "Why? Looking to leave? Because good riddance."

She rolled her eyes. "I have my eyes on that vacant space on the edge of town."

"The one near the Weird Sisters store? You sure you want those witches as neighbors?"

"Not that I have anything against witches, but it's two doors down. The rent is cheap. We can get in before the area is fully revived."

"Well, you know my friend Alex owns the building. I'll put in a word with him."

"And I'll put in a word with my dad. You do the same." Sabrina held up her fist. Dennis bumped it.

A gesture they'd done without thinking since childhood. Maybe she and Dennis could have a fully formed adult relationship, after all.

"Now what's this I hear about you and Brandon Blake? Am I gonna have to threaten to whoop his ass like I did in high school?"

She groaned. "On that note, I'm out. Keep me informed."

Dennis called out another question as Sabrina rushed to the door. She didn't bother to answer.

* * * *

"Oh, this part of the country is so beautiful," Beatrice said. "I can see why Gabriel and Merit want to purchase a property here."

"All the decorations for autumn are just so charming, as well," Jasmine added.

"I can see why Gabe and Merit think this place is something special," Beatrice said.

"Gabe's always had a good eye," Jasmine said. "He got that from me."

Brandon tried to keep his heart neutral, even though he felt a little wistful at the Westmores' back and forth banter.

He'd mourned his mother for months before she'd died. The anticipatory grief meant that once she was actually gone, he felt relief that she was no longer suffering. Although now that more time had passed, little moments of grief would creep up on him.

After stopping for breakfast, they were on their way to Roanoke. With traffic, they should arrive in plenty of time for visiting hours to meet their granddaughter.

"Oh, is that the hospital?" Jasmine asked.

Brandon pulled up to a stop light and turned on his signal to turn into the hospital garage.

"It sure is. And we're right on time. Visiting hours start in just a few minutes."

At those words, Jasmine shattered apart like glass. The tears came out nowhere—just moments before, she'd been joking about the possible innuendo on a billboard they'd passed.

"Oh, Mum, do rein it in," Bea said. "You haven't even seen the baby yet."

"It's just so hard." Jasmine pulled a silk handkerchief from her bag. "Having my son, daughter-in-law, and now granddaughter so far away."

The light changed and Brandon turned into the garage. "You could move to the States."

That earned him a raucous round of laughter from the Westmores. "Oh, no. We like to visit but could never leave."

If he'd known the Westmores better, he'd have told Jasmine that she'd crafted herself a situation where it was unlikely that she could ever be happy. No wonder she was overbearing when she was here. She was trying to cram a year's worth of life into only a few weeks.

"Well, you'll have to make the best of it while you're here." He parked the car and unlocked the doors. "Just give me a text when you're ready to go."

"Oh, no," Bea said. "You're coming with. It's all hands on deck to keep Mum from making a spectacle of herself."

Brandon shook his head. There was a limit to his hospitality. One recent trip to the hospital was enough for him.

"As much as I'd love to, I hope you'll forgive me for passing. My father died in this hospital. It's still a place I'd rather not go if I don't have to."

Or unless he had moral support on hand, like the kind Sabrina provided. Funny, how this place hadn't seemed as imposing with her by his side.

He snapped out of his reverie when Bea placed her hand on his arm.

"Why didn't you say something? We never would've forced you to come here if we knew."

This earned a fresh round of wailing from Jasmine, and a grunt from George.

"Jazzy, stop making a spectacle of yourself. You're ruining the image of cold, unfeeling Brits everywhere."

Jasmine chuckled. "Oh, I'm sorry. I'm just menopausal, you know. I'm either weeping or so cross I'd like to burn the house down."

"Please don't," Brandon said. "At least while you're staying at the inn."

That earned him a smile and a quick squeeze on the hand from Jasmine. "We shouldn't be too long. We'll text you when we're ready, okay?"

The Westmores piled out of the car and Brandon turned the engine off.

After scrolling through his phone for a minute or two, negative thoughts swirled through his mind.

Was he doing the right thing, selling the Pumpkin? He'd always assumed he could never be happy in Falling Leaves. That his life's blood came in the form of concrete and skyscrapers. He'd been back in Falling Leaves for months now and was hardly miserable.

Stressed sure, but he didn't hate the town like he once had.

His phone rang. Grateful for the interruption, he quickly answered the call. Especially when he saw who was calling.

"Hello, Sabby. Miss me already?"

"Be careful, or I might leave some nails scattered along the floorboards in your room."

His laugh surprised him. "I'm up to date on my tetanus shot. You'll have to do better than that."

She chuckled before exhaling a long breath. "I had a reason for calling, you know. Not just to gab."

"Oh yeah? Did you think about what I proposed last night?"

He had. Who said they had to be forever? Clearly there was something between them. They weren't kids anymore. He wasn't sure if he could go on for months with the tension between them thick as concrete.

He wished he could be there in person to see her sputtering as she forced an answer. Eventually, she came up with nothing short of a pathetic, "You wish."

He laughed again. "Then what's up? Please don't tell me there's some new disaster. Or God forbid, another prank."

"No on both fronts. I was just going to ask if you could stop by one of my suppliers in town and pick up a few things for me. I told them you'd be by."

"You're telling me, not asking, exactly."

She exhaled. "I thought you were trying to get into my good graces. I mean, why would I even pretend to be in a fake relationship with someone who can't go on an errand a few blocks out of his way for me? You're getting a hell of a lot more out of this than I am, right? So far all I have is one lousy kiss and a migraine."

"How are you using that adjective there, Sabby? Lousy meaning it was bad, or that there was only one —"

"You're not going to just speed past the point without addressing it. I'm not getting much out of this. The least you can do is pick up some tile, Brando."

He tapped his fingers on the steering wheel. "I suppose that's a fair point. You're doing me a big favor."

She lowered her voice an octave, "Maybe, if you're lucky, I'll do something for you."

That word — *something* — hung heavily in the air with anticipation. It had come seemingly out of nowhere. Perhaps she'd considered his words more than she'd let on.

Their relationship had been serious before, seeing through all levels of intimacy. But they'd been kids then. It'd be different now.

"Where do I go and who do I talk to?"

She chuckled. "That's what I thought. I'll text you the info. I've got to get back to work. Bye."

She hung up before he could reply. He tossed his phone into the passenger's seat and smiled.

For the first time since his mom had taken ill, Brandon felt happy. Even if the happiness was fleeting, he could enjoy it while it lasted.

Chapter Sixteen

"Uh, Sabrina? You might want to watch where you're pointing that nail gun."

Sabrina blinked into focus. Carlos stood a few steps away from her, shielding himself with his arm.

She dropped the gun. "Sorry. The last thing I'd want to do is ruin that masterpiece made of flesh that is your face."

He chuckled. "Speaking of that, I hear you're in the running to be the Miss Autumn to my Mr."

Sabrina returned to work nailing up the side of the new front desk counter. "You're awfully confident. Sounds like you think you'll win again." She ducked under the counter and pulled off a cover on a plate of pumpkin rolls. She shoved half of one in her mouth and covered up the plate again.

"I mean, yeah?" He slipped into Spanish. "The town knows what it likes. And they like me." He brushed imaginary dust from his shoulders.

She snorted. "Your humility is one of the things I love about you, *hermano*. How's Yessica doing? I need to book an appointment to see her soon." Yessica owned a salon two towns over. Sabrina pointed at her hair. She was far past due for a cut and highlight.

"Hinting heavily about a ring. And buying a house. She's fallen in love with one of the vacant houses at the edge of town. It seems like a money pit to me."

"Well, we can walk through it with her, if you want. Give her a reality check."

"Hmm, maybe. She's bringing her nephew into town soon for practice for the Halloween pageant."

Conversation paused as Sabrina wiped her mouth. "Then give the lady what she wants. You're never going to find a woman who puts up with you better than she does." She gave him a playful slap on the arm before she wiped herself off.

From behind them, someone cleared their throat.

Brandon. Her heart flew up and out of her chest like a butterfly. The man really needed to wear a bell. Did they teach him how to creep like a mouse at that Ivy League university of his?

"Oh, you're back. Are the Westmores here?"

"They stayed in town overnight tonight. Gabriel will be bringing them back in the morning." His tone was sharp.

She realized what her playful kidding with Carlos must've looked to him, as they'd been speaking Spanish.

"Hey, can you get the wallpaper from the truck?" She turned to Carlos. "I want to be sure Brandon likes it before we hang it."

Carlos ducked his head and slipped out of the room.

"You already know I like the wallpaper." He crossed his arms across his chest.

That chest was a fair bit broader now than when they were kids. She coughed down a flirty remark, since he appeared to be in no mood.

"You really need to improve your Spanish if you want to thrive in your field."

He pouted. "I understand some. You two just talk too fast."

She took a step closer to him. His shoulders tensed up. She put her hand on his arm. "Do you really think I was flirting with my second in command on a job site?"

He shrugged. "You two are awfully chummy."

"We were talking about the house his girlfriend has fallen in love with."

He exhaled. "Everyone loves Carlos."

"Sounds like a sitcom," she replied. "I do love him. Like the annoying, pretty boy little brother I never asked for. Speaking of that, my annoying real-life older brother is coming to town next week. So, life's about to get even more hectic."

"Oh," Brandon said. "I'm sorry. I didn't mean to be jealous."

"Nothing to be jealous about. Everything's temporary, right?" She held his gaze.

Brandon's nod was curt. "Right."

Carlos, bless him, made a bit of a ruckus in entering the room to alert them to his presence.

"Ah, hand it over."

Carlos passed over the wallpaper roll and she dismissed him for the day. With the area taped off for construction, it was just Sabrina and Brandon in the space. Voices carried down the hall from The Frosted Squash.

Their gazes settled on one another. She wanted him to unburden her of the heavy wallpaper roll and kiss her. By the way he looked at her, it was something he was considering.

Despite her rough talk, she understood the spark between them was in no danger of extinguishing.

Laughter, carrying in through the ancient etched glass windows, brought Sabrina back to focus.

"Do you want to see the wallpaper, then? Because I'll charge a dollar a minute to take it down if you don't like it. Hanging wallpaper is a huge pain in the ass."

He exhaled. "Sure, I guess."

She edged around where the front desk sat haphazardly at an angle. They'd secure it in place after the wallpaper was installed. She unrolled a section of the wallpaper and placed it against the wall. She had to strain on her tiptoes to expose a fair section of the pattern.

"Well?"

His gaze shifted from the wallpaper to her face.

She groaned. "See, this is why I asked. You like to change your mind at the last minute."

She'd meant it as a light-hearted dig. Given the way Brandon's expression clouded over, he'd taken it as her dredging up decade's old history.

"That's not fair."

She released her grip on the wallpaper and rolled it back up. "I didn't mean it like that. I was only talking about the job. Sometimes you don't know you don't like something until you see it in person. I get it."

He exhaled. "Can we clear the air?"

She leaned over and set the wallpaper on the floor. "We can pick out another pattern, it's no big deal, Brandon."

"I like the wallpaper just fine, Sabrina. I'm talking about what happened when we were kids."

They'd danced around their shared history in the days since she'd started working at the Pumpkin. Maybe it was best to get it out there, so they could move on.

"I mean, I guess? I don't know if it'll change anything. It was a long time ago." She worried one hand over another.

"Well, I'm glad you think so. Because my idea of clearing the air had less to do with talking, and more to do with kissing."

He hooked a finger into the belt loop of her coveralls and pulled her into his arms.

Brandon pulled them into the small closet off the front desk where guest luggage was stored. He rested his hand on her cheek. "When you were taking Spanish in high school, I took French." He traced his index finger over her bottom lip. She gasped but made no attempt to move. Her eyes were half-closed, and her mouth parted open where he touched her.

He waited half a second. Just enough time for her to tell him no. Instead, she nudged herself closer to him.

"*Bisou* means kiss in French. How do you say it in Spanish?"

She swallowed. Her eyes stayed away from his. Her cheeks had taken on a beautiful blush.

"*Beso.*"

"Ah, so it's similar." He leaned forward and kissed her face. She smelled of a vague floral perfume — likely applied at the start of the day, many hours had passed by now — and fresh cut timber.

He brought his lips to the side of her cheek and brushed the softest kiss there. Her breath came out in one long exhale.

"I know I can't make up for the past. But I can't stop thinking about you. You've been on my mind since I got back to town." He cupped her head, and she leaned into his touch.

"Then why didn't you approach me? Would you have left town without saying a word?"

He brushed her hair free of her eyes. "Why didn't I approach you? Well, because until last week you were about as approachable as a Doberman with a mouth full of bees. I'm a man who knows his limits."

She laughed. "I'm not that bad." She snapped her mouth open and shut a couple of times, miming bees flying out.

"Your resting bitch face should be in the dictionary under the definition of the term."

She laughed again. "Okay, so I can hold a grudge. This is nothing new."

"Truth is, I didn't want to start something with you. It was better to turn the other way when you had someone sneak in for your daily pumpkin roll. Or when I saw you at the bookstore, or around town. It's not what I wanted."

"But it was easier."

He cupped the other side of her face with his left hand. "I'm starting to realize, easy is bullshit."

At that, he gathered the rest of his courage and brought her face toward his. She had to arch up to reach, her hands coming to his shoulders.

He'd dreamed about this — especially after the first time he'd seen her after years away. She was more beautiful now than before.

She leaned against him. He slid his hands down from her face to her waist, pulling her as close as he could.

He'd worried that if he'd ever got the chance to kiss her again, he'd find the magic had been snuffed out between them.

That had been a pointless thought, as she returned each kiss with fervor, making repeated gasping noises that he'd buried deep within the broken-down drawers in the rear of his brain. He'd never thought he'd hear her make a noise like this again, so it was better to forget.

Now, all he wanted to do was remember. He pressed his hands into the small of her back, holding her in place.

She moved her head to the side, breaking the kiss. "I'm gonna pass out if I don't get some oxygen. Give me a second."

"Only a second." He kissed the side of her face. "Now that we started, I don't want to stop."

She exhaled and looked over at him. "Before we go any further, can we agree that this is just for now? No matter what anyone else may think, we're just...friends with benefits. Nothing more. That's not my usual type of thing, but if it's this or nothing, I'll take it. Are we on the same page? Promise?"

Sabrina was one of the few women in his life that he could see settling down with. But they wanted very different things out of life. That didn't mean they couldn't enjoy each other in the meantime. "Okay. I agree. Friends with benefits. So, the fake dating turns real?"

She let out a dry laugh. "Kind of. You agreed to that easier than I thought you would."

"I think you'll find me to be a very amenable person, Sabrina."

This time her laugh was genuine. "Sure, whatever you say."

He tugged her back into his arms, so there was no space between them. "How about we talk less, kiss more?"

She kept her gaze on his, long enough he could see the tiny slivers of gold hidden in her dark brown eyes.

"I think I like that idea just fine."

He angled his head to kiss her. Just as every light in the inn went dark.

Chapter Seventeen

"You've got to be kidding me." Sabrina looked around the dimly lit room. It wasn't dark outside yet, but given the angle of the sun, and the low hanging porch, not much light filtered in through the inn's windows.

Brandon was reluctant to let her go. "Do you think it's the breaker?"

"Or maybe Old Levi, starting trouble again." Sabrina grinned.

Brandon groaned. "You don't really believe that. Nobody's actually seen that ghost, you know."

When Sabrina started to argue, he added, "Nobody sober. It's probably just the breaker."

"I'm glad you keep that cynicism to yourself during the ghost tours," she teased. "But yeah, I guess we'll have to venture into the ancient basement to find out." She tried to ease out of his grip. He was unrelenting.

"Do you want to crab walk down there, or what?" She mimed the motion.

"Hey, what's going on?" Adalyn called from the hall. "Do y'all know what's going on with the lights?"

"We're about to find out. Hopefully it's just a tripped breaker or something. We're not reworking the electrical until later in the renovation. I'm sure that's all it is."

"Or another prank," Brandon muttered to himself. He really should've called that security company Eleanor suggested to him. He'd have to move that to the top of his to-do list.

"I have six dozen pumpkin muffins in the oven for a catering order, so if you could make haste in getting the power back on, I'd appreciate it."

"On my way." Sabrina rifled through her overalls until she found the small, sturdy flashlight she kept in one of the pockets.

"I'll go with you," Brandon said. "Just to be sure there's nothing sinister in the basement."

She turned to face him. His face was half in shadow. He looked so handsome she wanted to kiss him again, and again and again.

"You must be feeling some type of way about me to come with."

He laughed. "I'm not that bad. It's not like I have a long list of fears or anything. I'm just not particularly fond of the dark."

She shook her head and started walking to the basement. "Remember the haunted hayride? Fourth grade? When that clown with a chainsaw appeared, you took off running like the devil was on your tail. We couldn't find you for nearly an hour afterwards. You about gave your mom a heart attack."

"Thanks for taking me back to the exact origin of the fear. I appreciate it."

Sabrina turned and placed her hand over his. "I'm sorry, I didn't know. You have nothing to be ashamed of. We all have fears. You know how I feel about frogs."

He laughed. "One ribbit and you're through the roof."

She pulled a face. "Gross."

"I was a kid. I'm fine now." He swallowed. "Honestly. Let's go."

She flung open the basement door and turned on her flashlight. "Here's a kiss for bravery." Her lips tingled against his stubbled cheek.

Then she took off down the stairs two at a time. She'd always been fearless. Growing up with two older brothers would do that to you. Brandon clung to the rail and made his way at a much slower pace.

"Which way is the breaker box, do you know?" She shone her flashlight across the musty, dark space. Pockets of sunlight eking in from one of the small windows cast small bits of light on the floor, not enough to illuminate the space.

"It's on the left, far back wall."

She extended her hand to him. He took it, and they set off.

"What's down here, anyway?" They passed towers of boxes leaning together, as if the slightest movement could topple them.

"A lot of Mom's old stuff. And Dad's, too. I need to go through it at some point." He exhaled, then coughed. "Ugh, it's so dusty down here. It's making my allergies act up."

"Well, I'll help you go through everything. We can cart the boxes out before the weather gets too cold. As from the smell of it, there might be a water leak down here somewhere."

Brandon grumbled. "That's just what I need."

"Luckily for you I'm already here, huh?" She scanned the flashlight around the room. "There's the breaker. But let me see if I can find the leak first. The last thing I want to do is find a live wire or something like that if there's standing water."

He stood by the door. "I'll wait here."

"What if there's a frog in there? You'd really leave me to my own devices?"

"Just shout ribbit, and I'll come running." He pulled his phone out of his pocket and shone the flashlight onto the floor. "Hurry back. I might have a surprise for you if you make it snappy."

"I have a nose like a bloodhound. I'll find it." She took off, through the narrow path of boxes. This really was a fire hazard. But she wouldn't push Brandon just yet about going through his parents' things. He wasn't the type to wear his heart on his sleeve, but the wound was still raw.

Her flashlight beam bounced off the floor and wall as she traversed the basement. The musty scent grew stronger the farther she walked. Her boot landed in a puddle. She shone the light down and found that the sump pump had overflowed.

She leaned down and attempted to manually run the pump. It kicked to life. The well drained about halfway before it sputtered to a stop again, meaning there was likely a clog somewhere in the plumbing line. An easy fix, hopefully.

"I'm making my way back to you, so need to freak out when I round the corner, okay?" Sabrina called.

"Ha, ha," Brandon replied. "What is it?"

It took her the rest of the journey to tell him what she'd seen.

"So, not a thousand-dollar emergency?"

She rounded the corner. Despite himself, he did jump a little.

She reached across and touched his arm. "Hopefully, not. I'll take a look at it before I leave. What was my surprise?"

He leaned forward and kissed her. She smiled against his mouth, allowing him several kisses before she laughed and turned away. This sensation wasn't one she'd forgotten. She couldn't quite believe that they were doing this again.

"I thought you wanted to get out of here?" She pried the metal breaker box door open. She ran her finger down the fuses until her finger brushed against something.

She lowered the flashlight. "What the hell is this?" She pulled out a small key attached to the last fuse.

Sabrina switched the fuses on, and the basement flooded with light. Brandon leaned over her and ran the key between his thumb and index finger.

"There's a little tag, look."

A tag was tied to the key, holding it into place on the fuse. He unraveled the string and pulled it off. He turned over the tag and in tiny text was written:

BROADMERE BOOKS. 8 PM.

"Okay, I repeat, what the hell?" Sabrina asked. "Did someone come down here to leave this key? I mean, I doubt the Broadmeres would be thrilled someone's handing out a key to their business."

Brandon pocketed it. "I mean, I guess so? Unless the Pumpkin really is haunted. Have there been any sightings of Old Levi lately?"

"Not that I've heard. Come on. If someone *was* down here, they left through the back exit."

Brandon was less concerned about this new mystery and more interested in Sabrina's snug overalls as she speedily moved through the basement.

"What are you going to do with the key?"

He stuck his hand in his pocket, his thumb brushing against it. "I'm going to go to Broadmere Books at eight o'clock, obviously."

Sabrina whirled around. "Since when do you run face first into danger?"

"You're coming too. And probably Eleanor. It seems a good idea to have a police presence with us. Besides, old man Broadmere isn't exactly a threat."

Edwin Broadmere was ninety-five if he was a day. Nobody was sure, as he'd lied about his age to enlist in WWII. His son Junior ran the store now. They both kept a low profile in town. They were friendly, but not the type to get wrapped up in any of the town's schemes.

Which made this new development all the more intriguing.

They reached the back stairs. Sabrina lowered her flashlight and looked for anything out of the ordinary.

"As dusty as this basement is, not a single footstep to be seen."

"Well, this entrance is used fairly regularly," he said. "The root cellar is in the rear. Adalyn stores her preserves and mad experiments down here."

Sabrina tapped her chin. "Hmm, maybe it was Adalyn who left the key for us to find."

"She told you herself she was in the middle of baking."

Sabrina shook her head. "I think we should take this seriously, Brandon. First the threat, now someone wants to meet you?"

He cupped her elbow. "Which is why we're going to bring Eleanor tonight. Come on, let's fix the sump pump while we're here."

They didn't talk much as they sorted out where the clog was coming from. Sabrina was beautiful while she concentrated, twin lines bunched up in between her brows.

She told him to run the pump, so he went back into the basement to run it.

Even before he alighted the steps, he could hear her whoop. "Got the clog!"

He ran up the stairs just as water rushed out of the pipe, into the back of the yard.

"I knew you could fix it," Brandon said.

"There ain't much I can't fix." She kicked up her country accent as she wiped her hands on her coveralls. "But now that it's fixed, I've gotta say, you don't seem very concerned about this new development. Which is out of character for you."

He chuckled. "Is that an accusation I hear, Sabrina?"

"Not exactly. I just mean you don't have to go through such grand gestures if you want to hang out with me."

He reached forward to brush a smudge from her cheek. "Duly noted. But I promise, I'm just as surprised as you are."

"Then I guess we should head to the police station, then."

They locked up the basement and walked around the long way into the house.

"It's a shame Falling Leaves is getting interesting as I'm on my way out of town," Brandon said.

Sabrina's smile faltered. "It's always been interesting. You just need more flash to keep your attention. We're never going to be the height of fashion or food. But at least we don't have the pretentious folks."

"I guess that's true." He batted her ponytail. "But we can have fun in the meantime, right?"

Sabrina shielded her eyes from the late afternoon sun. "Right. Maybe even after we find out what's going on at Broadmere Books." She leaned in and stood on her tiptoes. "If you're lucky."

Before he could reply, she let out a peal of laughter and took off toward her truck.

Chapter Eighteen

"What do you mean, we shouldn't contact the Broadmeres?" Sabrina hopped out of the truck and slammed the door. Brandon followed.

Sabrina had texted Eleanor on her way home, and the two of them pulled into the driveway at the same time.

Eleanor motioned for them to go inside. "Some things aren't meant to be discussed in front of the neighborhood, Sabrina."

Sabrina looked around, finding no one outside, save the three of them.

Knowing there was no point in arguing, she motioned for Brandon to follow. She hopped up onto the porch. The door was open. The stale scent of teenage boy BO lingered, which meant Dutch and his friends were probably stinking up his bedroom after basketball practice. A loud whooping of male voices confirmed this.

Eleanor closed the door and called up the stairs, "Y'all need to go home to your mothers."

Teenagers were never so obedient, but having the sheriff as roommate had its advantage. A herd of teenage boys took the stairs two by two, saying both hello and goodbye to them as they ran out the front door.

Dutch appeared at the top of the stairs once Eleanor had seen off the last of the boys.

"You need to light a candle, spray some air freshener, pray to Jesus or whatever, child. This house smells like a dormitory. I know they've got showers at that school."

Dutch blushed. "Ma, seriously."

"I could've said it while your boys were here. Now go on." She shooed at him, and he got to work.

"Oh, shit," Sabrina said. "I nearly forgot. Sebastian is coming, with Gretchen and the kids. They want to stay here."

To anyone else, this would've been major news. Eleanor merely shrugged. "I'll make up the guest suite for them tonight. When are they coming?"

Their conversation temporarily sidetracked regarding their new houseguests. Then Sabrina turned and remembered Brandon was there.

She sucked in a breath, at the thought of him not-so-subtly snooping through her living room bookshelves. As children, they'd always one-upped each other on their reading levels. Now, she favored reading genre fiction and business books, although Brandon likely still favored the classics.

"So, the Broadmeres? You were saying we shouldn't tell them someone is handing out the key to their business like party favors?"

Eleanor walked into the kitchen and flicked on the lights. "There are things in this town that you don't question. And getting a key to Broadmere Books is one of them."

Sabrina slapped the countertop. "What the hell are you talking about? I've lived in Falling Leaves my whole life. There's no mystery here."

Eleanor chuckled. "Every small town has its layers. You two just peeled back one. Go to the bookshop tonight. You won't be in any danger."

Brandon meandered into the kitchen. "How can you say that, after the threat I received the other day?"

She flung open the refrigerator door and pulled out the fixings for beef stew. "You staying for dinner, Brandon?"

Brandon cut a glance over to Sabrina.

"I'd love it if you stayed. But I wouldn't want to keep you from your work, if you need to be back at the inn," Sabrina said.

He waved a hand. "Babs is on duty. Besides, with construction, we don't have many guests. And the Westmores are out. It sounds like the perfect night for adventure."

Sabrina reached over and squeezed his hand while Eleanor's back was turned. "To me, it sounds like whoever set up this little adventure has insight into our lives."

"Maybe, maybe not," Brandon said.

Eleanor turned around. "So, have you two finally pulled your heads out of your butts and realized how cute you are together?"

Sabrina palmed her face. "Jesus, Eleanor. You're my best friend, not my mother. Save that sort of insight for the lady who birthed me, okay?"

Eleanor chuckled as she pulled out a big stock pot. "I'm just saying. Y'all are cute."

"Well, we're not dating or anything," Sabrina said quickly. She wanted Brandon to be sure she understood their agreement. "We're just having a little fun, since it's important the Westmores think we're dating."

What they got up to in their own time was nobody's business but theirs.

Eleanor shook her head. "I'm not even going to ask about that. So are y'all gonna keep up the charade once Sebastian gets here?"

Sabrina exchanged a look with Brandon. She hadn't thought about that. Her brother would be here in a few days. Hopefully, the Westmores would be gone by then.

"I mean, I guess we won't have a choice. Especially when Mom hears that Brandon was over. And you know she will. Inez lives down the street and she peers out her window with binoculars. I'm pretty sure she just installed one of those camera doorbells, too."

Eleanor sliced open a package of stew meat and set it in the pan. It sizzled as it started to cook. "I don't know, maybe it's because I'm older than y'all, but you youngin's have too many rules for things. Friends with benefits? Part-time partners? Whatever you call it, you two are dating."

Sabrina sputtered, trying to find a proper response to that. Brandon reached forward and grabbed her hand. He gave it a squeeze. "I guess you can call it that. But you know how people in this town are. They'll have us booked at the church for a June wedding."

Eleanor merely murmured. Knowing Eleanor, that meant that she didn't think it was such a far-off idea that the two of them *would* be having a June wedding.

As much as Sabrina loved the idea of settling down, they'd made things clear. Nothing serious.

That was the whole point of this. Sure, she was helping him maintain face with the Westmores. But Sabrina got to get Brandon out of her system, once and for all.

Even as she looked at him, she already felt her heart getting away from her. She hoped that these next few weeks — months at best — were something worth remembering. Then she could send him off for his next adventure in the big city. And perhaps it was time to let her mother start setting her up with a man who was just as into the small-town life as she was.

As long as *she* kept her expectations in check, other people could think whatever they wanted.

* * * *

"Should we case the joint?" Sabrina tapped her fingernails against the steering wheel. They were parked behind Broadmere Books. Eleanor said the key was to the rear door, not the front, although she wouldn't say how she knew.

He'd never thought Falling Leaves, Virginia would surprise him in any way. He thought he knew everything about every resident — down to the plot his ancestors lay in in the town cemetery. This mystery intrigued him. But more than that, this new partner in crime of his was alluring.

Brandon chuckled. "For what? Ghosts? Eleanor said we didn't need to worry. I believe her." He leaned forward and kissed the side of her neck. He'd had to swing by the Pumpkin to check on something and she'd met him there. Now she smelled like vanilla and a vague woody scent. The perfect perfume for her.

"Well, if you can be brave, so can I." She tapped her phone screen to check the time. "It's one to eight right now. Let's go."

They hopped out of the truck. The lights flashed as she locked it with the key fob. She rubbed her hands together nervously.

Brandon produced the key from his pocket. "I thought I was the scaredy-cat, not you?"

She whirled around. "I'm no scaredy-cat! I just can't believe you're so calm about this."

"It's eight o'clock. Let's find out what the mystery is all about then, huh?"

He pulled her in for a quick kiss on the cheek before inserting the key in the lock. As the door creaked open, there was a distant sound, not unlike the wail of the undead.

Sabrina took a step back. "I'm out."

Brandon laid a hand on her arm. "It's the kids practicing for the Halloween pageant." The town hall doors were thrown open on the cool night. A miniature zombie came tumbling out, into his mother's arms.

"Sheesh. I'll be giving this year's pageant a pass, then. Go ahead."

He'd half expected the door to not budge but it swung open easily. Of course, with an ominous creak. But they'd come this far. He'd truly be cowardly if they turned back now.

"Let's go, Sabrina." He extended a hand to her.

She swallowed and stepped forward to take it. Hand-in-hand, they walked into Broadmere Books. Brandon closed the door behind them, taking care to lock it.

He paused a moment to breathe in the aroma of the old bookshop. Housed in one of the oldest buildings in town, there was always a slightly musty odor, but it fought and lost out to the alluring aroma of old books. How many hours had he lost in this shop as a child?

The old shop was still as charming, fully decked out for Halloween. Jack-o-lanterns lit with electric candles led a path into the store.

He turned to Sabrina, who was clearly reminiscing, given the wistful look on her face.

"Even though I come here a few times a month, I still manage to find nostalgia for it."

He gave her hand a squeeze. "Me too."

"Where's the light switch?" Sabrina turned around. "Oh, there it is." She flicked on the lights. They were both surprised to find it wasn't the overhead lights that turned on, but instead the endless strings of fairy lights that wound around the endless bookshelves, and along the handrails leading to the second floor and basement levels.

"Oh." She looked around. "That doesn't seem scary. It's nice, actually."

Brandon's phone chimed with a text message. It was from an unknown number.

Take the stairs one flight down. Then your first left. The key will work on the last door there.

Sabrina peered over his shoulder. "I swear, if someone with a Michael Myers mask is waiting for us, they should know that I'm not going down without a fight." She mimed elbowing someone to the face.

He chuckled. "We'll fight 'em off together. Me, with my big meaty hands, and you, likely with some weapon you've hidden on your person."

Her eyes glinted in the dim light. She reached into her purse and pulled out a pen knife. "You do know me, after all."

"Our fate awaits, m'lady." He mimed doffing an imaginary top hat.

"Ew, never do that again. You remind me of that old internet meme."

He stopped on the first step. "What meme?"

She laughed. "You really are a hundred year old trapped in a twenty nine year old's body, Brandon Blake."

"I just never cared much about pop culture. You know this."

"Ah yes, the story where you checked George Clooney into one of your hotels and had to be told later who he was went around town for months."

Brandon shrugged. "There are other, better things worth occupying my time."

"Like playing chess in the park or reading snooty literary fiction? Anyway, I'll tell you about the meme later."

They came to the bottom of the stairs. He gave her a playful shove. "How about you don't mock me for my hobbies, and I don't mock you for your encyclopedic knowledge of Bravo's television line-up?"

"Deal. Now come on, if I want to meet my maker, I don't want my last words to be about *The Real Housewives of Salt Lake City*."

They took the first left, past the numerous meeting rooms that people used for gatherings since Falling

Leaves was too small to merit a library. Dull, overhead fluorescent lighting flickered above them.

"Here it is." Brandon came to a stop in front of the last door. Sabrina ducked in front of him and attempted to peer in, but the door was papered up.

"That seems like something a murderer would do. You can see into all the other rooms. I've never been in this room before, have you?"

Brandon slipped the key into the lock. "No. Only one way to find out what's inside, huh?"

Sabrina clutched her pen knife, just in case. Although he was pretty sure it was just for fun. Whatever this evening was, it wasn't meant to be sinister.

The door slipped open, revealing nothing but a dark space. Brandon blindly reached inside and fumbled around for a light switch.

"Ah, there it is."

The lights came on, and inside was not a meeting room, used by the biddies or other groups, but a small theater. Seating no more than twenty, chairs and a few sofas were scattered haphazardly around a large projection screen.

Here, more twinkle lights flickered, giving the room a warm, inviting glow.

Brandon laughed. "Look, there's a popcorn machine in the corner. It smells like someone's turned it on recently."

He led Sabrina over and found a bucket as the popcorn popped under the heater.

"Was there a schedule posted on the door? I wonder what film is playing tonight."

His phone chimed with a text, from the same unknown number.

Welcome to the Broadmere Film Club. Tonight's film will begin shortly. Please lock up at the conclusion of the film.

The screen lit up with the image of an hourglass, and a countdown clock.

"No wonder Eleanor told us not to worry," Sabrina said. "I can't believe I never heard about this. It's like *Fight Club* if it was wholesome. I wonder what film is showing."

"First rule still applies, though," Brandon said. "Do you think there's a projection booth somewhere?"

Sabrina looked around. "It doesn't look like it. But someone is probably here with us, so we should mind our P's & Q's."

No sooner had she finished the sentence than there was the bang of the back door slamming shut.

Chapter Nineteen

"What the hell was that?" Sabrina asked.

"I don't know. It would be like a serial killer to lure us into a false sense of security. Perhaps it's not too late to summon the zombie hoard."

"Not funny." Sabrina gave him a shove.

Maybe this wasn't going to be a wholesome evening after all. Sabrina didn't have time to fret, as a text came in on Brandon's phone, again from an unknown number.

That was our club leader, leaving for the evening. That old door sticks. You're alone. Please respect our space and a reminder of our one and only rule: you must not speak of this to anyone outside of the Club.

"See? It is like *Fight Club*," Sabrina said. "Except only for the two of us." She turned around to face him. "Were we set up here? And by who, do you think?"

Brandon pocketed his phone. "Who knows. I mean, we can leave if you're uncomfortable. We can hunt for the movie club culprits instead."

"No, I'm not that curious. I want to stay. We can sort out the mystery later. And who knows, maybe inquire about membership to the club."

"Hmm, I have a feeling it's not the sort of thing you ask for."

"Good point. We should be on our best behavior tonight."

He mimed a salute. "I wonder what great cinematic classic they'll be showing this evening."

Brandon picked up their popcorn tub, while Sabrina grabbed a drink from the cooler next to it. There was a small donation cup next to the cooler. She peeled a ten-dollar bill from her wallet and stuck it in.

The timer on the screen reached zero and the screen went black. She hurried over to the sofa to find her place next to Brandon. She passed him a drink and he settled the popcorn bucket between them.

"What do you think? Classic French cinema? Or a modern classic?"

The screen lit up with the opening credits and Sabrina let out a howling laugh. "I recognize that font. It's the last *Twilight* movie. Or wait, was it the second to last one in the series?"

"Wait, what? That awful vampire franchise?"

She rounded on him. "Don't be a snob, Brandon. We were teenagers when *Twilight* was popular. It's not like we were living glamorous lives or anything."

"Yeah, and I lost out on dates because I couldn't live up to some fictional hundred-year-old vampire. Even you were smitten."

"With the handsome British actor who played him, less so for the shimmering vampire," Sabrina added. "I was firmly Team Jacob."

He grabbed a handful of popcorn. "Well, this wasn't what I expected. Pity for me expecting high cinema from Falling Leaves."

She tossed a piece of popcorn at him. "Stop being a snob. I'm sorry this isn't some fancy indie theater in DC or New York. We must make do."

He turned to her as the movie started to play. "Hey, I didn't mean it like that. I'll admit I'm a bit of a film buff. I was taken off guard. I'm happy to watch frolicking vampires." He leaned in closer to her and brushed a kiss on her lips. "Especially if I'm with you."

The light caught Brandon's blue eyes.

"Okay, well, the vampires don't exactly frolic. They do play baseball, but that's a different movie..." She trailed off as he kissed her again. "I'm committed to seeing this film through and rating it for its artistic merit. Same as I would any other film."

They made it roughly five minutes into the film before Sabrina had to stop to explain things, as Brandon's *Twilight* knowledge was vague at best.

"I just don't understand how this merited five movies." He shoved a handful of popcorn into his mouth.

She turned to him. "Because you've never been a teenage girl."

He reached forward to gently bop her nose. "I'm starting to wonder if the film is the least important thing about tonight. As this is our first official date, huh?"

That...was a lie. Their first official date had been to the homecoming football game. Then the following day, the Homecoming dance. Brandon seemed to remember.

"I mean, our first official date since starting over." He angled toward her, his face cast in a bluish glow from the screen. "I don't want to forget about what happened. We had good times, to go along with the bad."

Sabrina reached for a handful of popcorn. "That's true."

"Let's turn our attention back to this fine piece of vampire cinema before I become even more lost than I already am."

He scooted closer to her and drew his arm around her shoulders. Her weight easily fell against him as if they'd always been meant to be close, like this.

They watched the movie in silence for no more than a couple of minutes before Brandon spoke again.

"I hate to break it to you, but this is a pretty terrible movie."

She let out a noise of mock-indignation. "And after I spent all that time explaining the intricacies of the plot!"

He laughed. "I'm sorry. But I'm starting to wonder if the movie wasn't necessarily the point of bringing us here tonight. Which makes me even more curious about who left the key."

"Did you ask Babs?"

"She was full of denials, of course. She's been in hospitality too many years, though. She's quite the excellent liar."

"Does it really matter, though? I mean, the rule of movie club is that you can't talk about movie club. I like the intrigue."

"I don't like an unsolved puzzle. That makes two, after the handkerchief incident."

"Yeah, tell me about it. I remember you tossing that sudoku book in the fireplace at the inn when you couldn't solve the last puzzle."

He set the popcorn bucket on the floor. "You really do know me well, huh? We have this shared history."

"There was kind of a large chunk of time we didn't talk to each other."

He ran his hand through his hair. "I can fill you in, if you want."

"I don't know, can you really hold a candle to Robert Pattinson?" She gestured to the screen.

She expected him to laugh or trade a barb of his own. He'd never admit it, but she knew he'd had a crush on Kristen Stewart when they were younger.

Instead, he gave her a determined look, and before she could take her next breath, he'd gathered her up into his arms and kissed her.

Sitting in the musty basement of a bookstore, watching a movie that was never going to be remembered for being a cinematic masterpiece, should be anything but magical.

But something struck him about this evening. As though someone had tempted fate to push the two of them together. As much as he was curious as to the person's identity, he knew it was the last important thing right now.

What mattered right now was the slow lean of Sabrina's body into the back of the couch as he deepened the kiss. She readjusted to accommodate his weight, her lips never leaving his. Her hands mapped the terrain from his back to his shoulders, until finally settling on his waist.

"Wait," he drew away from her. "Do you think we're really alone? I mean, if we're caught, there's no way they'll extend membership to us."

She exhaled. "This old building would betray anyone else's movements. And I doubt someone went through all the trouble to get us here, just to peep on us."

He lowered his mouth back to hers. "I don't know. You know what they say about small towns. Lots of perverts."

She leaned up to kiss him again. "It's not like we have an easy time being together without being spotted, anyway. I live with Eleanor, and my brother will be in town soon. You live at the inn."

He pushed her dark hair free from her face. "You have a point. Privacy is at a premium. And hey, even if there is a pervert peeping, it's pretty dark in here."

"Let's make good use of it." She fisted the collar of his sweater and brought him back to her.

The movie droned on while they kissed. Sabrina wasn't the only woman he'd kissed but she was the only one who made him feel like this. As though a fire had been lit at the center of his body and was spreading with each kiss.

She turned her head, and he kissed the exposed flesh of her neck. That made her exhale, one of his favorite sounds.

"I had to pack you up, like a box in the attic," she said. "Because remembering hurt too much. Especially after you left."

His kisses stopped. "I know you had to deal with the fallout on your own. I feel really shitty about that."

"I held a grudge for over a decade. I'm learning to lessen the reins. Hell, I may even let go of it all together if you keep kissing me."

Despite her light tone, there was some seriousness to what she was saying. No matter what happened when this ended, he wouldn't run away without a word.

Hell, maybe some part of him hoped that Sabrina would leave with him. That maybe once she saw the world outside of this tiny hamlet, she'd love it as much as he did.

He'd changed, maybe she could, too.

"You stopped kissing me again." She ran her fingers through his hair. "Do you want a penny for your thoughts? Or maybe a roll of them? Because you keep starting and stopping like Dad's old truck."

He leaned back. "Don't bring your dad into this."

She laughed. "I just mean you seem distracted. That's a little insulting."

"No, this has nothing to do with you." He cupped her face in his hands. "Well, maybe it does a little. I don't want to leave you high and dry, like I did last time. Dad had died right before I left. I wasn't in a good place."

Sabrina rested her head on his shoulder. "I know your dad's death was sudden."

A widow-maker heart attack had taken Bob Blake on the first sunny spring day of Brandon's senior year. He'd come home after kicking Sabrina's butt in debate club to find an ambulance in the driveway of the Pumpkin.

Everything after that was a blur.

"I feel like I used you as an escape, then. I wouldn't do that again, I promise."

She reached for his hand. "I think we're a lot clearer on where we stand, this go around. And we're not hormonal teenagers."

He intertwined his fingers through hers. "It was the sort of thing that kept me up at night. How I hurt you."

"I thought about you, too. But in between doing tie-cutting rituals involving candles I picked up at The Weird Sisters shop."

"I didn't think you dabbled in that sort of thing."

"Everyone in town goes to Tabitha and Esme at some point."

"Hmm, not everyone."

"Only because you're a non-believer in all things supernatural. Which is an odd combination, given that you're scared of the dark."

"There are very real things that can hide in the dark." He touched her cheek.

"Including me." She leapt forward and tackled him, trailing a line of kisses on his face before she pushed him onto the couch.

She leaned back so she could see his face. "Enough of talking about the past. We went from hot and heavy to Dr. Phil's couch pretty quick."

"I don't want to hurt you again, Sabrina. It would kill me."

"As long as you keep being honest with me, we'll be fine, Brandon. I promise. I mean, especially since you'll owe Ellis & Daughter some serious change once the renovation is completed."

He drew her in for a kiss.

"You can put a tracking device on me if you want. I'm not leaving for a bit. Construction just started. I promised Mom I'd oversee the whole process. I don't want her haunting my dreams if I disobey her."

She rested her head against his chest. He wrapped his free arm around her. "I thought you didn't believe in that kind of stuff?"

"Eh, I think my mother would find a way."

She kissed his cheek. "Can we stop talking and get back to kissing?"

A loud noise on the screen made him jump. She leaned forward and kissed him again. "It's just a movie. But I'm here, in the flesh. If I wasn't so worried about the possible placement of cameras around this place, we could potentially do more than that."

That got his thoughts back in the right place. They fell back onto the couch and resumed kissing. If prompted at gunpoint, he'd never be able to state what happened in the movie.

Chapter Twenty

Breakfast at the Over Easy was not an invitation one turned down without a mammoth guilt trip. Five o'clock in the morning was far too early to deal with the biddies.

But she was in a good mood after spending the evening with Brandon. A happiness that even her mother's needling couldn't ruin.

Besides, she had a busy day ahead of her. Even though it was just her and Carlos working, they should be able to finish off the new front desk. There was a short punch-list to finish the lobby and front entrance project. Then they'd be taking things outside for the next phase of the project before the weather chilled too much — fixing the porch, painting, and window repair. Thankfully, the roof had been replaced only a few years before, so she didn't have to worry about that.

Sabrina arrived at the Over Easy just as Inez was unlocking the front door. Even though the sun had only started to lighten the sky, there was a line outside.

If you asked Inez, it was because her food was the best in town. That was true. But also, she was the only game for the early risers in town. The closest drive-thru was nearly twenty minutes outside of town.

"Oh, good. I'm glad you're already here. I was worried I'd have to hunt you down." Lainey linked arms with Sabrina.

"Shh, Mom. Coffee."

That caused Lainey to chuckle. "I bet you need coffee, especially after what you've been getting up to."

"You know better than to believe this town's gossip mill." Sabrina gave a pointed glance at Inez, making her way into the kitchen.

"I didn't *hear* this news from anyone. I spotted this scoop with my own eyes."

"The ones in your head or the binoculars you carry around?" Sabrina countered.

Inez muttered something unintelligible as she wandered into the kitchen.

Sabrina groaned and scooched to the center of the booth. Her mother—never one for personal space— came to rest right next to her. She dropped her elbows onto the table and peered at Sabrina.

"How about you tell me why I saw your truck outside of Broadmere Books last night? After closing?"

Did her mother know about movie club? Jeez, she hadn't been expected to be put on the spot this soon. Especially before coffee.

So, Sabrina did what she did best. She distracted. Luckily, Lainey was easy to distract.

"I'm assuming you've heard your first born is coming to town soon."

Lainey blinked. "Oh, yes, of course. Although I'm a little miffed they want to stay with you."

"Do you think Dad wants the kids underfoot when he's hobbling about? Besides, you know how Dad and Sebastian can grate on each other's nerves."

There was an old wound between them. Their father had always expected Sebastian to take over the business. After all, her father had inherited it from Sabrina's grandfather. Uncle Gordon had worked there for a while before deciding he preferred the hardware business.

Inez came by to fill their coffee cups. Once she was topped up, Sabrina held the cup under her nose, inhaling the intoxicating scent.

"I suppose you have a point. Do you have the dates firmed up, yet? I hope he'll be here in time for the pageant. Have you talked to Caleb?"

"I haven't heard from him, but I'm sure I will soon. I'll try to give him a call and see when he's planning on coming up. Knowing him, he'll push all the kids into that RV he's rigged up to run on alternative fuel. Then he'll park it in your driveway."

Caleb was an environmental scientist who eschewed most forms of transportation, save the train, his electric car and ancient RV.

"Oh, dear. How about I give him a call, then. That thing is an eyesore. It looks like the RV they cooked meth in on that TV show."

Sabrina chuckled as the other biddies began to file in.

"What a treat to have you here so early," Babs said. "I'm surprised you don't have bags under your eyes big enough to travel to Europe in. Oh, youth."

"Oh, yes, that new relationship feeling. I barely remember how that feels," Tiffany said.

Sabrina cut a glance around the table at the biddies. "Would y'all know anything about the key that was left for Brandon and me at the Pumpkin yesterday?"

Suddenly, everyone was very interested in the menu — even though their standard orders hadn't changed in nearly a decade.

"Hmm, did everyone get their flyers for the pumpkin decorating contest? We need to blanket the town by this afternoon," Lainey said. "We need to be sure to have enough entries before judging at the Miss Autumn pageant."

Everyone started to speak about the pumpkin decorating contest at once, until Tinesha's voice cut through the din.

"What key? I didn't hear anything about a key."

If there was an innocent member of the biddies, it was Tinesha. She had a busy job as a nurse manager in Roanoke. She didn't have the time to get wrapped up in their schemes.

Sabrina started to explain when Inez appeared at the table with her order pad in hand and a pencil tucked behind her ear.

"Everyone ready to order?" The timing felt a little too coincidental.

The biddies likely had something to do with movie club. But given the rules of the club, and the fact that this group could withstand grilling from a team of grizzled detectives and not break, it was better to let it drop.

Once Inez scurried away from the table, Lainey embraced Sabrina's silence and went into full pageant mode.

"Don't forget about the pageant meeting tonight at town hall. It starts right at six o'clock."

Sabrina let out a groan that should've been inaudible, given the rising volume inside the café. Give it to her mother to pick up on anything and everything.

"Oh, stop. It's just an introductory meeting for the contestants. A chance to mingle and to discuss what needs to be done before the pageant. It's hardly a Miss Virginia pageant."

Sabrina braced herself for an incoming tangent about her mother's time in the Miss Virginia pageant, back in the eighties. Thankfully, Tiffany saved them all, by launching into the latest scandal in town hall — someone had been sabotaging the parking meters in front of the courthouse.

"It's an act of sabotage," she said. "At least that's what Mayor Ford says. There's going to be a meeting about it soon."

"I'm sure it'll be a rowdy one," Sabrina said. "You know how many folks in this town are desperately in need of a hobby."

"Well, don't be surprised if his feathers are all ruffled at the pageant meeting tonight. Especially with the cider festival kicking off next weekend."

These petty little squabbles kept life interesting in Falling Leaves. She couldn't imagine living in a big city, where you never talked to your neighbors.

Her smile faltered when she remembered that Brandon didn't share her views. He'd hated the town's gossip mill since the first day he'd arrived in second grade, and he'd become the latest curiosity.

If she passed on this latest bit of town gossip, he'd likely roll his eyes.

He'd been honest with her, all along. This thing of theirs was for fun — while it lasted.

* * * *

With the construction crew only working a half-day on Saturday, Brandon hadn't the chance to see Sabrina. He'd had a staff meeting with his department heads in the morning. The sale had been the top topic of conversation, just as it'd been when they'd first heard about it.

He couldn't blame everyone for their worries. Now that construction was well under way, it was hard to ignore that the Pumpkin would soon be under new ownership.

Despite him telling them that he would fight to keep them on, and that worst-case scenario was generous severances, it wasn't like there were a lot of similar jobs in town.

By the time the meeting had let out, Sabrina had wrapped up work. She'd texted him, saying she'd see him at the pageant meeting that evening.

He'd forgotten all about it and had told the Westmores he'd dine with them. Thankfully, they were amenable to the change of plans and insisted on tagging along to the meeting.

"Are we ready to head over, then?" Jasmine Westmore appeared in the doorway.

She was all aglow after spending time with her brand-new grandbaby. When he'd asked how long they'd be staying in town, the answer he'd received was vague.

They were clearly in no hurry to leave. It was a good thing he and Sabrina were getting along so well.

"Give me a moment and we'll walk over together."

Bea appeared behind her mother. "Rumor has it Sabrina is one of the contestants. *And* that hunky contractor of hers is one of the contestants for Mr. Autumn."

"Carlos is usually the only contestant. It's a running joke. You've seen him. No one can compare." Brandon stood from his desk. "Besides, Carlos has a girlfriend. He's like a brother to Sabrina."

"Oh, you're no fun." Bea briefly stuck out her tongue before her mother could chastise her.

They met up with George in the lobby and left for the town hall, although not before Babs placed to-go cups of apple cider in their hands.

She obviously wanted to play up to the relations of the Pumpkin's possible new owners.

Her views had changed most of all. She seemed to accept the reality of the Pumpkin passing out of the Blake family, once and for all. It was bittersweet — but it needed to be done. The Pumpkin wasn't his dream. The mountain lodge was. He may never achieve that dream. But he knew well enough that running the Pumpkin would never make him happy.

The Westmores followed Brandon down the steps. Jasmine nearly tripped on one of the loose boards on the last step. Brandon reached out to catch her arm.

"Sorry about that. The outdoor work is next on the docket for the renovations."

"Oh, it's fine. I wasn't paying attention to where I was going. I was distracted by that beautiful oak tree, starting to change colors."

"This is a rather charming town, isn't it?" George put in. "Even more so dolled up for Halloween."

"I suppose," Brandon said.

"Spoken like someone who grew up in a small town and got out as soon as they could," Bea said. "Gabriel was like that."

"I grew up in Washington, DC. Well, for the first seven years of my life, that is. Then my grandmother died, and my parents moved to Falling Leaves to take over the inn."

"Oh," Bea said. "You're very much a reluctant small-town guy."

Maybe it was Sabrina's influence, but as they walked through downtown, Brandon found himself *charmed*. Where he usually saw tooth-achingly sweet window displays, everything placed just so, now he saw the enchantment.

It hadn't exactly been this charming when he'd been growing up. The town had gone all in on the haunted vibe to excuse the derelict downtown.

Now, in a few years, the whole town would look like something out of a postcard. The kind that folks traveled for miles to see.

"My family's all gone now. There's nothing keeping me here."

"Except for Sabrina," Jasmine said.

He looked up to find Jasmine gazing at him skeptically. Of course, Jasmine didn't know the truth about his and Sabrina's agreement. He needed to back pedal. And fast.

He cleared his throat. "Sabrina lives and breathes this town. I don't. So…it's a challenge."

"Hmm." Jasmine toed at a fallen leaf with the edge of her boot. "Seems to me like if it was the real thing, you'd try to make it work, no matter what."

Brandon choked down a cough. He had to bring this back, before they got the wrong idea. The last thing he wanted was for them to catch onto the lie. Even though it wasn't much of one anymore. He'd date Sabrina in a heartbeat, but he couldn't blame her for being hesitant.

"We're trying to make it work," he said softly. "But life isn't always that simple."

"Gabriel and Merit made it work for nearly two years before they were reunited," George said. "With an ocean separating them. You two could, too."

"There might be an ocean between us soon, too." Brandon hadn't told anyone about the job in Paris — not even Sabrina. He knew if she did, that would be the end of them. Him returning to DC was one thing. Considering a move to another continent was another.

All he needed was a few more days, to convince her that he was fully committed while he was here — then he'd tell her. It wasn't a sure thing anyway. There was no sense in upsetting her over nothing. Especially when things were so new between them.

"Well, that's a little different, I suppose. But you can still make it work if you want to." Jasmine's tone had cooled somewhat.

Conversation shifted to the new baby for the remainder of the walk. Brandon walked ahead of the Westmores, and they didn't include him in the conversation. He'd clearly fouled things up.

Brandon was caught up in his thoughts, trying to find a way to reassure the Westmores he wasn't the type to cut out on a woman he supposedly loved.

Well, he did love Sabrina. That was the problem. He'd never stopped. But he'd sealed off that part of his heart for so long, it was hard to open it again. It wasn't like he'd even dated since things ended with Cassandra.

They walked into the town hall. Sabrina sat at the rear of the room with her mother. She turned and their eyes locked. She smiled and waved.

That small bit of encouragement—her acknowledging him in public—had his feet moving before his brain could catch up. Before he could talk himself out of it, he walked straight up to her and kissed her.

Chapter Twenty-One

The room went quiet as a pin. She could feel twenty sets of eyes boring into the back of her skull.

Which wasn't to say that the kiss was bad. Unfortunately, the opposite was true.

She managed to pull away from Brandon in a way that wouldn't arouse suspicion. She placed her hand on the back of his head and drew their heads together.

"What the hell are you doing?" Her whisper cut like a knife.

He turned so his face was nestled against her shoulder and hissed into her ear. "I'll explain later. The whole town knows we're together, anyway. Maybe this will stop all the talk."

"Um, hello?" Lainey tapped on Sabrina's shoulder. "What was that little display all about?"

Brandon stepped back. Although he kept a grip on her hand. For his own comfort or for hers, she wasn't sure.

"Oh, I think I know," Jasmine said. She gave Brandon a little punch on the arm before introducing herself to Lainey. Her mother was quickly enamored by the glamorous Jasmine Westmore, so her questioning ended there.

Not everyone was so quick to let the subject drop. The clamor in the room rose up again, with several people proclaiming, "I knew it!" And another saying, "'Bout time you two took things public!"

Angela Jones stepped forward. "Don't think that little stunt is going to win you Miss Autumn, Sabrina. I'm favored to win. Again." She flipped her auburn locks over one shoulder.

Sabrina would rather slurp a denim jacket through a straw than have this conversation.

She gripped Brandon's hand tightly. "I have to talk to my, err…boyfriend for a moment. Don't start the meeting without me."

Angela scoffed at the dismissal but didn't protest when Sabrina turned to leave.

Even though Brandon was hardly a small man, she had no problem nearly dragging his arm out of the socket while she led the two of them outside.

It smelled like autumn—that aroma of fallen leaves and the sharp crispness of the season turning over for good. They wouldn't have many warm days left in the year.

She tugged Brandon down the front steps, toward a bench off to the side of the town hall.

"Jesus, Sabrina. You about pulled my arm out of the socket." He extracted his hand from her grip and rotated his arm. The fabric of his sweater bunched around his biceps as he moved.

She found herself transfixed by the movement before she snapped back to focus. "How did you expect me to react? A little warning would've been nice.

Especially now that Angela thinks this is a ruse to steal her title. Like I'd care enough to do that."

"Miss Autumn is all she has. She's threatened by you." He stepped forward and cupped her cheek. "By your beauty."

"Oh, stop." Although she couldn't deny she was flattered, she also knew he was trying to dig himself out of the hole he'd created.

He motioned for them to sit on the bench. She dropped onto it, arms folded.

"I didn't have time. Things took a quick southward turn with the Westmores. I might've given them the impression that things weren't as serious between us as they originally thought. They didn't take that well."

"Why would they care?" As much as she loved small town life, Sabrina was growing rapidly tired of everyone's input into…whatever she could call what she and Brandon were doing.

She swallowed down a lump in her throat.

"Because we're knee-deep into this lie now. How do you think the Westmores will feel if they find out the truth? They'll start to question my judgment in everything. I could lose out on the sale."

Her heart dropped like a stone falling from a cliff. "Of course, the sale. Your ticket to starting your new life. Or going back to the one you had." Her knee nervously jogged against his.

He reached out to stop it. "I thought we were on the same page. If we're not, then let's make a show of breaking up, right now. Before things get out of hand."

If they did that, then this would end. She was the sensible sort. The kind to always lead with her head. But just this once, she couldn't manage it.

"I don't want to do that."

He leaned closer to her, so his head rested against hers. "I was hoping you'd say that."

She closed her eyes and breathed in the scent of him. Masculine, sophisticated. He was the fancier of the two of them — the kind to spend money on a bespoke suit or a custom cologne.

She brushed her lips against the side of his face. This was something she could get used to.

"So now everyone knows," he said.

"But they don't really," she said. "They'll think one thing, when the truth is different."

She wouldn't be left high and dry again. He'd promised her that.

"That won't happen again, Sabrina. I promise."

This was the moment she could call it off for good. But she didn't want to. He might not be staying but she could at least give him a proper goodbye. So that when he finally did leave for good, she could fully move on.

With no regrets.

"Are y'all coming?" Lainey called from the doorway. "We need to get started sometime."

"We'll be right there!" Sabrina called.

Lainey leaned out to get a look at them before returning inside.

Brandon raised his head and looked at her. "Let's just allow things to unfold naturally, okay?"

She reached for his hand and gave it a squeeze. "Okay."

He leaned in for a kiss. "You know, the upside to everyone knowing is that we don't have to sneak around. Do you want to come by, afterwards?"

She chuckled. "Typical man, going from zero to a hundred."

"I didn't mean what you think I did. I only meant that if your truck is in front of the inn, no one will think anything of it. There's nothing to hide, anymore."

She stood and extended her hand to him. "I suppose there's a silver lining for everything."

He took her hand and they turned toward the hall. "Let's get this atrocity over with. Then we'll talk about extracurricular plans."

His only response was a burst of warm laughter against her cheek.

* * * *

Brandon barely heard a word of the meeting. He didn't feel guilty for tuning out the goings-on, as his presence was mostly ceremonial.

Growing up, he'd been the pageant errand boy, doing whatever was asked of him by his mother and the other organizers. Not much had changed.

He left with a list a mile long of things that would need to be purchased for the sets before the next meeting. A job far more suited to Sabrina than him.

Thankfully, she took pity on them. "I'll leave the list with Uncle Gord. He or Dennis will pull everything for you. You can just pick up the stuff in the Pumpkin's van today or tomorrow."

"Thank you. I mean, I'm not a total idiot, but I don't know what half this list is."

"Hey, I'm the handy one in this fake relationship. I'll take care of it."

He brushed his hand against hers. "I thought we decided we were done with faking."

She reached for the key fob for her truck and unlocked it. "What happened to friends with benefits? That's real, right? The only thing we're pretending is that we're in a committed relationship. That's only when the Westmores are around."

They paused as they climbed into the truck. Once the doors were closed behind them, Brandon said, "I never really wanted that. I only suggested it as a...compromise." He reached forward and grabbed her leg. "I never stopped caring for you, Sabrina. I had a crush on you all those years before we dated. After, whenever I came to town, I'd always hope I'd see you. Even if it meant risking you running me off the road or TPing the inn."

"It hurt too much, to see you. Especially after you returned for good when your mom got sick. Hence why I avoided the inn." She reached forward to press the truck's start engine button.

"I hurt you. I promise that won't happen again."

The truck whirred to life. The wipers came on automatically as a steady rain began to fall.

"Guess we got in just in time." Brandon gestured to the group of people pouring out of the hall.

"Luck has a way of working out, from time to time."

He gave her knee a squeeze. He longed to touch her skin To make up for past mistakes and years passed.

But he couldn't hurt her again.

"Nothing's really changed for me. Only that we don't have to sneak around."

"Put on your seatbelt."

He released his grip on her and did as asked.

She threw the truck into reverse. "I appreciate your honesty—about what we're doing, and that you don't want to hurt me. But the reality is, I will be hurt, eventually. DC and Falling Leaves aren't exactly commutable."

Let alone Paris. He should tell her about it now. To Sabrina, DC might as well be Paris. She'd made it clear that long-distance was off the table, after what he'd done when they were kids.

He didn't blame her for that.

The rain came down in buckets, bouncing off the roof of the truck. "Jesus, let's just go back to my place," she said. "Shorter drive, and I can park in the garage. I can barely see anything."

The wipers swished across the windshield. Even though they both knew the route like the back of their hands, Sabrina took the journey at a fifteen mile an hour pace.

"It hasn't rained like this in forever. I hope the gutters at the Pumpkin can handle it," Brandon said.

"I guess we'll see tomorrow, huh?"

"You don't work on Sundays."

She turned onto Jackson Street. "Like you were ever going to wait a day to tell me your gutters were billowing in the wind. Even if we weren't fraternizing in our off-hours."

Brandon laughed. "I suppose you have a point. I'm glad we're working on the outside next."

She pulled into the driveway and hit the button on the automatic garage door opener. The garage was separate from the house, but covered with a portico, so they wouldn't get too wet on their walk.

"Is Eleanor working?"

"Oh, I forgot. Dutch had an out-of-town basketball game tonight. He's on a traveling team. They're staying in Harrisonburg tonight."

"So, we have the house to ourselves?"

She cut the engine and turned to him. "It would appear that way." She grinned like a devil before she made off for the door.

Chapter Twenty-Two

Sabrina flicked the light switch on and off, to no avail.

"Ah, shit. Looks like the power's out. I'll have to see if it's just a breaker or if it's the grid. And somehow, I doubt I'm going to find a key attached to my breaker box for the second day in a row."

Brandon laughed. "I'm pretty sure that was Babs' doing, by the way. She won't admit it. I didn't press the issue much, though. She agreed to run the ghost tours for the rest of the season for me."

"So much for mystery in this town."

"Hey, I'm surprised there was even a hint of it."

She sighed. Falling Leaves had its own kind of magic. She wished that Brandon could see it.

Brandon peered across the window. "The street's dark. It must've happened right after we got home. Should we light up some of the jack-o-lanterns on the front porch?"

"Eleanor would kill me. She spent hours carving them. We better gather the supplies, then." She took off for the kitchen. "Turn your flashlight on your phone. I wouldn't want you to fall. Or step on one of the cats. I'm sure they're around here somewhere."

"You have cats?"

"Yep, Sarah and Jareth. They're about six months old. I found them on a job site."

He chuckled. "You still love that movie, huh?"

"Obviously."

She loved all things fantasy. After all, she'd grown up thinking she'd lived in a town not unlike the one in *Labyrinth*. Although she'd grown out of the hope that one day a David Bowie-like goblin king would steal her away.

"I'm going to run downstairs to check that nothing's amiss. The basement tends to leak in the rain, no matter what I do."

"Hundred plus year-old houses will do that." He paused. "Do you need me to come?"

She pulled the box of emergency supplies out of the cabinet and set them on the counter. "No. My basement is creepy enough with the lights on, let alone for someone with an aversion to the dark." She flicked on a flashlight and handed it to him. "Wait here."

She grabbed one of her own and headed for the stairs. She tried to ignore the shadows the light cast on the wall. As she reached the bottom step, a nearby clap of thunder had the flashlight roll out of her grip.

"Jesus," she murmured to herself.

Thankfully, it didn't roll far. She picked it up and scanned around the basement. She double checked the breaker, confirming the outage came from the main line.

"All clear downstairs!"

His reply was muffled at first, before he laughed. "Uh, I think I found your cats?"

She hurried the rest of the way up the stairs. Brandon had set up a circle of candles around the sofa in the living room. Some on the old stone mantle, coffee table and even a couple on the floor.

Jareth was batting at the flame of one of them. "Uh, that's not a good idea, with kittens."

Brandon grabbed one of the candles, and she got the other. "I figured they'd be hiding until the storm ended."

Another clap of thunder had the kittens scrambling for purchase on the hardwood floor before darting under the sofa.

Sabrina laughed. "It's probably safer for all of us if they stay under there." Her gaze met Brandon's and they both smiled. He looked handsome in the soft, warm glow of the candles. The flames reflected in his glasses.

Her stomach did a somersault. She nervously turned toward the kitchen.

"Do you want something to drink? I have some wine and I think we have some of the charcuterie board that Eleanor made yesterday left over."

His stomach grumbled in response. "I'll get on that, then."

She turned to leave. Brandon dropped to the floor and stuck one hand under the sofa. "It'll be okay, kitty. It's a storm. It'll pass, eventually."

Jareth's head popped out briefly for a rub before another grumble of thunder had him darting back under the couch.

She couldn't hide her smile. Her mother always said you couldn't trust a man who didn't like animals. And Brandon always had—even though he'd never had a pet himself, as his mom had been allergic.

"He'll be eating out of your hand before you know it."

"I don't doubt that. Oh, this must be Sarah. Hi, pretty girl."

His voice faded as she slipped into the kitchen. She pulled out her phone to inspect the dark refrigerator. It took her just as long to find wine glasses, napkins and cutlery. Even though it was her kitchen, Eleanor did most of the cooking and had arranged things to her liking.

She pulled everything onto a tray and returned to the living room. Both cats had emerged from their hiding spaces and were rolled onto their backs.

"This seems like a trap." He pointed to the bare kitten bellies.

"Sometimes it is, sometimes it isn't. Depends on their mood. Luckily, you won't have to find out."

They both rolled over and hopped up, having caught the scent of the charcuterie board.

"Ah, the fun of eating when you have animals. It's akin to guarding your food in prison."

Brandon reached over to take the wine glasses from her as the kittens started up a howl.

"Uh, I can see that."

After Brandon poured the wine, she handed the board to him before breaking off small pieces of cheese and tossing them to the kittens.

"Hopefully that will occupy them for longer than twenty seconds."

They settled onto the floor, the sofa at their backs. Brandon raised his glass. "A toast. To power outages."

She chuckled. "Hopefully tomorrow won't make three times a charm."

"How about this" — he closed the space between them — "if there's an outage tomorrow, I'll owe you a kiss?"

She drew her thumb down the bridge of his nose. "What if I want that kiss now, instead?"

"I'll kiss you on the lips," Brandon said. "In good time." He caught her hand and kissed her palm.

"You're no fun." Her laugh was light. Perhaps in an effort to hide her disappointment?

He set his wine glass down and scooted closer to her, until their knees touched. "I've been thinking. About you and me. How we were each other's first."

Sabrina lowered her gaze, the light catching on her long lashes. "First nemesis, first and only boy I punched on the playground. First person I beat in debate club..." She trailed off when his hand landed on her knees.

His memories traced back to the treehouse on the rear of the Pumpkin's property. Back when they were kids, there'd been nothing but a field there. It was where they'd met in private — to keep their reputations as rivals in place. Then later, it was where privacy had taken on a different meaning.

A night full of firsts — not unlike this one, with candles and a storm brewing outside.

"Are you okay? You look a million miles away."

He trailed a hand up to meet hers. She intertwined her fingers with his. "I was thinking about the treehouse."

Her eyes lit up. "Oh. I remember now. I cried when a storm took down the tree a few years ago. Those were good times." She shifted her weight toward him. "And you say this town has no magic. That treehouse was magical."

Brandon squeezed her hand. "They were. Before life got…complicated."

She fell quiet, likely caught up in her own version of events.

"I didn't mean to drop a bomb on the mood. I was only mentioning it because of the candles, and dark room."

Lightning flashed across the sky. "You didn't ruin anything. Those were good times. I'd forgotten about them." She paused. "Well, not so much forgot, than I forced myself not to think about them. They still existed, in the musty corners of my brain."

"I get that."

They both fell quiet again, until the kittens scuttling up the stairs drew their attention.

"I figured they'd be back under the bed once their curiosity was sated," Sabrina said. "Let me make sure they're settled, and I'll be right back." She rose to standing, pausing as Brandon continued speaking.

"I understand, having a phobia myself." He chuckled to himself. "Sometimes I wonder if it's just tied to this town because that's where it started. I'm not afraid of the dark when I'm in my condo back in DC. Falling Leaves brings up some buried trauma within me, I guess."

She leaned forward and ruffled his hair. "I mean, you moved here from the big city when you were a kid. Both of your parents died here."

He let out a morose laugh. "Well, when you put it that way."

"Hold that thought. I'll be right back."

She hurried up the stairs. While she was gone, Brandon fell into his thoughts.

His condo was currently being sublet by a friend of a friend. Another dangling string in his life that would have to be tidied up, one way or another.

He hated this feeling of limbo — but especially when it came to Sabrina.

Sabrina came down the stairs two at a time, talking a mile a minute. "If we're talking about phobias and this town, Falling Leaves *does* have its share of creepy things. Old Levi sightings. Doors that open on their own. Creaky old floors. I grew up in a house that my grandma died in. So, when anything weird happened, I'd tell her to stop her foolin' around."

Brandon smiled. "I remember. Your grandma died not long after I came to town."

"Yeah, back when you were still in your 'I'm from DC, this place sucks' mode." She settled next to him once again.

He shifted a leg forward, so it rested against hers. "To be fair, I never really got out of that mode."

She laughed. "At least you admit it! Tell me, what magic is in DC? It's a city chock full of politicos and monuments. Everyone is from somewhere else, including you. You probably don't even know your neighbors."

"Hey, yes I do. The Jacksons have lived next door to me for years. I even feed their cat for them when they go on vacation."

She brought her hands to her face in mock-shock. "Well, color me corrected."

They smiled and the heaviness in the room evaporated. "Maybe if I'd grown up here, I'd be in love with it the way you are. I think growing up in a city just formed me. I get itchy when I'm out of the city for too long. It's too quiet out here."

"So quiet you can hear your blood moving through your body, on some nights."

"I think that's the first negative thing I've ever heard you say about Falling Leaves." He gave her a gentle poke in the side.

"Look, I get the appeal of big cities. In small doses, that is. There's a lot to do. You don't have to drive to get where you want to go. I know I was being snarky earlier, but DC does have its charms. There's tons of museums, culture, great food. But I couldn't see myself living there, long term."

There it was—the elephant in the room. She couldn't leave. He couldn't stay. It was good they were both on the same page.

"Oh, I almost forgot." She dug into her jeans pocket. "Remember this?"

She handed over a golden locket. A flash of memory hit him like a truck. He remembered buying that locket for Sabrina. His mother helping him pick it out. It was a rare bright spot in that dark time after his father died.

"I'm surprised you still have it." He turned it over, finding the delicate engraving of their initials along the back of the locket. The swooping flourishes of the *B&S* merged under the letters.

"I put it into a box and forgot about it. Until recently." She drew her finger over the chain. "It's the only jewelry a man has ever bought for me. I mean, outside my family."

He arched a brow. "I find that hard to believe."

"Like I said, I haven't dated many people seriously." She snapped the locket up in her hand and shoved it back in her pocket.

He leaned forward and caught her chin in his hand. "Look, we spend an awful lot of time dwelling in the past or worrying about the future. How about we focus on now?"

She tilted her head to the side. Her hair tumbled over her shoulders, revealing a slice of her neck. He longed to lunge for her and kiss her there.

He wasn't sure if this was a relationship or not, but he knew one thing. Wherever Sabrina led, he'd follow. He owed her that much, seeing as he'd been the one to implode their relationship last time.

"Now sounds good." She came forward onto her hands, so she was leaning over him. Her lips brushed against his. "As fun as this is, it looks like the rain is letting up some. And we have a busy day tomorrow, installing the final finishes on the lobby and stairwell. We both need to be on our best game."

He kissed her gently. "Damn you, for making so much sense."

She settled forward so she was in his lap. He wrapped his arms around her and gave her a light kiss on her neck. She exhaled through smiling lips.

"How about since the whole town knows about us, we have our first official date soon? Dinner at Luci's?"

"I don't know, it's hard to get a table on short notice there." She nudged closer to him.

"Massimo owes me a favor. I got him a discounted rate at my hotel for his anniversary overnight stay in DC a few months back. It still might take a few days, though."

Luci's was a tiny place—only ten tables—with a renowned reputation that stretched far outside of Falling Leaves. Normally, it could take weeks, if not months to land a reservation.

"Give me the time, and the place, and I'll be there." She laughed as she snuggled against him. "Oh wait, I already know the place."

He held her close as the rain carried on outside.

"I thought I was driving you home."

He kissed the side of her face. "You make a compelling argument towards staying."

She turned so they were nose-to-nose. "I didn't say anything."

He smiled. "You just existing is convincing me. Everything about you is something special. The way you smell…" He brought his face to the back of her ear, enjoying the sharp intake of breath as he kissed her there. "The way you feel…" He trailed a hand down her shoulder. "The way—"

"You're gonna make me crazy if you keep this going." She shifted in his lap. "Early day and all, tomorrow. You should go. Besides, it gives us something to look forward to, huh?"

Before he could answer, she eased out of his lap. He reached for her as the power came back on.

He shielded his face against the light. "Well, that certainly is a mood killer."

Sabrina groaned. "All the more things to look forward to later, huh?"

"You're right." He rose from the sofa and followed her to the door.

"Do you need me to drive you back?"

He shook his head. "No, because we both know where it'll go. I'm going to embrace having something to look forward to." He captured her chin and brought their mouths together.

She leaned against him—their chests crashing together, her arm looping around his waist—before he ended the kiss.

"Besides, the walk in the bracing October air will do me good." He reached down to brush his fingers against her cheek.

"I'll see you tomorrow. But I'll be thinking about you tonight."

She shoved an umbrella into his hands. "So unfair!"

He shrugged. "You're the one that said good things come to those who wait."

She leaned against the door. "Not in those words, but yes. You should go. Text me when you get home. Wouldn't want you to have a run-in with the handkerchief bandit."

"I can handle myself. Goodnight, Sabrina."

She stepped back inside and started to close the door. "Night, Brando."

Brandon smiled all the way home. Once he was in his room, he couldn't resist returning fire.

See you in the morning, Sabby.

He put his phone on 'do not disturb' and called it a night.

Chapter Twenty-Three

Despite her newfound happiness with Brandon, life carried on. Over the next week, Sabrina barely had a moment with him, despite the two of them working no more than a few hundred yards from one another most of the time.

The Westmores were in no hurry to leave. Not that Sabrina could blame them. Baby Lakyn was doing better but wouldn't be leaving NICU for at least another week.

Sabrina had a jumble of her own balls tossed into the air. Her father was being a stubborn jackass and refusing to get up for his required ambulation every day. He was in such a foul mood, Sabrina hadn't found the time to talk to him about the future of the business.

Her mother was stressed, so that meant Sabrina was, too. She tried to help as much as she could. But her mother had that wonderful mom-like quality where she bemoaned never having help, but then no matter what Sabrina did, it wasn't up to her standards. Thank

God, she had the pageant to keep her busy and out of Sabrina's hair most of the time.

Added to the chaos of the last week was Sebastian and Gretchen's arrival. Eleanor had seen to the guest suite being set up for them since Sabrina had been slammed with work at the Pumpkin.

At least with Sebastian, Gretchen and the boys around, there was more help for her parents. Her brother Caleb would be arriving by the end of the weekend, as well.

She'd be expected to put in her family time. As much as she loved having her brothers in town, time with Brandon was precious. She wanted to spend every second with him, especially as they'd spent a total of an hour together all week.

They were both looking forward to their first official date as soon as work wrapped up for the day. But first, she had to get Carlos off the roof.

Sabrina kept one hand on the ladder and called up to him. "That gutter is hanging on for dear life, be careful!"

They'd fixed the gutter on the far side of the roof at the beginning of the week. Of course the wind had to pull down another that morning.

He clung to the side of one of the turrets and yelled back something half in English, half in Spanish. It took her mind a moment to translate. He thought the gutter removal should be put off until the full crew was back on Monday.

"You're probably right," she called back. "Get down from there."

"There she is! Look, boys, it's Aunty Sabrina!"

Sabrina whirled around to find her mother, brother, sister-in-law, and nephews piling out of her mother's SUV.

She stepped to the side as Carlos shimmied down the ladder.

"You know better than to sneak up on someone on a job site, Mom."

Her mother didn't respond, instead she passed Graham over to Sabrina. This was a tactic to avoid confrontation, as her mother knew she adored Graham. Blonde curls and big green eyes, he was the most precious toddler she'd ever seen.

"Hi, baby." She pulled him in close for a tussle of his curls.

"Graham says he wants Aunty Sabrina to come to dinner with us," Lainey said. "We're going to Roanoke. So, get changed and let's go."

"You don't have to," Gretchen added. "You must be tired from work."

Sebastian walked over to one of the loose boards on the porch. "When are you going to get around to fixing this? It's a trip hazard."

Sabrina exhaled into the crook of Graham's neck. She wanted to tell her older brother that he'd forfeited his right to his unasked-for opinion when he turned his nose up at the business. To assure her sister-in-law that she knew she had no part in her mother's plans. And to tell her mother to butt out.

"Well?" Lainey said. "Hurry up. I'm sure Carlos can mind things."

Carlos was busy leading Caden around the front garden. Children, just like everyone else, gravitated toward him.

"I'm not going to Roanoke. I have other plans."

"Cancel them," Lainey snapped. When she was stressed, everyone felt the brunt of it. She usually knew better than to pull stunts on Sabrina. She wasn't afraid of her mother's wrath.

That said, she didn't feel like getting into it with her mother on the front lawn. Reluctantly, she passed Graham back to his mother and stepped up close to Lainey.

"I have plans with Brandon. I'm not canceling anything."

"Brandon?" Sebastian asked. "Blake? I thought you two hated each other."

Lainey's mouth opened and closed. A slow smile spread across her face. "Have him come along, then. He's practically family, anyway."

"Mom, no. It's our first official date. I don't need hangers-on. We'll have dinner another day, okay?"

Lainey opened her mouth to argue. She didn't get a chance to speak. Brandon beat her to it.

"Sorry, Lainey. I'm going to have back Sabrina up on this one." He stood on the top step of the porch, his arms folded across his chest. His white dress shirt stretched across his biceps. His sleeves were rolled up to the elbow, revealing forearms dusted with golden hair, catching the light afternoon light.

As he stood there, some part of her heart elevated and lodged in the base of her throat.

"Oh, fine," Lainey said. "I am so happy you two kids are seeing each other. But I'm saying it now—dinner Sunday night at the Ellises. No excuses."

Sebastian stepped forward to shake Brandon's hand. "Sorry about your mom, Brandon. She was a spectacular lady."

Sabrina caught the flash of grief on Brandon's face. "Thanks, man. She really was something."

"Well, we should get going. Caden will pitch a fit if he doesn't eat on time," Gretchen said.

As if on cue, the little terror ran around the corner. "Hi, Aunt Sabrina!" He shouted as he bolted straight for the car, with Gretchen and Sebastian giving chase.

Lainey threw her arms up in the air. "I guess that's my cue. Don't forget, dinner on Sunday. You can't get out of it since pageant rehearsal is right before."

Sabrina waved her mother off. "We'll be there." Once Lainey turned to leave, Sabrina stepped onto the porch. "We will, right?"

He leaned forward to place his hands on her shoulders. "With bells on."

She stepped onto the edge of the step. "I mean, are the bells necessary? There's enough noise, with all the Ellises under one roof."

"The bells were metaphorical." He reached for the end of her ponytail. "You should get changed. I'll pick you up at six."

"Pick me up? We can walk to Luci's from my house."

"What kind of date would I be if I didn't pick you up in my fancy ride?"

She laughed then they both fell silent, likely remembering the old junker he'd had in high school — lovingly referred to as 'the shitbox'.

"I should hurry, then."

"You do that." He grinned before opening the door.

Sabrina didn't stop smiling as she met up with Carlos to gather the rest of their tools.

"*Hermana*, you look happy," he said. "Like you're lit up from the inside."

"I am happy. He's a good man."

"Then if he's a good man, he'll stay. This inn will stay his."

Her smile faded a fraction. "I don't know about that. I don't want to worry about the future too much."

Carlos knew her well enough to leave it alone. She drove home, pushing the negative thoughts out of her head. This night was the start of something, not the end.

* * * *

It felt like high school all over again. Only this time, Brandon didn't have to make nice with Mr. and Mrs. Ellis before taking Sabrina out.

Now, he had to contend with Eleanor and Dutch.

The kid was only sixteen, but already towered over Brandon. Impressive, since Brandon was six feet tall. He stood on the porch, between him and the front door.

"What are your intentions with Aunt Sabrina?" Dutch puffed up his chest.

"Oh, knock it off, junior." Eleanor appeared from behind Dutch. "Come on in, Brandon."

Dutch stepped to the side and Brandon entered Sabrina's house. Eleanor was in the middle of cooking dinner and the aroma was intriguing.

"What's for dinner?"

"I'll do the asking questions here, mister." Eleanor closed the front door with a bang.

Brandon swung around to face her. Both she and Dutch broke out into laughter.

"Your face! I wish I had my camera," Eleanor said.

He held both hands aloft. "You *are* the town sheriff. Excuse me for leaping to conclusions."

She reached behind her to gather up her long hair into a ponytail. "You have nothing to fear with us. I like you, especially for her."

The kittens came tumbling down the stairs, drawing their attention.

"Ah, she must be on her way. She's like the former Queen of England. Although instead of Corgis, the kittens announce her arrival."

Brandon laughed. "Animals have been following Sabrina around since we were kids. She once rescued a den of bunnies from the school bully during recess."

He bent over to rub Jareth's tawny head. He stood up on his hind legs and rubbed against Brandon's hand.

Sabrina's legs came into view first, in elegant black high heels. Her dress came next, dark blue, lightening in color until it reached a sky blue on her chest.

Her long hair was free around her shoulders, showing off its slight natural wave.

"Wow," Brandon said. And he meant it. She looked fantastic. Despite his best effort, eyes were drawn to the way her dress hugged —

"Your dad used to look at me like that," Eleanor said to Dutch, who pulled a face.

"The taco meat is gonna burn, Mom."

"Oh, shit." She scuttled toward the kitchen. "Have a good time, you two!"

Dutch lingered behind a moment. "You look really pretty, Aunt Sabrina." Before she could thank him for the compliment, he added, "I didn't think you remembered what it was like to wear a dress." He chuckled and ran into the kitchen before Sabrina could swing at him.

"You little jerk!" She pursed her lips. "More like a big jerk. Although to me, he'll always be the same age he was when I met him — eight years old." She turned to Brandon and looked at him.

Now it was his turn to fall under a scrutinizing gaze. "I'd say you clean up nice, but you always look good. Is the suit new?"

The dark suit had been buried in his closet. One he'd bought for his DC job before Mom had gotten worse.

"Newish."

She brushed her hand across his biceps. "You can really tell that you get your suits custom tailored."

He nudged his glasses up his nose. "Is that a compliment?"

"A subtle one, yes." She opened the hall closet. "It's such a nice night. Can we walk? It's only a few blocks."

"You'll be okay in those shoes?"

She tugged a coat off the hanger. "If I'm not, you'll be there to catch me, right?"

"Yes. No guarantee we'll both be standing if you fall, though."

She laughed. "Fair enough. I'll make my way over the cobbles carefully."

He opened the door. "After you."

She grinned and walked out of the front door, her high heels making a pleasing sound on the wooden front porch. He closed the door behind them and offered his arm.

"Shall we?"

Chapter Twenty-Four

Obviously, the term 'slack-jawed yokels' was originated by someone who'd grown up in a small town.

Even though the news of Sabrina and Brandon dating had gone around and back along the gossip circuits, they were the star attraction at Luci's. No one was subtle as they stopped to stare.

Brandon kept his hand firmly on the small of her back as they made their way through the restaurant. She felt like sticking her tongue out at the gawkers. That news would make its way to her mother within seconds. It wasn't a hill worth dying on.

Thankfully, Massimo and Stephanie, the owners, had seated them in the most private booth in the place, in a dim corner with a single Edison dangling above their table. At the center of the table was an arrangement of fall flowers in a mason jar.

"Thankfully I'm familiar with the menu, because I can't see a thing." Brandon lowered his glasses for a better look. "Aren't I a little young to need reading glasses?"

Sabrina gave his knee a squeeze under the table, causing him to drop the menu, face up on the table. They looked at each other and laughed.

"I look like the blind little old man I'm halfway to being."

She leaned forward and nuzzled her cheek against his. "Glasses are underrated. Especially on you."

He grabbed her hand. "Not everyone thinks that. I'm glad you've got a thing for guys with glasses."

She rested her head on his shoulder. "I don't, not really. Just you."

Stephanie appeared at their table, dropping off a carafe of wine and quickly taking their orders before disappearing again.

Brandon reached for his glass and swirled it around before giving it a sniff.

"Ooh, you're so fancy. I bet by one sniff you can tell me everything about the wine, including the name of the winemaker." She was teasing — but she knew there was more than a kernel of truth to her statement.

"I dabble a bit. But I won't bore you with those kinds of arbitrary facts."

It was one of those details that spiked her insecurity. He was sophisticated, with bespoke suits and hundred-dollar haircuts. She looked down at her hands, where the hastily applied nail polish gathered on her cuticles. She should've taken her mother up on her offer for a manicure.

"You all right?" He snaked his arm around her shoulders. She relaxed at his touch.

"I'm fine." She reached for her wine glass. She gave it a swirl before she downed a mighty sip.

Brandon grinned at her. She half-expected him to chastise her. To tell her that wine wasn't beer — her alcohol of choice.

Instead, he only smiled. "You like it?"

She pulled a face. "I remember now why I don't drink much wine. I don't like that aftertaste."

"Trips to wineries scratched off the list, then."

She dabbed the corner of her mouth with her napkin. "Already planning future dates, huh?"

Before he could answer, a familiar voice carried over the top of their booth. "I had to see it for myself. Look at the happy couple!"

Inez clapped her hands together. She was hardly dressed for the atmosphere of Falling Leaves' fanciest eatery. She still had on her apron with the café logo embroidered on the front.

"You really didn't have to," Sabrina said. "Did my mother send you?"

The subtle shrug of her left shoulder told Sabrina all she needed to know.

"You've seen, you can stop your gawking now. And put away the phone before I do it for you."

Inez lowered her phone and spoke to Sabrina in Spanish. "Don't ruin this before it has a chance to start."

"Mind your business," Sabrina responded in English.

Brandon let out a dry laugh. "I really need to learn Spanish, huh?"

"Only if you stay," Inez said before she turned to leave.

Sabrina reached for her wine glass and downed the rest of the contents. "I'm starting to understand why you were so eager to have this town in your rear view. It can be exhausting to be under the microscope."

"You know as well as I do, they'll move onto the next thing soon enough."

Stephanie appeared with their appetizers. "I've seen Inez out. You know how she can be."

"Like the annoying second mom none of us asked for?"

Stephanie laughed. "Yes. But we don't want to get on her shit list, or we'll be banned from the café."

"Like when she banned me for a full month after I learned as many Spanish curse words as I could."

"I heard about that," Brandon said.

Stephanie slipped away, having done her job to lighten the mood.

"Do you like being a face in the crowd when you're in the city?"

He reached for the plates and placed one in front of each of them. "Kind of. It can get lonely, sometimes. But it's better than everyone knowing your business. Or still treating you like you're a kid."

She reached for a piece of focaccia and slipped it through the flavored olive oil.

"I can see the appeal of that."

"Y'know, I want to say something. If I'm off base, tell me. It's not like we've not said worse to each other."

She broke off a piece of bread and motioned for him to go on.

"Sometimes I wonder if you're so determined to stay here because your brothers were so quick to leave. I know your work makes you happy, but you could do that anywhere."

He probably had a point. But he also had an interest in getting her to entertain the idea of leaving Falling Leaves.

"I suppose. I don't want to leave Mom and Dad alone. It's why I put up with my mother's behavior. She'd be so upset if I left."

"You can't set yourself on fire to keep someone else warm. You have to do whatever makes you happiest." He leaned forward and touched her hand. "If that means staying here, then that's fine. But do it because it's what *you* want. Not to make your parents happy."

She exhaled. "This is kinda heavy first date conversation. How are those Hokies doing, huh?"

Brandon laughed. "You know I'm not one to keep up with Virginia Tech sports. And this is *not* our first date."

"Semantics. And oh, I forgot. You have a fancier alma mater."

They shared a smile before he leaned his head against hers. "Fair enough. I'll turn the tide. I have a surprise for after dinner."

"Oh?"

He raised an eyebrow. "You'll have to wait until dinner's over to see what it is."

"I can wait. We've waited this long, right?"

He grabbed her hand and kissed it. "Right."

* * * *

"You're passing on dessert? Are you sure you're all right?" Stephanie reached forward to touch Brandon's forehead, which made Sabrina roar with laughter.

"I have plans for dessert, so just the check please." Brandon ducked away from Stephanie.

Stephanie arched a brow before presenting the billfold. He handed her his credit card without looking at it and she left again.

"I would've gone halfsies with you," Sabrina said.

"You can get our next date." Because there would be, no doubt. He'd had a great time, and the night wasn't over yet.

She blushed and looked away. He liked seeing Sabrina grow shy—normally she was no shrinking violet.

They quickly settled the bill and soon enough were walking back to her house.

"So, any hints?"

"None."

"You're no fun." Her mouth turned into a beautiful pout.

He turned to her. "All will be revealed, soon enough."

They stopped at the house long enough to pick up Brandon's car. Thankfully, the house was dark, so they didn't have to worry about running into Eleanor or Dutch.

"Do I need anything? Coat? A map? Give me something here."

He pressed the ignition start on the SUV and it roared to life. "You're overestimating the surprise. You should really stop reading so many fantasy books." He turned to her before she had a chance to react. "I'm just kidding. Read whatever makes you happy."

"I can't help that I have a big imagination." She smoothed a pleat in her dress.

"I love that about you. I just don't want to disappoint you."

"I know you really don't have passage to a fairy land or something fanciful. My imagination gets ahead of me."

He felt guilty of that himself, as a flash of a possible future passed in front of his eyes. The two of them getting married in a courtyard filled with willow trees, fairy lights and the bride wearing a crown with flowers and crystals woven into them.

He exhaled as the image dissolved inside his mind. He had to remember what this was. It had an expiration date.

The drive was short, and they pulled in front of the Pumpkin. He cut the engine. "See? I told you to lower your expectations."

"Stop selling yourself short." She unbuckled her seatbelt and they met in front of the SUV. He took her hand. She started to lead them toward the front door but he gently pulled her onto the stone path that led into the back garden.

"Oh, so the surprise lies outside. Good to know."

"Hopefully there won't be any screaming handkerchief surprises, like the last time we were here together."

"I doubt it, but this time I'm wearing heels. I can nail 'em with one." She mimed taking off her shoe and throwing it like a football.

He squeezed her hand. "I bet you could."

Brandon swallowed and hoped that the staff had set up the surprise like he'd asked. He already felt like he was failing her a little, not having a wardrobe with passage to a secret land. Even though that was outside of the realm of possibility, he wanted to give her a taste of it.

But as they rounded the corner, his worries quickly unraveled. They'd done what he'd asked and more.

"Oh my God!"

She clasped her hands together as she looked around the back garden. Like his daydream, fairy lights were strung from trees. Lanterns lined the path to the gazebo, which had a warm glow emanating from inside.

"Is this you being romantic?" She turned to face him.

"What else would it be? I can be romantic. I've been known to melt a heart or two."

She placed her hand on his chest. "Or three."

They shared a smile before turning toward the gazebo. It was nicer than a typical gazebo, with The Frosted Squash using it for private gatherings.

He reached for the screen door handle and opened the door for her. "After you, my lady."

He couldn't take his eyes off her as she stepped inside. Her mouth dropped open in awe.

The room was dimly lit with a constellation of fairy lights intertwined in the beams. A warm, orangey-blue hue emanated from the heater set up by the table.

"No wonder you wanted me to pass on dessert."

She walked in front of the small buffet table Adalyn had set up piled with different treats. From Sabrina's favorite pumpkin rolls to the Pumpkin's famous bourbon pecan pie.

"How are we possibly going to eat all this?" She rubbed her hand over her stomach.

"Whatever's left won't go to waste. Don't feel like you have to stuff yourself."

She reached for a plate. "A chocolate fountain?"

At the edge of the table, a small fountain bubbled up chocolate. She reached for a marshmallow and set it under the flow until it was covered. She reminded him of her childlike form. The two of them at a birthday party, bickering under the table while they shoved cake in their mouths.

He drew his thumb across her chin to scoop up the chocolate. "It's considered a crime within the town limits to let chocolate go to waste." He dipped his finger in her mouth.

She began to cough. "Jesus, a little warning would be nice."

"Sorry. I got ahead of myself." He wiped off his hand. "I know it's not a fairy land. But this is as close as I could get with our earthly tethers."

She shook her head. "If I'd had any idea you were this romantic, I wouldn't have wasted so much time caught up in an old version of you."

"Let's not focus on what we can't change."

She nodded. "Sometimes I forget that you know me better than just about anyone."

He reached for the pie server. "I *did*. Then I lost you, along the way. But we're finding each other again, right?"

"Right."

"I like that term, finding. As if even though we have this shared history, there's still a lot to discover between us."

Sabrina reached for the whip cream and shotgunned a mouthful. Now it was Brandon's turn to sputter like a fool.

She pressed more whip cream into her mouth. "Tell your staff not to reuse that container. That wasn't very sanitary of me."

He placed his finger on her lips. "Don't worry. I think I'll remember."

The two of them sat on a bench at the rear of the gazebo. He balanced his pie plate on his knee.

"Thank you for this, Brandon. This is the nicest thing anyone's ever done for me."

"Well, you've surely not dated anyone of merit since I've left." He scooped pie into his mouth.

"No, there was never anyone like you. That's half the problem." She paused while she took a bite. "And kind of why I agreed to doing this if I'm honest. I won't tie you down to a life you don't want. That's not good for either of us. But by doing whatever "this" is" — she made quotation marks with her free hand — "I think I'll be able to let you go."

It stung a bit, to know her reasoning. But it made sense. Or maybe it would have at one time. He wasn't so sure anymore.

"I suppose life will lead us where we're meant to be, hmm?"

"If we're lucky."

They finished their pie and sat together on the bench. As much as Brandon wanted to invite her upstairs, her admission made him hesitant.

Even if he left, there was more between them than a simple roll in the hay. He wanted it to be special.

For both their sakes.

Chapter Twenty-Five

Less than six hours after she'd left the Pumpkin, she was back. Thankfully, it was Saturday, so the workload was lighter. Carlos had arranged for a sub-contractor to come on Monday to install the new gutters. In the meantime, the two of them kept busy knocking a few small jobs off the punch list. A soft, steady rain fell outside, keeping them inside.

Even though she knew Brandon was off property — taking the Westmores back to Roanoke to visit their granddaughter — her head turned every time she thought she heard someone approach.

"Sabrina."

Carlos' voice cut through her daydream. "Yeah?"

"Is it straight or not? The level keeps sliding back and forth." She looked up to find him with a level on top of one of the photos lining the stairs. They'd reframed a lot of the old photos and replaced a few of the creepy ones with more benign photos of jack-o-lanterns and friendly ghosts.

"It's straight. And even if it's not, it adds to the charm of the place."

He handed her the level and screwed in the picture hanger. "You seem a million miles away. Is your dad okay?"

Guests mingled around, watching them, so he'd switched to Spanish.

"Hmm? Oh, Dad's just fine. Other than being stubborn about doing his therapy, but I'm working on that. We're going over there tomorrow for dinner. Caleb is arriving late tonight, I think."

"We? Did you use the right word there, *jefa*?"

It wasn't uncommon for the two of them to take the piss out of each other for their second language skills. But this time, she'd used the right word.

"Brandon's coming."

Carlos hopped off the ladder. "So last night went well, I see."

More than well. Not that she'd been on many dates over the years, but it'd been the best. Dinner had been wonderful. After had been even better.

They'd left it before she'd wanted to. Perhaps the promise of more after the long day they had ahead of them. Work, then pageant rehearsal. Then a busy Sunday with her family.

And him.

"I don't want to rush this. I know I won't be here forever, but there's no reason for breakneck speed. You're worth waiting for." He'd whispered the words against her cheek.

Carlos' chuckle brought her back to the present again. "That dreamy look on your face answers that question for me."

"I'm happy."

He placed the next photo on the wall. "I'm glad to hear it. So, is this one straight?"

"As an arrow."

They worked hanging up the rest of the photos before calling it a day. Brandon hadn't returned by the time she left, so she headed home for a little R&R before pageant practice.

She was so caught up in her own happiness that it took her until she pulled into the drive to remember that her brother, sister-in-law and nephews were staying with her. She'd already been read the riot act from Sebastian that they hadn't seen much of her since arriving.

So much for retreating to her bathroom for a bubble bath.

She pulled her truck onto the street, behind Sebastian's rental car. Eleanor's squad car was missing, and if Dutch had half a brain, he was out, too.

She barely made it to the door before it swung open. "There she is, finally gracing us with her presence," Sebastian said.

"I'm gonna start calling you Mom if you insist on acting like her."

Childish laughter carried down the stairs from the guest suite. Thank God for her nephews.

She stepped inside and sat down on the bench by the front door and began pulling off her boots.

"I'm just saying, you've hardly been home. Kind of defeats the purpose of staying with you."

She tugged her boot off and tilted it upside down. Several pebbles tinkled onto the tile. "It's not like I was getting a mani-pedi. I was working."

The business was always a sore point between them. Some part of Sabrina knew that Sebastian had probably hoped that Ellis & Son would end when Dad retired. Then his guilt could be assuaged, and they could all move on. He'd been less than pleased when Sabrina had stepped in to take over.

"Spending time with your boyfriend, more like."

She tugged on the laces of her left boot. "What crawled up your ass and died? Nobody forced you to come back. And if you're going to be a sour ass grump all the time, you can go stay with Mom and Dad." She dumped out the pebbles from her other boot and reached for the broom and dustpan.

"You'd really kick us out?" Sebastian balked.

"There's no us. Gretchen and the boys can stay." She swept up the mess and held the dustpan aloft. "You and Dad would be on each other's last nerve before sunset."

Sebastian sighed. "I just don't know what to do with myself. I'm not used to having free time."

She walked past him to dump the dustpan in the guest bath trash. "There it is. The source of your asshole-ish ennui."

"All right, all right," he griped.

She returned the broom to the coat closet and beckoned her brother to follow her into the kitchen. Without asking, she began pulling down boxes from the cabinet. When Sebastian was stressed, he baked.

"Here's the supplies. Have at it."

He rolled his eyes. "I don't need to bake."

"Sure, you do. I have a big kitchen that wouldn't get any use if Eleanor didn't live with me. So, have at it."

He half-heartedly began rifling through the contents. "I should tell you something."

Sabrina kept her eyes on her older brother. He wasn't the confiding type. At least, not with her.

"What's up?"

"I sold the startup. That's a big reason why we're here for an extended stay. To get the house fixed up, and ready for whatever's next."

Sabrina exhaled and settled onto the bar stool next to her brother. "That's big news. Did you tell Mom and Dad?"

He produced a bag of fancy chocolate chips that Eleanor must've bought.

"No, because you know what they'd say. Move back here."

A burst of laughter floated down the steps. Gretchen and the boys were play-acting dinosaurs.

"You could be happy here. Lord knows it'd cost you a lot less to live here. The boys would grow up happy, just like we did."

He pulled out another bag of shredded coconut and brown sugar. "I don't know."

"You could open a bakery. With as much money you've made, it wouldn't even need to make a profit."

He snorted at that. "Every business venture needs to be profitable. But I did notice there is room in the market. Over Easy offers more diner fare, and The Frosted Squash is more of an upscale brunch and dinner sort of spot. I think a small bakery would do well here."

"So, explore the idea. Don't you want to see your boys grow up? Working in finance isn't exactly low stress."

He pulled vanilla extract and a few more small ingredients out of the container and stood. "What's Brandon's deal, then? He was just like me, wanting to get out of here from the time he could string a sentence together."

"That's a bit hyperbolic. He didn't move here until second grade."

"You know what I mean. Where are your cookie sheets?" He started opening cabinets.

She opened the lower cabinet closest to the oven and pulled out the rack she'd installed for easy storage. More for Eleanor's benefit than her own.

"What about Brandon? Is he staying this time around?"

There was the nine-thousand-pound elephant, squeezing itself back into the room again.

"I doubt it. He has a life waiting back for him in DC."

"Parchment paper?" He extended his hand.

She retrieved it for him. "Are you making cookies?"

"Dark chocolate coconut. Gretchen's favorite." His face lit up at her name.

"Ten years and you two are still like kids."

"I see that with you and Brandon, too. You could be the real thing."

She exhaled. This was the last thing she wanted to talk about, especially with Sebastian of all people.

"I'll leave you to your cookies." She paused. "If you did decide to stay, we'd be thrilled to have you. And there's no saying you'd have to stay forever. Maybe until the boys graduate high school."

"That's an option." He tore off pieces of parchment. "Do you know who the best realtor is in town? There's a space I'd like to look at."

Sabrina clasped her hands together. "Really?"

"Don't get your hopes up."

"I'll get you Debbie's contact info. But hands off the property two doors down from The Weird Sisters mystical shop. I've had my eye on it for a while."

Sebastian opened a drawer and pulled out measuring spoons. "For what? Dad doesn't want to move the business?"

"Well, he might not have a choice. Uncle Gordon is going to be retiring soon. Dennis wants to have a proper office when he takes over."

Hence why he was working on his father. Sabrina just needed to start working on her dad. She hoped to get a look inside the space sometime soon, but there was no point if her father wouldn't consider it.

She worried that her father would make some declarative statement and decide to retire from the business. As much as Sabrina prided herself on the work she did, she wasn't quite ready to go on her own just yet.

Sebastian chuckled. "I'm surprised Uncle Gordo would allow Dennis to take over. He's always been the one with a loose screw."

To his credit, Dennis had worked hard over the last year to prove his worth, and she told her brother as much.

"Well, maybe things can change. Dennis can get his shit together. And maybe I'll move back to Falling Leaves."

"Just don't go getting Mom and Dad's hopes up about me and Brandon. We're just having a good time, for as long as it lasts."

He chuckled to himself. "Whatever you say, kiddo."

* * * *

If he had to hear one more off-key rendition of *This is Halloween*, Brandon was going to throw himself down the stairs. Although to be fair, Carlos had an amazing singing voice and outshone everyone. No wonder no one ever ran against him in the pageant.

The only saving grace was Sabrina's take on the choreography. Much to her mother's annoyance, she had two left feet. When the rest of the contestants went right, Sabrina went left. Once, almost falling off the stage.

He couldn't help himself, he laughed. She mimed her finger slicing across her neck.

He couldn't help but marvel at how things changed but also stayed the same. They'd been kids in this very same town hall, working on various pageants, festivals and concerts together.

"You look happy." Jasmine dropped into the seat next to him.

Funny, how this had all started as some sort of ruse to keep the Westmores' interest in the Pumpkin. He'd started to waffle about what he really wanted.

"I am happy. This silly little town can grow on you."

She flipped her blonde hair over one shoulder. "So much so that you're thinking of staying? Gabriel told me he wanted to stop by next week to see the progress on the renovations."

Obviously, Merit and Gabriel had been busy with their newborn, so he hadn't been in touch with them. He'd also let Cassandra's two most recent calls go to voicemail. He knew she'd only be needling him about the sale. He had nothing to tell her.

About the sale or Paris.

"I look forward to updating him."

"Sabrina, I swear." Lainey slapped a hand to her forehead as she dropped her prop.

Jasmine nudged him with her elbow. "I wonder if you'd find someone in the big city who makes you smile the way she does."

That was the rub. He doubted he ever would. Sabrina had always existed in the back of his brain. A distant love, laced with regret.

Now, all he felt was love. Leaving wouldn't be so easy.

But it'd have to be done, eventually. He'd grown less sure about the job in Paris. It wasn't a conscious choice he'd made. He'd gone from spending his rare idle moments to looking for apartments in the City of Light, to scouring the internet for mountain lodge properties.

Not that he'd had any luck on that front.

"You're probably right about that."

"Between you and me"—Jasmine had to raise her voice to be heard over the commotion of the choreography falling apart—"I think this place is spectacular. Maybe you're starting to realize that, too."

He managed a small smile. "You might be onto something."

Sabrina jumped off the stage. Her dark costume billowed behind her as she ran to him. "Let's get out of here before they notice."

"Your mother will kill you." Brandon pointed to where Lainey was talking things over with the pageant coordinators.

"She's killed me a hundred times already. Come on." She extended her hand, and he rose from his seat. They ran out the side door, giggling like kids.

"Wait a second." He paused at a fuse box on their way out. He flung it open and switched one of the fuses back and forth.

"Oh no, is that Old Levi again, causing trouble?" he called.

Inside, chaos broke out as everyone ran around to see if they could get a glimpse at Falling Leaves' resident ghost.

Brandon grabbed Sabrina's hand and they ran away.

They ran half a block before they realized no one was chasing them and slowed their pace. "Do you have a ghost tour tonight?"

He shook his head. "No, with occupancy so low, we probably will have one last one for Halloween and that'll be it for the season. Then it'll be time for sleigh rides." He shook his head.

"You look almost nostalgic. I mean, you invoked Old Levi's name back there. I thought you didn't believe in him?"

Brandon shrugged. "I don't, not really. I just wanted a distraction that would keep your mother from chasing after us."

"Well, we're here."

They'd come to stop in front of the Pumpkin, half in tatters with the renovation work on pause for the rest of the weekend. Plastic sheeting covered the gutters and one of the roof turrets.

He turned to look at her, her face made-up with the type of glittery make-up she'd never wear outside of the pageant. She was wild and spectacular.

"Do you want to come upstairs?" He kept his gaze on her. He half expected her to bolt.

Instead, she said, "Are you sure?"

"I've never been surer of anything in my life."

She ducked her head as he took her hand. They walked around the Pumpkin to the side entrance.

"After you."

She whirled around on him, a smile on her face. "You just want to look up my dress."

"Well, duh," he said. "It's an appetizer for things to come."

She laughed and leaned forward to take off her heels. Then she took off up the stairs. He closed the door behind them and followed her.

He half-slid into her at the top of the stairs. Their arms came around each other, at first to steady one another.

She drew her hands to the back of his neck, pulling him in for a kiss. He wrapped one arm around her while he fumbled in his pocket for his keys with the other.

She reached in for a kiss, her lips brushing against his as they moved together down the hall. His keys dropped to the floor and he cursed under his breath.

"This is almost as bad as that time in your car. Remember when you nearly put the car in drive, pulling me over into your lap?"

He swiped the keys and swiftly inserted the right one into the lock. "Don't remind me."

She leaned in to give his hand a squeeze. "We have a lot of good memories together, huh?"

He turned, finding her gaze already on him. "We do. Now it's time to make new ones."

He grabbed her face in his hands as the door fell open. They tumbled through it together, before he kicked it closed.

Chapter Twenty-Six

Sabrina wasn't the type to wake up in beds that weren't her own. As her eyes blinked open, she was momentarily alarmed. Until she took in the familiar lace curtains, half-covering the window. The striped wallpaper, soon to be for the fire once they began tackling that phase of renovations.

Oh, and the man lying next to her. Brandon looked almost unrecognizable without his glasses. But he was somehow even more handsome, his fretful face relaxed in sleep.

She fell back onto the pillow and rolled onto her side. She watched the subtle rise and fall of his chest. Last night wasn't the first time — after all, they'd been each other's first, many moons ago — but it was like a return to a place she'd forced herself to forget.

It'd been too painful to think of those moments when they'd snuck away together. Lying under the stars in the bed of her old beater truck. The perfect bliss of that first love.

Their first love had been too perfect to last. Maybe twice, she'd get lucky. He didn't seem so eager to leave now.

At first, she'd overhear him telling Babs or Javier how he was eager to get back to his job at Hotel Blaque. That he missed being just a metro ride from anything exciting in the city. Now, he didn't mention his previous life as much. That didn't mean he was keen to stay in Falling Leaves, though.

And she didn't want him to resent her. That would be worse than him leaving. For him to stay for her and be miserable.

She traced her fingertips from his shoulder, down his biceps to his forearm. He stirred at her touch, his eyes lazily opening.

"Were you staring at me while I slept?" His deep voice was crackly from disuse.

"So what if I was?" She hitched up onto her elbow. "You looked peaceful."

He brought a hand to his face and yawned. "Peaceful is not a word usually associated with me."

"Well, duh. That's why it's nice to watch you sleep. All the day's worries are absent from your face."

He snorted. "That may be true, but my brain wasn't at rest. I was in the middle of dreaming that a horde of spiders were climbing all over me."

"Probably because of this." She ran her fingertips over him once again.

"Yep, that's probably why. Before that, I was walking through the world's longest hallway." He laughed to himself. "Oh. no, I've become one of those people who talks about their dreams."

"There's nothing wrong with that. Although I don't remember mine. I slept soundly." She leaned over him.

"Thanks to you." She leaned over for a kiss, morning breath be damned.

Luckily, he didn't seem to mind. He pushed her hair back from her face as he broke the kiss.

"What do we have to do today?"

Her heart leapt at *we*. Like they were a solidified unit.

"We have dinner at my parents'. Well, more like linner. Dad dozes out early since his surgery."

"How is he doing, anyhow? Will he be back on the jobsite soon?"

"Not if he doesn't keep moving. Stubborn old goat. I'll get on him while we're there."

"Do we need to bring anything?"

"Just ourselves. Maybe some anti-anxiety meds for Mom. You know how she takes on too much and won't let anyone help her."

"I do know. She used to drive my mom crazy."

Sabrina rested her head on Brandon's chest. "Would she be happy? About us, I mean?"

He traced his hand down her bare arm. "Oh, you know my mom and your mom would be planning our wedding."

They laughed but said nothing. She kept her gaze out of the window, wanting to say the words. To address the ongoing elephant in the room. She should — to fully protect her heart.

He wouldn't skip town like he had over a decade before. But he would leave. And she'd have to carry on, somehow. She glanced over at Brandon, finding that he'd dozed off again.

Poor thing had been running on caffeine and adrenaline for days. She wasn't surprised he was so tired.

Her phone buzzed with a text. She sighed, grateful for the distraction from her thoughts. Not wanting to untangle herself from him, she blindly reached for her phone. Only two people would be texting her this early — her mother or father.

The text was from the former.

Your brother is here with the kids. Did he tell you he and Olivia are separated?

She sat up with a start. Caleb was an enigma wrapped in bacon. He was exactly the type of person to drop a bomb like that and act surprised when you questioned him about it.

"Everything okay?" Brandon murmured.

"Dinner is going to be interesting, that's for sure."

She'd have to pick up a six-pack on the way.

* * * *

"Are you sure we didn't need to bring anything? I mean, other than the beer?"

Brandon and Sabrina stood shoulder to shoulder on her parents' front porch. He wasn't sure why he was nervous. The Blakes and the Ellises had been friends for decades. Even after he and Sabrina had ended things, their parents had stayed friends.

But he felt like he was a kid again, standing on the porch, waiting for Mr. Ellis and being grateful that Sabrina's older brothers had already moved out of the house. He knew Sebastian was staying with Sabrina, and judging by the ramshackle RV in the driveway, Caleb and his brood had arrived.

The door swung open, revealing a harried Mrs. Ellis.

"Oh, thank God you're here. I'm about to lose my ever-loving mind." She ushered them inside.

It took all of a half a second for understanding to dawn on Brandon why Mrs. Ellis was halfway to madness.

The Ellis men were in a heated discussion, apparently about Caleb's separation. Which was news to him.

"So, you let her take off with someone else?" Mr. Ellis said.

Caleb sighed and dropped onto the sofa. "Olivia is going through some things right now. It's better for everyone. She'll be home when we're there, to take care of the girls." Caleb ran a hand through his longish, dark hair.

He'd always smelled like patchouli, weed and nag champa. As he rose to greet them, Brandon thought to himself that not much had changed.

"Well, I'm glad to see some smiling faces. They're only being nice to the kids and not me."

"Oh, hush," Mrs. Ellis said. "You can't blame us for being shocked. To tell us that you're separated and that our daughter-in-law is a lesbian!"

"She's not a lesbian, Mom. She's bisexual. I always knew that. We never told you and Dad, because, well" — he gestured at them with his hand — "you aren't exactly taking it well."

"I haven't said a word on the subject," Mr. Ellis said.

Brandon cut a look to Sabrina. She didn't appear surprised by this news, either. Not that it mattered to Brandon.

Not unless he didn't know them nearly as well as he'd thought.

There was a cry from the other room where the children were playing, and Caleb walked off to investigate, followed by Mrs. Ellis.

"I guess we're not the big story tonight," Brandon whispered to Sabrina.

Sabrina grinned and gave him an elbow in the ribs. "I guess not."

Before he could ask more about the current situation, a little girl tore through the doorway.

"Aunty Sabrina!" She leapt into Sabrina's arms without waiting for Sabrina to prepare to catch her. Brandon leaned forward to assist, but Sabrina picked up the little girl with no problems.

"Poppy is a little acrobat. I'm used to her throwing herself at me."

The sweet little girl rested her head against Sabrina's shoulder and smiled at him.

"Who're you?"

"I'm Brandon. A friend of your aunt's."

Her grin spread. "A boyfriend?"

Sabrina rolled her eyes. "Don't go getting ahead of yourself there, kid."

Before Poppy could ask what that meant, Mrs. Ellis returned with a toddler in her arms. "Can you take her? I have to have a word with her father."

The little girl was thrust into Brandon's arms. He held her like a bomb, about to go off.

"She's a little girl, she doesn't bite." Sabrina shifted Poppy over to one arm and reached out to stroke her cheek. "This is Emerson. The baby of the family. How are you doing, Emmy?"

She replied by yawning, then babbling against Brandon's shoulder. He relaxed when he realized she wasn't going to make a leap for it, not like her older sister.

"She needs a nap. Come on, help me get her down. Then we'll rescue Caleb."

Poppy dropped to the floor and took off with a shot. He passed Emerson over to Sabrina and followed her up the stairs to where Mrs. Ellis had set up a makeshift nursery and playroom for the grandkids.

"Can you get the light?"

He paused to flick on a light by the crib. Sabrina laid Emerson down. She was half-asleep already, so it didn't take much effort for her to fall asleep. Sabrina pulled a blanket over the little girl and turned on the baby monitor.

She didn't leave right away, instead stood over the crib, watching Emerson breathe.

"I haven't seen her since she was a tiny thing. It makes me wish my brothers lived closer."

Brandon stood next to her. "I guess kids are in your future, huh?"

She turned to him. "I've always wanted a kid or two, maybe someday. You?"

As an only child, he'd never known what it was like to grow up with siblings. He found himself relatively neutral about children.

"I won't lie and say I've given it a lot of thought. It's tough to raise kids when you work crazy hours in hospitality."

Her smile cracked a little. Just enough that most people wouldn't notice. He knew her too well for that.

"Well, good thing you'll be headed back to the big city, right?"

He wanted to tell her that he was less sure about what he wanted with each passing day. How in such a short amount of time, she'd changed his mind about everything he thought he wanted. He was the type to fret every decision.

But not this one. This wasn't the time, though, not with Ellises hiding around every corner.

Mrs. Ellis appeared in the doorway. "There you two are. Come on, supper's on." She leaned in the doorway. "Is the baby down?"

"Put her down myself," Sabrina whispered.

"You're so good with children," her mother replied. She gave Brandon a knowing glance before leaving the room.

He followed Sabrina down the stairs, wanting to tell her how he was feeling. But soon he was dragged back into the midst of the Ellis chaos tornado and the moment had passed.

He found himself at the long, battered wooden table in the Ellises' dining room. He remembered when Mr. Ellis had made it, back when he and Sabrina were in the tenth grade. Conversation rolled through topics like the pageant — quickly coming up next weekend — the cider festival, Sebastian's possible move back to Falling Leaves.

He'd thought that they could potentially get through the evening without an interrogation. Until Caleb, of all people, started the conversation.

"So, looks like you two finally found your way back to one another, huh?" He grinned before his face flashed into a mask of pain. "Ow! Who kicked me?" He reached under the table to rub at his leg.

"Thanks for repaying my earlier kindness by allowing me to be examined under the microscope."

"I am very fond of microscopes, little sis." Caleb reached for the plate of mashed potatoes.

Sabrina groaned and shook her head. "Well, what do you want to know?"

"That you don't already?" Brandon added.

Sabrina looked over at him, shocked. Under the table, she squeezed his hand.

"Ooh, spicy," Sebastian said. "You're not the shy kid you once were, Brandon."

He turned to Sabrina. "I guess I'm not."

One of the kids wailed for juice, and the topic turned again. Sabrina looked at him, a wide smile on her face.

"You're no shrinking violet."

He shrugged. "Thought you knew that about me." He leaned across the table and swiped a kiss across her lips before he could lose courage.

This felt like the beginning of something that he didn't want to turn his back on. Or he could be getting ahead of himself.

Either way, he had to have a big think about what he wanted. Because a night like this—with a found family and a woman he'd never stopped loving—wasn't something he'd be so quick to give up.

Chapter Twenty-Seven

"I don't think you've stopped smiling since Sunday night."

Sabrina glanced over at her father. He'd asked if she could take him to his follow-up appointment to his doctor's. Sabrina wanted to be sure he was recovering as he should be. Especially since he'd promised her that he was getting in his activity as directed by the doctor. They sat alone in the waiting room at his surgeon's office.

"You say that like I'm some miserable old cow who never does anything but scowl."

He laughed. "No, you're saying that. I just mean you're happy, is all."

"I am."

He flipped the page in the magazine he was half-reading. "Why do I feel like there's a but coming there?"

She pointed to the article he was reading. "Looks like the housing market is set to improve, huh?"

He peered at her over the top of the magazine. "Way to dodge the question there, Sabrina."

"I shall continue to dodge it, then. Have you started clearing out the office space above Loose Screw? Dennis harassed me at the grocery store a couple nights ago about it. He's angling to have his own office, instead of making an old two-by-four work as a desk."

This was a half-truth, but a lead in for the much-needed conversation with her father.

Her father glowered. "I don't see why I have to move. It's—"

"It's time for a fresh start, Dad. Uncle Gordo is retiring soon. Dennis wants his own office. It's only fair."

He grumbled again before letting a rather large sigh escape. "Oh, fine. I'll start going through the office. Fair enough?"

"And I'll meet with the realtor about renting a proper office space. I have my eye on a space I think will work perfectly. A home base for us, but also a place to meet with clients. No more running meetings out of truck beds. They can come to us."

He started to argue with her, but as luck would have it, the medical assistant came out to take him back. She wheeled him through the door before closing the door behind him.

While she waited, she mentally reviewed the day's punch list. New gutters were being installed, along with the finishing touches for the painting on the porch and front side of the house. The final stage of the outdoor work would be to replace the cracked and broken windows. She'd commissioned an artist in Roanoke to make a beautiful stained-glass window that would illuminate the lobby on sunny days.

She wondered if work would even carry on that far, as the Westmores seemed eager to talk to Brandon. Would they just cut him a check, and that would be the end of it?

They danced around the subject, both swerving when they got too close. But the reality was, they'd have to talk about it eventually. Unless they wanted to have another misunderstanding, like the one that had caused their first breakup. She wasn't sure how long she'd sat there, lost in her thoughts, when Inez dropped into the seat next to her.

"You look like a bird shit in your shoe."

Sabrina swiveled her head to look at the other woman. "That's a very specific observation."

Inez stowed her reading glasses in her purse. "Little girl, I've known you since you took your first breath. I know you better than you know yourself."

The last thing she wanted was Inez's input into...anything. She was worse than her mother.

"How's the final planning going for the biddies' charity project?"

Every year, the biddies held a pumpkin decorating contest, with proceeds going to the local food bank.

"Oh, I could run it naked and blindfolded at this point. What's the cause for your wicked puss, young lady?"

Sabrina reached for a magazine. "Nothing. I hate doctor's offices. That's the extent of it."

Inez clicked her tongue against her teeth. "Well, it can't have anything to do with you and Brandon. You two are finally getting along, as you were always meant to."

"Finally? What's that supposed to mean?"

She raised her shoulder in a half-shrug. "I just mean you two kids were always the perfect couple. Well, once you got over the bickering and moved onto better things. We've all been waiting for this since he returned to town."

"Perfect couples don't exist." She paused. "Everyone thought Caleb and Olivia were and look at them now."

Again, Inez shrugged. She likely knew the entire story from Lainey. The biddies had a group chat that read more like the ticker along the bottom of a newscast, it was updated so frequently.

"Those two will figure things out. Just like you and Brandon will, too."

"Sounds like Caleb and Olivia already have. Besides, what's to figure out? I want to stay, and he wants to leave."

Inez touched her boot against Sabrina's shoe. "Does he, though? Have you asked him?"

Sabrina opened, then closed her mouth. Inez chuckled. "I thought you didn't. You might want to try that, darlin'."

The door to the exam rooms opened and her father was wheeled out by the assistant.

"That was fast," Sabrina said.

"I'm healing up like a champ." The assistant left him to Sabrina's care, and she thanked the young woman.

"He just needs to make sure to get to physical therapy," the assistant called over her shoulder.

Her father muttered something under his breath before turning to Inez. "What are you doing here? Are you finally getting that old hip looked at?"

"Like I'd have time for that." She rose to stand. Sabrina didn't miss the wince as she shifted her weight onto her right side. "I just knew Sabrina was here, and I wanted to talk to her. I'll see you both later."

Without another word, she strode out of the front door.

Sabrina turned to her father. "Are you really doing all right?"

"Would I lie to you?" He held up his hands. "I promise I'm getting the movement I need for recovery. You'll be dealing with me back at the job site before you know it."

She came around him to wheel him out. "You mean like how you lied to me about having the surgery in the first place. You need to go to physical therapy, Dad. Don't make me call the office to find out when your appointments are."

"I'll go. Hopefully, by the new year I'll be back to bossing you around, like I never left." He reached for a bottle of soda from the cup holder. "We'll talk more about the office space later. I want to go home and nap now."

Sabrina knew when to leave well enough alone. Her thoughts turned to the business as she drove her father home. By the new year, they'd be done with Pumpkin and onto some new job. Hopefully.

It might be a good idea if she and Brandon had a chat—just to be sure they were both still on the same page.

* * * *

"There you are. I've been looking everywhere for you."

Brandon was eyeballs-deep into clearing out the second-floor guest rooms for the next phase. It would likely be one of the best parts of the renovation. He and Sabrina had a trip to Roanoke planned to pick out new furnishings for the room.

He looked up, surprised to find Gabriel Westmore in the doorway.

"Hello there, Gabriel." Brandon rose to his feet and brushed the dust from his knees. "Pardon my appearance. We're hitting the mid-way point in the renovations now. Which means it's time to tackle the rooms."

Gabriel leaned in the doorway. "I saw how fast work is coming along. The outside looks brand new. Less like a haunted house, and more like a charming — if slightly spooky — inn."

He laughed. "I hope that doesn't change things. Were you and Merit hoping for the haunted house route?" He pushed a chair to the side. "How is she, and the baby, by the way?"

"She's been out of the hospital for a few days now. Little Lakyn is improving faster than originally thought, as well. I'm hoping we'll be headed home before the end of the week." Gabriel ran his hand over the newly laid wallpaper. "And no, it doesn't change things. We do our research before we purchase any property. Falling Leaves has a bit of kitsch about it, with it being the most haunted town in the Commonwealth and all that. Keeping the Pumpkin as is will keep guests interested in that lore."

Part of Brandon would be sad to lose the Westmores. He'd grown used to their charms. And without them, who knows if he and Sabrina would've figured things out on their own.

"That's excellent news."

Gabriel smiled. "I'm just here to retrieve my family for the evening. But I did want to let you know that Merit and I will be looking to have a meeting with you before we leave town."

Brandon drummed his fingers along the back of a wingback chair. "Oh?"

"We don't want to leave Falling Leaves without deciding about the Pumpkin. I think it's best for everyone involved. It's been nice to see how renovations are progressing while we've been here."

Brandon blinked. He should feel...something right now. Either dread or excitement at the thought of the Pumpkin's fate.

"You all right, mate?" Gabriel prompted.

He snapped out of his reverie. "Sorry, yeah. I got distracted thinking about tile there for a second." A lie, capped off with a laugh. "That should work. I look forward to talking to you both when you're available."

Gabriel reached out to shake his hand. "I'm hoping it'll be beneficial for both of us. I'll let you know the particulars later."

Gabriel turned to leave and Brandon threw himself back into work, not stopping until the whole room was packed up and ready to be moved.

He stopped off at The Frosted Squash for a treat. Sabrina had already left for the day, but they had plans to meet up later.

He was idly scrolling through social media when a text came in from Cassandra.

Are you alive??? Or have you forgotten all about me and the Paris job?

Brandon sighed and tapped on the message. It wasn't like him to not respond to texts. Especially about something as important as his possible next job. He sent off a curt reply saying he'd be in touch then muted notifications for the conversation.

He would be, whether he liked it or not. He was reluctant to move outside of the comfy little bubble he and Sabrina had crafted for themselves.

But eventually, reality would intrude.

Chapter Twenty-Eight

"One last time! And a one and a two!"

Sabrina stood in the back of the group of Miss Autumn contestants, hoping not to draw the wrath of the pageant's ancient choreographer, Miss June.

She'd practiced the stupid dance no less than a hundred times in her living room, until she'd driven the entire household to the brink of insanity. Not because she cared about winning. More that she didn't want to end up making an ass of herself in front of the town.

And maybe trying to coordinate her limbs was a way to keep her mind off what was going on with Brandon.

After tonight's practice, they were taking a drive out to the edge of town for a bonfire — the final event of the town's cider festival. It was part of her plan to show Brandon the magic of Falling Leaves. Not that it would make him stay. No, that was a decision he had to come to on his own. This was for creating memories, nothing more.

At least that's what she told herself.

"Sabrina Ellis, you almost ran into Angela!" Miss June called. "Keep to time!" She clapped her hands together.

Sabrina grumbled to herself and kept up with the routine well enough until Miss June called for a break.

"You know, the talent portion is a big part of the overall score," Angela said. "It's not too late for you to drop out."

Sabrina didn't look up as she unlaced her dance shoes. "It's also not too late for you to develop a personality outside of this competition."

Angela scoffed and turned on her heel. They'd known each other for over twenty years. She should really know by now that Sabrina wasn't the type to return a jab like that.

"You okay, there?" Brandon walked up to them.

Sabrina grinned and lowered herself to the edge of the stage. She dangled her legs over the side.

"Dancing's never been my thing. Miss June knows that, since she kicked me out of dance class in the fourth grade when I refused to do a routine to *I'm a Little Teapot* and danced to Britney Spears, instead."

Brandon chuckled. "I remember that. It was the talk of the town for a full day."

She shrugged. "I'm used to being part of the gossip mill. Everyone is at some point."

He hopped up on the stage next to her. People milled about, but most escaped the stuffy atmosphere of the hall for the beautiful autumn evening.

"Especially when you go your own way. Like us." He gave her a subtle elbow in the ribs.

"Exactly." She gestured to the note in his hand. "Another to-do list from the committee?"

He looked down at his hand. "Ah, no. I was going to stop off at the sheriff's office before we leave for the bonfire. There was another note at the Pumpkin today."

"Shit, really? What does it say?"

Brandon shrugged. "I don't know, it all seems kind of anti-climactic now."

Sabrina reached over to snatch it. "Just when I thought all that was behind us." She scrunched up her face. "'*It's not too late*'? What the hell is that supposed to mean? That sounds like some Scooby Doo shit."

He took the note back from her and put it in his jacket pocket. "Got me. The first note was all about 'we know what you did' and now that it's not too late? If they're trying to threaten me, they're not doing a very good job of it."

"Yeah, the threats are as vague as a fortune cookie."

He shrugged. "I figured we should hand it over to Eleanor, but I don't know if there's much that can be done about it."

"I'm just confused about it all. Like, if you're going to threaten someone, be more specific. They don't even address you by name, so technically, the threats could be for anyone."

He ran his hands down the front of his jeans. "I'm pretty sure they're for me. But whatever. I'm not worried. If someone has something to say to me, eventually they'll tire of notes and say it to my face."

She reached her arm around his shoulders. "I'll be there, to have your back, if it comes to that."

He put his arm around her waist and pulled her close. "I'm glad you have my back."

"Aww, look at you two," Caleb said. He had Emerson on his hip. "Looks like the family might be gaining a new member soon, huh?"

With his own life's crisis, Sabrina hadn't had time to fill her older brother in the ins and outs of her relationship with Brandon.

"Oh, don't scare him off. It's bad enough I have a giant for a father, that both my big brothers are back in town can be kind of terrifying for anyone."

If Brandon was bothered by Caleb's implications, he didn't show it. "They did scare the bejesus out of me when I was a kid. Not so much anymore."

Caleb laughed. "I'm glad to hear it. I don't want to be that stereotypical big brother, protecting my little sister. Mainly because she can protect herself."

Miss June returned to the room and clapped her hands. "Contestants, places. Everyone else, off my stage!" She leveled a rheumy glance at Brandon.

He snuck a kiss and hopped off the stage. "I'll see you after."

Sabrina forced herself up and wished the time would go faster. Not only to get out of this torturous rehearsal, but so she and Brandon could finally put everything out in the open.

* * * *

"Here you go." Brandon passed a cup of cider to Sabrina.

She accepted it and took a sip. "Ah, I forgot how good the festival cider is."

He lowered himself on a log next to her. The bonfire was the final event of the Cider Festival. He'd been so busy he hadn't been able to attend any of the other festivities. It was the same every year, with bands full of banjos and fiddles, different types of cider and stalls selling baked goods and crafts.

He'd once hated the sameness of this place. How every year, the same events took place, each year indistinguishable from the next.

He sipped his cider and gazed over at Sabrina, her face warm from the firelight. Now, he wasn't sure hate was the right word.

"Eleanor seemed to take the threat seriously, huh?"

He shrugged. "I just wish if someone had it out for me, they'd say it to my face. I'm over the cryptic BS."

"Let's go all horror movie, then." She stood up and gestured. "Where are you, huh? Show yourself!" Cider sloshed out of her cup as she drew curious stares from people on nearby logs.

He laughed. "I don't know if I want to tempt fate."

She sat on the bench next to him and rested her knee against his. "That's a funny word, fate."

He turned to her. "You look like you have something to say."

She sipped her cider and looked at the bonfire. There was nothing but the murmur of nearby conversation and the snap and crackle of the fire for a few moments until she turned to him.

She clenched her hands together before speaking. "I think it's time to be honest with one another, Brandon."

He nudged his glasses up. "I wasn't aware we were lying."

She turned to him. "I mean about…whatever this is between us. We've been ignoring the herd of elephants in the room."

"By elephants, do you mean the sale of the inn and my inevitable departure?" He found himself drawn to the fire. He hadn't been expecting this conversation.

She let out a hollow laugh. "Inevitable departure sounds like the name of some depressing British period piece." She sipped her cider. "But yeah, that's what I meant."

He nudged his boot into the moss in front of his foot. "We can't close the distance between us. Falling Leaves will always be here."

"And I don't want to leave. Ever." She huffed out a breath. "You don't want to stay."

He drained the rest of his cider and set the empty cup at his feet. "That was the truth, once upon a time. Now, I'm not so sure."

Her eyes widened. He'd surprised himself with that admission, so he knew she had to be shocked, as well. "So, what, you're not going to sell the Pumpkin?"

He hadn't thought that far yet. All he knew was that he didn't want to leave Sabrina.

Part of this conversation had been spurred on by a phone conversation he'd had with his boss at Hotel Blaque, Jamal. He wouldn't hold his job past the new year. So, if he wanted to return to the comfortable life he'd had before his mother had gotten sick, it was time to act.

He also needed to address the Paris job once and for all. Once the sale was final, it would be time to move on to his next opportunity.

"I don't know. Gabriel wants to talk about the sale soon, before they leave town."

"If they want to buy, will you leave sooner?"

"Maybe. If I want my old job back, I'll have to."

That fact hung between them like a fly caught in a spiderweb.

She exhaled. "A desire to stay isn't enough, Brandon. If you want to do this…we can't do this halfway." She turned away from him. The wind took her hair and whipped it in front of her face.

He caught her shoulder and turned her around. "You're right. I have to figure things out on my own."

She reached for his hand. "This feels like that funny little word, fate. You and me, always orbiting one another." She squeezed his hand so hard his bones ached. "But I know this time, if you leave, there will be nothing to bring you back. I'll have to move on."

The thought of passing through town to check in on the Pumpkin and finding her married to some man who could never love her the way he did made his stomach turn.

"I'll meet with Gabriel in the next day or so. I'll figure it out, Sabrina."

"If you sell the Pumpkin, why would you stay? Falling Leaves isn't exactly a hotbed of opportunity. And Roanoke doesn't have any fancy hotels, like the kind you worked in."

"There you are, being the weight to my balloon." Her eyes narrowed and he reached forward to grab her face. "I mean that in the best way. Sometimes I'm too pie in the sky. I don't think about the details. I figure it'll happen, or it won't."

"You need to, Brandon. I want you to stay. But I don't want you to force your square peg into a round hole. I want you to be happy. Would running the Pumpkin make you happy?"

He lowered his hands. "Honestly, the Pumpkin runs itself, especially with Babs. I'd be bored."

Sabrina managed a small nod. "I see."

"That doesn't mean I'd have to live in the big city to be happy. You know my old dream?"

She leaned back on the log. "The one where you'd be bitten by a radioactive spider and become a small-town superhero? I don't think that's very realistic."

He laughed. "A different dream. One that's realistic. The mountain retreat. Do you remember that?"

Her gaze carried to the sky. "The cabins in the mountains? A treehouse lodge? Oh yeah, I remember. You haven't talked about that in a while, though."

"If I sold, I'd have money. I could maybe look into starting my own business. Luckily, I know a contractor who's pretty good."

She smiled. "Are you serious?"

"I am. But I'd have to find a property nearby. So far nothing's come up. Ideally, I'd find an existing resort. I don't have the kind of budget to build a place from the ground up."

"I understand. We're not quite free and clear, then."

He squeezed her hands. "Life is rarely like that."

In the distance, someone took up a fiddle and people got up to dance.

Brandon stood and offered his hand. "Shall we?"

She stood. "Do you still have two left feet?"

"One and a half, at best."

"So we're both terrible dancers. Not much has changed." She chuckled and Brandon brought her in close. He'd never felt happier than he had these past few weeks. Now all he needed was the final pieces of the puzzle to fall into place.

Chapter Twenty-Nine

"Is that a gargoyle?" Brandon bent over to get a better look at the newly installed drain spout.

Sabrina found herself momentarily distracted by the way his khakis clung to his backside.

"Yeah, a friend of a friend of Carlos' made it. Isn't it cool?"

Brandon gave the gargoyle a pat on the head before standing. "I shall call him Grim."

She laughed. "It's fitting, since Halloween is right around the corner."

He looped an arm around her waist. "You're going to help me hand out candy on Halloween night, right? You know we get trick-or-treaters from all over, thanks to our display. It'll be all hands-on deck."

She smiled. "Don't you have employees for those tasks?"

Brandon's face fell like a punctured balloon. "Oh. I mean, I do, I just thought it could be fun."

She snuck up on him and gave him a hug. "Obviously, I'll help. I still have a Victorian lady costume from some Halloween past hidden in my closet."

He snuck a kiss on her cheek. "Good. I think it'll be fun."

Sabrina's phone chimed with a text. She pulled it from her overalls and groaned when she saw it was from her mother.

The pageant starts at 8 sharp tonight. You need to be there no later than six. Don't be late!

"Like I could forget," Sabrina muttered to herself. Her truck was packed with all her pageant supplies. She'd be headed over there as soon as she wrapped up work.

Brandon peered at her over his shoulder. "Ah, tonight's the night, I almost forgot. What with the Westmores stopping by, that's taken up a lot of my thoughts."

Sabrina typed out a brief reply to her mother. "They're leaving tonight, then?"

"Yeah, they're stopping off to pick up the rest of the clan and then head back to Nashville."

"I've gotten used to them being around. I'll miss their accents."

"They already promised we could stay with them if we ever go to England."

Sabrina shoved her phone into her closest overall pocket. "We, huh? I don't even have a passport."

He nuzzled her closer. "Easily remedied."

She sighed against him. "What time is it?"

"Quarter to four."

She turned so they were nose to nose. "I should probably get a shower before I head over to the hall for pageant prep. And I don't really feel like going home. Eleanor is cooking for Dutch and his teammates."

"Say no more. Get your things out of the truck and meet me upstairs."

"That sounds like an alluring proposition."

He brought his mouth to her neck. "That's because it is. Now hurry, because I know your mother will come over here if you're even a second late."

She ran off to her truck to gather her things. She'd do her hair and make-up before heading over to town hall. Her mother had all her pageant wear with her, since she didn't trust Sabrina with them.

She locked up her truck and ran back inside. She ran into Javier and Adalyn at the new front desk, chatting.

"Where are you running off to?" Adalyn asked.

"I'm getting ready here for the pageant."

"Oh yeah," Javier said. "Wouldn't it be funny if both you and Carlos won?"

Sabrina turned to the stairs. "Now we both know that's not going to happen, but I appreciate your faith in me. Carlos doesn't need it."

She waved and took off to the third floor, toward Brandon's private quarters. As she approached the door, she heard him ending a conversation.

"Well, that sounds exciting. We'll discuss particulars when you arrive, then?"

She nudged open the door and Brandon waved her in. She closed the door behind her as he wrapped up his call.

"Well, the Westmores are on the way. Gabriel sounds rather optimistic."

"That's a good thing. Have you thought any more about your dream project?" She sat on the bench at the edge of the bed and began tugging off her boots.

"I have. But I didn't want to get too far ahead of myself." He slid onto the bench next to her. "You know, we have a little time before we're needed elsewhere."

Her boot flopped to the side. "Oh, yeah? And how would you like to fill the time? Discussing the events that led up to World War I, perhaps? I'm something of an expert in the area. Did you know that History was my minor in college?"

He captured her face and kissed her. The surprise of the kiss knocked her sideways and she fell into his arms. He caught her easily and wrapped his arms around her, tugging her closer until there was no space left between them. There was no place else she'd rather be.

He broke the kiss. She dropped her head to his shoulder.

"I think we both know what I was referring to. Although I wouldn't be against having in-depth conversations about history. At a later date, though."

She chuckled and reached up to draw her hand across his biceps. "I'll start work on my presentation now, then."

They both laughed as she scooted to the side and began to work on her overall buttons. "I hope you know what you're committing to. I take my presentations seriously."

He turned his wrist toward him and began working off one of his cufflinks. "You say this like I didn't lose to you twice in debate club in high school."

She tugged down the straps on her overalls. "And it would've been three times if you hadn't been such an apple polisher to Mr. Gerard."

He began to unbutton his shirt. "As much as I enjoy our shared jaunt down memory lane, I think it's time for something else, don't you?" He offered her hand and led her to the bed.

She followed with no hesitation.

He shouldered his way out of his shirt before he caught her hand in his and brought it to his lips. "How do you have such soft hands for someone in your line of work?"

"Are you really after my skincare routine right now? I mean, I'm happy to share. But—"

He cut her off with a kiss. "I was merely paying you a compliment. Y'know, to impress you with my smooth moves."

She threaded her fingers into his. "Oh, I see."

He tugged her back onto the bed. The fell onto it in a tumble of arms and legs.

She extracted her limbs from underneath him and drew her arms around his neck.

"A little warning would've been nice."

"Then I would've missed out on that lovely look of surprise on your face."

She drew her hand across the freckled plane of his back. "I suppose I can't argue with that."

"Let me jot that down. That's the one thing you *won't* argue with me about."

"Ha, ha." She shimmied a hand between their bodies, until she caught the top button on his trousers.

He inhaled sharply, causing her to chuckle. "How about we stop with the chit-chat and move things along, hmm?"

He grinned like a devil before he said, "Deal."

* * * *

He was sure Sabrina would hear it from her mother. Brandon had been reluctant to let her out of bed until the last possible moment. As a result, her hair was only half-done, and she'd gotten no further than her eyeliner and mascara before she'd had to rush out of the door.

"If she reads me the riot act, you'll have to make it up to me later," she said before she swept out of the room.

"We both know you'd never let her get the chance. Besides, I'm sure she factored your lateness into her schedule."

Sabrina laughed. "You're probably right. See you over there. Good luck with your meeting!"

Brandon checked his watch. He had just enough time for a quick shower before the Westmores were due to arrive. Where once he would've dreaded a meeting like this—knowing if they didn't want to sell, he'd be stuck—now he looked forward to it.

The Pumpkin had never looked better and they weren't even halfway done with renovations. Not even the vague threats he'd received put a dampener on his optimism.

Things were changing. For the better. But he still had a big decision left to make. If he stayed, his life in DC would have to be wrapped up. And he'd have to let Cassandra know that the job in Paris was a no-go. He'd put off answering her, mainly because he knew once he did, that life was over for good.

Old habits died hard. His ingrained hatred for Falling Leaves wouldn't vanish overnight, even if being with Sabrina reminded him of everything he loved about this place.

Once Sabrina left, he put on a suit and slicked his hair back. He had just enough time to meet with the Westmores before he was due at the town hall to help with the pageant.

When he made his way downstairs, he found Jasmine, George and Beatrice packed and ready to go.

"You'll be rid of us soon," Bea said.

"It's been lovely having you here," Brandon said truthfully. "I'm sure you're eager to get back to England now."

Beatrice shrugged at the same time Jasmine said, "Very much so."

"Not so eager, Bea?" her father asked.

"I like it here. And to be frank, it's been a nice break from the same old same old."

Brandon knew that Beatrice was in a job she was less than thrilled about—in commercial real estate in London.

"Well, when you're tired of London, you're tired of life," Jasmine said.

"I guess I'm tired of life, then." She brushed her blonde hair free of her eyes.

"Oh, Bea. Now's not the time for melancholy," George said.

Before Bea could continue, Gabriel and Merit arrived. There was a fair amount of fussing as they pulled baby Lakyn out of her car seat.

Until recently, one baby had been as good as another to Brandon. Now, he could see the charm. Lakyn had a shock of her mother's red hair, and her tiny fists were balled up, as though she was already angry at the world.

"Let's get her inside," Merit said.

A few moments later, Jasmine had swept away the baby, and Merit and Gabriel were ensconced in the conference room with Brandon. Gabriel pulled out his laptop. Likely, a good sign. If they were just here to say 'smell you later', he doubted he'd have gone to the effort.

"We know you've got places to be, and so do we," Merit said. "So we'll keep this short and sweet."

Brandon lowered himself into the nearest chair. This was it—the moment he'd been looking forward to since his mother had gotten ill. This should be his ticket to freedom.

So why did he feel so neutral about it all?

Gabriel pushed his laptop over. "Excuse the roughness of the proposal. I drafted it on the drive over. This is our offer to buy the Peculiar Pumpkin."

Brandon exhaled as he looked over the offer. It was more than fair. The amount would pay off the Ellises for the construction, as well as the mortgage.

There would possibly be enough left over for him to consider that dream mountain lodge project of his.

"Well?" Gabriel prompted. "You've been staring at the screen in silence for well on a minute now, Brandon."

Brandon snapped to attention. "Sorry about that. I think the offer is very fair. I'll have to have my attorney look it over."

Gabriel reached over to scroll down to the terms and conditions. "The Pumpkin has become a special project for us."

Merit laughed. "Yeah, that and we've all kind of fallen in love with Falling Leaves. We're debating whether we'll move to town to see over the business directly."

Brandon nudged his glasses up his nose. "Really? I thought you were more about the city life?"

"That was before we had Lakyn." She shrugged. "It'd likely be next year before the sale took place anyway."

Meaning he had to make some decisions about the next chapter of his life—sooner rather than later.

"Well, that's acceptable, since that was the plan after all."

Gabriel smiled. "Have your attorney look things over and talk to your staff. We'll plan on having a video conference next week to settle things, one way or another."

Brandon nodded absently. "Of course. You'd keep all the staff on, right?"

"We don't make a habit of shaking things up," Merit said. A baby's cry had her raising from her seat. "That's my cue to leave. We'll talk soon, Brandon. I hope we can come to a mutually beneficial agreement."

Gabriel began to pack up his laptop. "What'll you do, if you sell? Will you go back to DC?"

"I'm leaning towards staying, actually."

"Really? Then why sell at all?"

Brandon walked over to the window. "The Pumpkin was my parents' thing. I always resented it a bit. It was never my dream."

"Then what is your dream?"

Brandon paused. He'd never spoken about this dream. Mainly because it felt so out of left field for him. He cleared his throat. "A resort. In the mountains."

Gabriel slung his laptop bag over one shoulder. "Huh. That's interesting."

Brandon rubbed his face. "Why do you say that?"

"I may have a lead on that front. Let me get in touch with a colleague."

"At eight p.m. on a Friday?"

"You'd be surprised who answers my calls."

Brandon's eyebrows shot up. "Seriously? I've been looking all over for a property. I haven't found anything decent east of the Mississippi."

"Don't get your hopes up, then. I'm not exactly sure where this property is located. Besides, just because we're settling down doesn't mean we're getting out of the hotel business. We're always looking for new opportunities. I'll be in touch when I have more information." Gabriel and Brandon shook hands and he saw the Westmores out.

Once their car vanished around the corner, Brandon exhaled. Maybe he was about to get everything he wanted, after all.

Chapter Thirty

"If you laugh, I'm gonna push you off a ladder come Monday." Sabrina edged for space in the mirror with all the other contestants. Including the lone male contestant—Carlos.

Her mother had insisted on doing her hair. And it'd never been as close to God as it was right now.

Carlos snickered. "I've just never seen your hair so...fluffy before. Is that the right word?"

She angled a glare at him. "There's nothing fluffy about me, and you know it. Just because you never have any competition doesn't mean you can stand there and harass us."

"Sabrina, what are you doing to your hair? It looked perfect!" Lainey came behind Sabrina and started to fluff what her daughter had flattened.

"Mom, look around. Nobody else's hair is this big. Just because it worked for you in the eighties doesn't mean it'll work for me now."

Lainey sighed. "Carlos, tell her she looks beautiful."

"I'm not going to lie to your mother," Carlos told Sabrina in Spanish before turning to the door.

"Where's he going?" Lainey cried.

"He didn't want to lie to you, Mom. Even Carlos can tell the hair isn't doing me any favors."

"I really need to learn Spanish," Lainey groused, before turning back to Sabrina. "Oh, fine. Re-do your hair. Break your mother's heart."

"Don't you have a pumpkin decorating contest to judge?"

The pumpkins had been set up outside the town hall. Some of them were downright terrifying. Knowing her mother, the most wholesome would get her vote.

"Inez and Tinesha are overseeing that. They know I'm busy with you."

"Mrs. Ellis, the dressing room is for contestants only," Angela said.

Lainey rolled her eyes. "Oh, fine. I'll see you out there."

Once she was gone, Angela cut Sabrina a glance. "You're welcome."

"That's the first nice thing you've ever done for me, Angela."

Angela leaned forward to touch up her eyeliner. "Not true. I came to your birthday party in the seventh grade. Even though it was at a laser tag place, instead of somewhere civilized."

"Tomboys gonna tomboy." Sabrina stepped back and took herself in. Now that her hair was back to a style she'd wear, she had to admit that she looked rather elegant. She doubted she'd end up as anything but an also-ran, but she was glad she'd entered the pageant. It was good to push yourself, every now and again.

She slipped out of the dressing room and snuck to the side of the stage. She pulled the curtain to the side and peered out.

The hall started to fill up. She scanned the room for Brandon, and found him pushing in her father's wheelchair. The two of them were animatedly chatting about something, until her uncle, Dennis, and Dennis' second baby mama, Brooklyn, came in with the kids.

Eleanor and Dutch sat in the front row with several of his teammates. She knew the boys were there for blackmail material, nothing more, so she had to make sure she didn't embarrass herself too badly.

Her brothers and their kids brought up the rear. Her heart swelled. She was grateful her family was here to see her—even if she'd likely become the butt of jokes for years to come—but seeing Brandon with them just felt right.

A tug on her elbow had her spinning around. "Get backstage. We're about to start," Miss June groused.

Sabrina considered a snarky reply. Then she remembered this pageant was Miss June's baby. And even though the woman could be prickly, it was because she cared so much.

She swept the curtain back and snuck into the hallway behind the stage where contestants had begun lining up. Sabrina went to the back, where she and the fellow 'no chancers', as they called themselves, congregated. They'd all been strong-armed into the pageant by their mothers and were doing it to make them happy.

"I swear, I'm going to repeat this choreography in my sleep," one of them murmured.

Luckily for Sabrina, she had other things to occupy her mind. Like Brandon.

"All right, everyone, house lights go down in two minutes! Unless there's an act of God declared, nobody moves from their spot, got it?" Miss June called.

Sabrina hugged the wall and chatted with the other contestants until they were called to the stage.

She wasn't that nervous. As long as she didn't eat shit in front of the entire town, she'd be fine. Being at the back of the bunch, even if she did fall, as long as she recovered herself, she'd hopefully escape notice.

The Falling Leaves High School band began to butcher an old Ariana Grande hit. This was the contestants' cue for their introductions and first number. As they went onto the stage, Miss June and Brandon handed them umbrellas that they'd twirl as they introduced themselves.

Brandon grinned as he handed her umbrella over. "Knock 'em dead. But not literally." He pointed to the umbrella.

"Ha, ha." She pulled a face before she stepped out onto the stage. She followed the other contestants around the stage, before stopping at Mayor Ford, who thrust a microphone in her face.

A light switched on inside her and she put on her best fake smile.

"Hi, I'm Sabrina! And my favorite thing about fall is jumping into a pile of leaves."

Her family erupted into cheers as she spun her umbrella and took to the back of the stage. *Maybe this won't be so bad, after all.*

* * * *

Even though Brandon was busy running around assisting Miss June and the other pageant coordinators, he was able to catch the highlight of Sabrina's performance, her talent. She sang a spot-on version of Taylor Swift's *Betty*. She'd always had a beautiful voice, so it wasn't a surprise that she'd nailed it.

He wondered if she might pull out and win it after all. Then she nearly slipped on the hem of her beautiful autumnal dress while being passed off from the only contestant for Mr. Autumn—Carlos—during a dance routine.

When her number wasn't called to compete in the final dance number and interview portion of the competition, he snuck backstage.

He caught Sabrina right before she slipped inside. "Hey."

She turned to him. Her lovely face was slicked with sweat, and her hair had started to shift out of place.

"If you make a joke at my expense, I will ensure that every door at the Pumpkin sticks when you open it."

He chuckled and pulled her in close, away from the contestants filing in the dressing room.

"Look, we all can't be good at everything. You had to have a flaw, right? It's only fair."

Her eye roll was mighty. "I'm just glad I didn't end up with my dress over my head or something else super embarrassing. I don't want to be a viral video."

"Well, you *can* end up with your dress over your head. But that'll be later, with just the two of us."

She gave his arm a punch. "Ha, ha, very funny."

Miss June appeared from around the corner and furiously gestured at Brandon.

"I'll see you after." He kissed her before taking off.

During the final portion of the pageant, Brandon was put in charge of arranging the flowers, crowns and trophy. Every contestant received a wrist corsage, with the final three contestants receiving the bigger prizes.

It was all a bit over the top for a small-town pageant, but nobody did anything halfway in Falling Leaves.

Right before crowning the winner, he caught sight of Sabrina again. She'd changed into her final look — a simple dark purple prom dress that Lainey had altered to fit her perfectly.

In a room full of women dressed to the nines, she was the only ten he could see.

"I guess we should be glad you're not judging the competition," Miss June said. "We all know who'd you choose as your winner." She passed off a wrist corsage to him. "Here, you can give this to your girl."

He grinned and took it from her. He slipped through the crowd until he found Sabrina.

"M'lady, your corsage."

She looked down at the corsage blankly at first. Then he remembered that they'd done this before — senior prom. Right before they'd broken up the first time.

"Hopefully this will end differently than the last time I bought you one of these."

Her laugh reassured him. She extended her wrist. "Did you pick out the prettiest one for me?"

"Nothing less for my lady."

Her smile didn't quite reach her eyes. "As it should be."

Miss June called everyone onto the stage again. Brandon took a moment to look at himself in the mirror, since he'd be helping Miss June hand out the bouquets and crowns.

Angela and the other finalists did one last sweep around the stage. He kept his eyes glued to Sabrina, standing in the rear of the stage.

Once Angela had predictably been crowned for the umpteenth year in a row, there was a final sashay across the stage before the curtain fell.

He exhaled. His work for the night was done. He made his way into the crowd. Sabrina and the rest of her family would be going to a late dinner at Luci's, and he didn't want to miss out.

He'd nearly made it to Sabrina when a voice called out his name. He ignored it at first, thinking he was having some sort of auditory hallucination. Then he turned and found he hadn't imagined it.

Cassandra was in Falling Leaves. Her expression was dark enough to let him know he was in a world full of trouble.

Chapter Thirty-One

Sabrina's gaze followed the elegant woman making a beeline for Brandon.

"Who is that and why is she shouting Brandon's name like a lunatic?" Lainey asked.

"I don't know," Sabrina admitted. She could do nothing but nervously pick at her dress as the woman approached Brandon. She gripped Brandon's elbow and led him out the side door.

"Uh, what the hell?" Sebastian asked. "Is that his girlfriend or something? That better not be the case." He didn't wait for Sabrina to reply. "I'm going to find out."

In full protective older brother mode, Sebastian rounded up Caleb and the two of them took off.

Sabrina was stunned to the spot. Was this another woman? Her stomach roiled at the thought.

"Oh, Lord," Lainey said.

"Push me out there, Lainey," her father said. "I want to stop those boys from doing something stupid."

Her mother was miffed that the night had not gone in Sabrina's favor, so she grabbed onto the back of her father's wheelchair and pushed him through the crowd. Thankfully, not many people seemed to notice the disturbance, so that was a small victory.

Sabrina struggled with getting her father's chair through the doorway. That gave her enough time to overhear what was going on.

"What do you mean, you didn't tell anyone about the job in Paris? It's all but a done deal."

Paris?

Sabrina's stomach dropped like a stone. She'd almost hoped he'd cheated on her. That would've been easier to take. That he'd led her on when he'd been planning on leaving not just Falling Leaves, but the country, was somehow worse.

Sabrina nudged the wheelchair through the door, and it pushed through—nearly making her father tumble out of the chair. Everyone pivoted toward them.

Once she'd ensured her father was okay, she turned to Brandon. "What's this about Paris?" It felt like her mouth was full of cotton as she forced the words out.

The woman let out a dry laugh. "Oh, this is the childhood ex. Sabrina, is it?" She flicked her sheet of smooth blonde hair over one shoulder.

Sabrina was in no mood to dole out Southern hospitality. "And you are?" she countered.

"I'm Cassandra. Brandon's ex-girlfriend, but more relevant to this conversation is that I'm a headhunter in the hospitality industry. Brandon had an interview for a job in Paris. They'd gotten in touch, to check in on progress on the inn. Because that's the only thing the opportunity is hinging on—the sale of the inn so he can start his new job in Paris."

She looked Sabrina up and down. "I suppose *she's* why you're having second thoughts. Come on, B. You must know you'll never be happy in a town like this."

Sabrina cut a glance to Brandon, who kept his head down. She didn't want to get into an argument in front of her family, or the smug Cassandra.

"Towns like this have more charm than Paris. It's not all fairy tales," Sebastian snapped.

Kinda rich coming from her brother who'd escaped as soon as he could.

Cassandra chuckled. "I'm sure you'd know, having seen it on TV?"

"Having lived there for a year," Sebastian roared. "We're not all yokels." Although Sabrina almost laughed as his southwest Virginia drawl came out a little when he was angry.

"Son," their father said. "Take a breath."

With those words, the group disassembled. Cassandra's phone rang, and her brothers took off with their father, leaving just her and Brandon standing together.

"So? Are you just going to stand there, or do you have anything to say?" Sabrina said.

Brandon exhaled. "This isn't what it looks like, Sabrina. I promise, I can explain."

Cassandra ran back over to them. "Were you going to tell me you accepted an offer from the Westmores to purchase the inn? Jesus, B. Now once the lawyers approve the sale, you have nothing standing in your way. I'm going to call Paris. What time is it there?" She took off to her fancy sedan, parked at the curb.

Brandon did nothing to stop her.

Tears welled in Sabrina's eyes.

"You sold the inn, too? Wow, you're just full of secrets." She wiped her tears away. She looked down at the streaks of makeup on her hand and scrunched up her face.

Brandon met her gaze. "I can explain. Just give me a chance."

She bent over to take off her shoes. With everything wrong at the moment, her aching feet was one small problem she could tackle.

"This feels a lot like that post prom break-up, all those years ago." She looked down at her reimagined prom dress. "It's kind of fitting, huh?"

He stepped closer to her. "Please, let me explain. It's not—"

"Cassandra's right, Brandon. I think we were both fooling ourselves. You'd hate being stuck in Falling Leaves, eventually. You should go to Paris. I think you'd be happier there."

"But—"

"I'll be sure work is finished on the inn. Just give me some space if you see me there, okay?"

The tears she'd been holding in began to fall. He called after her as she ran but didn't stop her.

She ran barefoot all the way home.

Cassandra stepped out of the passenger's side of her luxury car.

"Damned time zones. I guess they're asleep or something now."

Brandon stood on the curb. "Why are you here, Cass? Are you that desperate for the commission for my placement?"

Her door closed with a slam. "Seriously? You stop answering my calls and texts for days, so I drive *hours* out to this hick, middle of nowhere town and you think it's because I care about money? Was I that terrible of a girlfriend?"

Cassandra was a better friend than she'd been a girlfriend. Brandon had gone MIA on her. Not exactly a trait he usually exemplified. He was reliable to a fault.

She angled her hand up to the streetlight. A large diamond glinted in the light. "Bernard and I just got engaged. I'm not here for the money."

Bernard oversaw a hedge fund or something. So, she was right about the money.

He exhaled. "I'm sorry. You were just doing what you thought was right. Like a good friend."

And she was — being a friend to the Brandon that she thought she knew. The one who felt like he was wearing an itchy, three-sizes-too-small sweater the longer he stayed in Falling Leaves. Watching his mother slowly die, Sabrina avoiding him, and becoming part of the neighborhood gossip mill had worn him down.

Now, he understood why Sabrina loved this place. And why he'd probably never be fully happy living and working in the small town, but that didn't mean that he had to leave it.

Cassandra leaned against the car. "I'm guessing it's a good thing no one answered the phone in Paris."

He exhaled. "I can't go to Paris, Cassie. The inn is going to sell, that's true. But you know I've always had the dream of starting my own place."

Her eyes sparkled at that. "The mountain retreat? I remember." She exhaled. "Well, if you go that route, then call me. I'll scour the east coast for the best people for you." She arched up off the car and walked over to him.

"In the meantime, give Sabrina time to cool off. You don't come off looking good here, my dude. I know I showed up at the wrong time and that didn't help things. But you're the one keeping secrets."

He nodded. "I know. She must think history is repeating itself."

Her smart watch beeped with a notification. She turned her wrist toward her. "That's Bertie. He wants me to spend the night here and come back in the morning. Apparently, there's a vicious storm on the way. Can you spare a room at the inn?"

"Of course. As long as I can pick your brain over dinner. About future projects, and well, Sabrina."

She chuckled at that. "It's a deal."

Chapter Thirty-Two

Rain and branches rattled against the windowpane, making Sabrina feel like the weather was responding to her dark mood.

Or perhaps she just read too many fantasy books. She lay in her dark room, with her cats on either side of her.

Luckily for her, Eleanor and Dutch had left right after the pageant for another one of Dutch's away travel basketball games on the other side of the state. Sebastian, Gretchen and the kids were likely still at her parents' house.

Lainey Ellis was a pain in the ass, but she was pretty good about respecting that no meant no when it really mattered. Before Sabrina stowed her phone, she noticed a text from Brandon.

I know your mind must be all over the place, thinking I betrayed you. Please give me a chance to explain in the morning. I'll see you at the inn for our design meeting, at nine.

She tossed her phone in the nightstand drawer and slammed it. This was why she'd not wanted to pursue things with Brandon. There were still several weeks left of renovations. It would be a lot harder to avoid him when they were under the same roof. But maybe if the sale was official, he'd leave her to it and head back to DC. *Or Paris.* It hardly mattered now.

It wasn't as if she could quit the job, or even pass over work to her father. He was improving but was in no shape to oversee a job site. She needed to prove to her father that it was time to expand the business. Quitting their biggest job in a year would show him the opposite.

Not that she even wanted to. She loved her life. She'd been upfront with Brandon since the beginning.

She felt so stupid. Like maybe this second chance was what she and Brandon deserved. Now she realized that nothing had changed, except they were both older.

Brandon would never be happy in Falling Leaves. And she could never make him stay. It was too large a sacrifice.

She rolled over onto her side and clutched her pillow. She felt a forgotten, now familiar sadness swallow her.

The thought of having to face everyone for a second time, after Brandon left town. How stupid was she, to date the man who'd broken her heart, not once, but twice?

"Hey."

She jumped and rolled over, finding her brother standing in the doorway.

"Sebastian. You scared the shit out of me."

He flicked on the light. "I would've thought you'd have heard the kids tearing up the stairs."

Now that he mentioned it, she could hear the kids, and Gretchen calling after them.

He closed the door behind him. "I was going to send them in here to cheer you up, but you kind of look like the last frame in a horror film right now, sis."

She found her feet and walked into the bathroom. As much as she wanted to admit it, her brother was right. Her cheeks were stained with streaks of black.

Sabrina began washing off her face. Sebastian stood in the doorway.

"Do you want me to beat him up for you? I mean, I am pushing forty, so I don't think I punch as hard as I used to. But I can try."

"I don't hate him. I know I should. But I can't force him to stay. He has a job lined up in Paris, of all places." She tossed one makeup wipe and reached for another one. "Like Falling Leaves could ever compare."

Sebastian came around her and propped himself up on the vanity. "You never understood how stifling this town can be. You always loved it, warts and all."

She looked down at the washcloth, smeared with makeup. "I understand. It's why it's best that Brandon leaves. No wonder he didn't want to tell me about the job. I would've steered clear of him if he had."

"Maybe he didn't tell you because he didn't want to take it, Sabrina. I don't know, I get the feeling that maybe Brandon is over his big city phase."

Sabrina snorted at that. "How would you know?"

"Because I am." He met her gaze in the mirror. "Are you okay with having us for neighbors? Because

Gretchen and I are considering putting an offer on one of the most tattered ladies."

Sabrina swung around. "The pink one on the corner of Jackson and Forest Glen?"

He nodded. "We need to do a complete tour of the inside before we make an offer, though You never know what's hiding inside."

Sabrina shook her head. "It's been sitting empty for decades. It'll be one hell of a project."

"We'll go back to San Francisco for a few months after the New Year, to settle up our life there. You can make it habitable for us in that time. Especially as Dad said you're killing it on the job at The Peculiar Pumpkin."

Sabrina's cheeks colored. Her father doled out compliments sparingly—not because he was cruel, but he'd always pushed her to do better than the last job.

"Well, that's good news, then. I'd love to have you guys as neighbors. And having another job lined up is even better."

Sebastian hopped off the vanity. "Maybe, things will be okay after all, kiddo."

She wiped the remaining mascara from her eyes. "Don't go getting too ahead of yourself just yet."

No matter what, she would not be made a fool of twice. She was finished being Brandon's back-up plan.

She'd never have the flash of a job in Paris, or even DC. If that's what he was after, they'd never be happy together.

But she'd hear him out, at least. If only because they still had weeks of work ahead of them at the inn.

* * * *

Brandon couldn't sleep. He and Cassandra had talked over dinner about the mountain retreat. He should've felt grateful for her expertise. Instead, he wondered what the point of it all was. Since she was the only guest and had long retired, he found himself wandering the floors, like his parents used to do. Back then, they'd been full of their own worries, even though he'd been oblivious to them.

They'd tell him later that they worried they made the right choice taking over the Pumpkin from his grandparents. Ripping him out of his life in the city. Especially as until they'd fully embraced the Halloween-kitsch of the inn, they'd struggled financially.

Then his mother had paced alone, after his father had died. Brandon had taken up his own pacing after returning to help care for her in the final months of her life.

Now, the habit was hard to break. Even though he was full up on worries of his own.

He'd messed up. And he didn't know if there was a way to fix it.

He turned toward the landing on the second floor and made for the lobby. He marveled at the hard work Sabrina had put in.

He exhaled as he stepped on the landing. He should see what leftovers Adalyn had stored in the small fridge. It was a staff perk, and a way that excess food didn't go wasted.

He passed through the library, down the hallway and into The Frosted Squash. He paused at the door, finding a light illuminated inside. He looked down at what he was wearing—a T-shirt and loose pair of lounge pants with herd of deranged looking moose on them.

It was after eleven. If one of his staff was inside, there was nothing untoward about him being dressed this way.

He pushed open the door just as a crashing sound came from the bakery. Maybe once, Brandon would've been the type to run from the Pumpkin's spectral scares. But his recent run-ins with threats of one manner or another had him eager to potentially catch the culprit.

He closed the door and crept on his tiptoes to the bakery. There was further clattering as the potential culprit moved around.

Brandon ducked around the corner and leapt behind the wall leading into the bakery.

He found Babs, covered in flour. He snickered despite himself. He kind of wished he had his phone to take a photo. His delight faded when he realized the person he wanted to send the photo to first — Sabrina — wasn't speaking to him.

He stepped toward the bakery, just as Inez waltzed through the back door, muttering in Spanish. She switched to English before turning to Babs.

"You were supposed to leave the last note, not make a huge mess. This is going to take all night to clean up."

"Note?" Brandon hadn't meant to say the word out loud. He'd spoken loud enough to catch Inez's attention. She peered out the door and caught him. "Have you two been leaving the notes? Why would you do that?"

Inez and Babs exchanged a glance. Inez laughed and drew her finger through the flour on Babs' cheek.

"Well, since you're here, help us clean up. Then we'll explain."

Chapter Thirty-Three

"Wait a minute. You want me to help you clean up a mess I didn't make while you explain how — more importantly, why — you decided to start a smear campaign against me?"

"Yeah, that's what she said." Babs thrust a broom at him. "Get to sweeping."

Inez chuckled. "We were going to reveal ourselves soon enough. Although we'd hoped under better circumstances."

"I doubt Babs planned a flour explosion. Especially not in Adalyn's kitchen. You know how she likes things just so."

"I've known her longer than you have," Babs groused.

Brandon leaned on the broom. "What gives, then? You've been having me thinking that half the town hates me."

"Nobody hates you," Inez said. "We were just following your mother's wishes."

Brandon swung the broom around and began sweeping. "What do you mean? I've seen her will. I'm pretty sure I would've noticed if there was a clause instructing you two to terrorize me."

"That wasn't what this was, and you know it," Babs said.

"Uh, that first note? With the screaming? It scared the crap out of me." Brandon swept so aggressively a cloud of flour swirled around his feet.

"Oh, that," Inez said. "Lainey stepped into a pile of dog poop in her nice leather boots. That's why she was screaming."

"Wait, Sabrina's mom was in on this too?"

"All the biddies were, in some way or another," Inez said.

"But why?" Brandon let the broom rest against the wall.

Babs motioned for him to carry on sweeping. He did, with reluctance—if he stopped, Babs wouldn't tell him anything.

"At first, it was to get you to reconsider selling. The first note? Was in reference to the fact that you'd been in touch with potential buyers for the inn. We knew about it and wanted you to know that."

"Uh, do you have any idea how incredibly hostile that sounded? It's like the beginning of a horror movie."

"We realize that now," Inez said. "It wasn't our intention." She had the decency to appear regretful, at least.

He bent over to sweep the mess into the dustpan. "It was a wasted effort, anyway. Mom supported me selling."

"I mean, I guess she did. Because she knew you'd be miserable. But then as things went along, and you and Sabrina were getting along, we took creative liberty with the messages."

Brandon dumped his dustpan into the bin. "Well, that seems all for naught now."

"Ah, so you're gonna run away, just like you did last time?" Babs said.

"I didn't run away. Sabrina and I both left Falling Leaves after high school."

"While that's technically true, we all know you fled town after your dad died. You didn't say a proper goodbye to anyone, let alone Sabrina."

Brandon threw down the broom. "I came back every Christmas break until I finished school, then three times a year after that, until Mom died. I don't appreciate your rewriting of history."

They were right about one thing, though. He'd left without speaking to Sabrina. Could he blame her if she thought history was repeating itself? Ugh, he was an idiot.

He turned to leave. From behind him, he heard Babs and Inez frantically whispering.

"All right, all right, let's let cooler heads prevail," Babs said. "Our tempers are all a little high right now."

He spun around. "Why are *your* tempers high? I'm the one who should be pissed right now. You butted into my life in a manner so grandiose I had to get the police involved. I have every right to sell the inn." He clenched his fists. "You also shouldn't have meddled into my relationship with Sabrina."

Babs exhaled. "We did everything because your mother asked us to, before she died."

He rolled his eyes. "Likely excuse, since Mom isn't here to defend herself."

Babs slammed down a piece of paper onto the countertop, sending up a cloud of flour. "Here. The last note. Read it."

He snatched it off the counter. He waved it a time or two to remove the flour then opened the envelope. He knew immediately that this note was different.

His mother's handwriting had gotten shaky near the end, so the message was brief.

Brandon my love,
I had to try. I understand if you want to sell. Don't be mad at the biddies—especially Babs & Inez. They were just doing what I asked them to do. I figured one last push from the great beyond couldn't hurt.
Love you,
Mom

Tears formed in Brandon's eyes. He'd had months to prepare for his mother's death. Maybe that's why after she'd gone, he'd shoved his grief away, thinking he'd deal with it properly once he returned to DC. After all, he was overdue for a session with his therapist.

This letter brought all those feelings to the surface.

"Well?" Inez said. "She never let us read that one. What did it say?"

He thought about being petty and hiding the note away. The biddies knew everything in town. This one secret he wanted to keep. Although knowing Babs, she'd snoop until she found it.

"She told me she had to try. But she understands if I sell."

Babs' usually stern expression wavered. "So, are you? Going to sell?"

"The Westmores are good people, Babs. I can assure you that very little will change if they take over. They buy businesses that are already working. It doesn't make sense for them to shift things around."

"So that's a yes." She turned away.

"Would you rather me stay here? When even Mom said she didn't want me to be miserable?"

All he received was silence from both women.

He whipped off his glasses and rubbed his eyes. "Look, I don't expect you'll ever understand why I want to sell. I'm not asking you to. I'm just asking for a little compassion. It's hard, being here, with both of my parents gone now."

He'd never said those words out loud. Mainly because he still had a hard time believing his mother was gone.

"I understand," Inez said. "But if you want to leave, you should do it soon. Go back to DC. We'll overlook the construction until the sale happens."

"I don't know that I want to go back to DC. Or Paris. Or anywhere else." He inhaled the biggest breath he'd ever taken. "I think I want to stay."

Babs' eyes widened. "Then why on earth would you sell?"

He looked around the kitchen. He'd had endless memories. Some happy, a lot of recent ones were very painful.

"Because this was never my dream. I have another one."

"And that is?" Babs prodded.

He didn't want to play twenty questions with them about his mountain retreat idea. "Not relevant at the moment."

He was surprised when they let it drop. "If you're going to stay, are you going to try to work things out with Sabrina?" Inez asked.

"I'd want to. I texted her, asking if she wanted to talk things out. She hasn't responded."

"I can see how she'd think that. You goofed up a bit there," Babs said.

Brandon reached for a rag to wipe down the countertop. "I can always count on you to see the bright side, Babs."

"Oh, shut it. If you really want to stay, we'll help you fix this."

He let out a dry laugh. "Why would I want your help? After you all boggled Mom's plans?"

Babs started to speak, but Inez talked over her. "It was our idea to leave the key for you to go to the movie club. So, you owe us for that."

Brandon chuckled. "I'll give you that, it was a nice touch."

"So, will you let us help?" Babs said.

He exhaled. "Yes."

Cat-like grins spread on both women's faces. "Excellent. Let's clean up the rest of this mess, or Adalyn will have our heads. Then we have some scheming to do."

Chapter Thirty-Four

Sabrina knew the pity party was fully underway when her parents showed up at her house early Sunday morning. She'd spent most of the day Saturday wallowing in her darkened bedroom. She'd planned on spending the rest of the weekend there, ignoring Halloween all together.

She thought about letting them rot on the porch. Her guilt about the effort it must've taken to get her father up the steps had her reconsidering. Plus, the last thing she wanted was for more gossip to spread around town, so she let them in. It was a hassle to get Dad's wheelchair in over the threshold, which only annoyed all three of them.

"I know y'all are early risers, but you don't tend to make unannounced visits this early." Sabrina wiped sweat from her brow.

"Well, we had some news," Lainey said.

"Worth the early arrival? It'd better be something spectacular."

"You can stay home today, Sabrina. I'll look things over at the Pumpkin. Here, we brought you pumpkin rolls to enjoy on your day off." He eased the plate onto the counter.

She knew she should drop by the Pumpkin today, just to rip the bandage off. Once she'd had a cup of coffee and a little more time to wallow.

She couldn't expect things to just stop at the job site. She had to put on her big girl panties and deal with it.

Her father, still in a wheelchair, showing up and telling her to stay at home, was more annoying than anything.

"Are you insinuating that my romantic status has something to do with how well I do my job? I'm capable of running a job like this."

"No, he's suggesting that he wants to get out of the house for an hour or two. I figured you could come with me to the Halloween party for the kids at Inez's. It's not every year I have all my grandchildren here. I'll need help corralling them."

"I'd rather just go to work, honestly. Being at a big party in front of half the town is not my idea of fun. Especially after the public humiliation I suffered Friday night."

"If it was that public, how come I didn't get the particulars until I talked with Inez this morning? We both know that wouldn't have happened if your so-called humiliation was as public as you thought."

Sabrina fussed with her tool belt. "If Inez knows, then everyone else does, too."

Lainey threw up her hands. "If you want to continue to mope, you can do that."

"I'd rather just go to work if it's all the same. This is an important job for us."

"There's another important job on the docket, too." Sebastian appeared at the top of the stairs.

"We're meeting the realtor at the new house. Dad was going to go with me, but since he and Mom are in full meddle mode, how about you come, instead? I could use your professional advice."

So grateful to not be stuck with either of her parents, the biddies or worse yet, Brandon, Sabrina would've agreed to just about anything.

"Oh, fine," Lainey said. "Let me see my grandkids. What costumes do you think they want to wear?"

Lainey trudged up the stairs, and soon the sound of her and Sebastian's voices drifted away.

Her father cleared his throat. "I'm not meddling, Sabrina. I wanted to get to the job site. I'm going crazy trapped at home. Your mother is bad enough on her own, but with your brother and kids, it's just a little too...loud for my tastes." He gently touched his knee. "Besides, the physical therapist says I need to get out of this chair and start using my cane more. So, I'm going to do that."

She started to make a smart-assed comment about him actually listening to a medical professional for once, but she stopped herself. "Dad, I'm fine. Honestly. I slept it off. Brandon never said he was staying. I was the foolish one for getting attached."

He'd hinted at it, sure, but he'd never said the words, *"I'm giving up the life I've always led for you, to stay in this hick town, Sabrina."*

She couldn't even really be mad at him.

She'd let her fantasies get ahead of her. She should've known better. She should be mad at herself, and no one else.

"I don't think he meant to mislead you, darling. You two have always had something special. But your timing's always been off."

She sat on the bench in the front entryway. "Special isn't always good enough. I can't force him to stay. If the inn is in the process of being sold, and he has a job on the other side of the world, what's keeping him here?"

"You are, darlin'."

She let her boot drop on the floor. "That's not enough, and we know it."

He wheeled his chair around, so he was facing her. "If the shoe was on the other foot, and he was asking you to move, would you?"

Sabrina started to argue, and her father held up his hand. "I know you're going to mention the business. Let's assume that's not an issue. If you had nothing but me and your mother holding you here, would you go?"

"If you put it that way, then…" She exhaled. "Yeah. I'd go."

"Well, maybe he's thinking the same thing, right about now. You two should talk."

She shook her head. "Not right now. It's all a little too raw."

He leaned over and clasped her hand. "Well, let a little time pass, then. Don't rush it."

She rested her head back against the wall. "If I give it too much time, he'll just leave. Like he did last time."

"It's not fair to hold that against him. You were kids. His dad had just died."

She fell forward so her elbows rested on her knees. "I really don't want to talk about this anymore."

"Okay, so we won't. Don't worry about the Pumpkin today. We'll see you tonight when we take the kids trick-or-treating. Then maybe we can talk more about your plans for the business."

That was a small positive. He was at least willing to discuss the future now. "Thanks, Dad."

His smile was tired. "Anything for you, darlin'."

* * * *

Everything was moving fast, and for once, Brandon didn't have time to fret.

He'd emailed the proposal to his attorney to look over the Westmores' proposal. His attorney promised to have it reviewed by COB Monday. When he texted Gabriel an update, Brandon had been surprised when his phone had almost immediately started to ring. Odd, considering it was Sunday.

Brandon sat in the Pumpkin's driveway, oddly nervous. Had the Westmores changed their minds already?

"How are you doing, Brandon?" Gabriel asked.

"I've been better, honestly." He paused. "Sorry, you don't want to hear about my personal problems."

"Adult conversation of any kind would be welcomed. What's going on?"

Brandon laughed. "You wouldn't believe me if I told you."

A baby's cry from the background had Gabriel pausing for a moment before he returned to the line.

"Try me."

The story burst out of him like water roaring downstream. More than a minute passed before Gabriel got a word in edgewise.

"Roll it back there, mate. You two started this whole thing because of Merit and I?"

"Well, it was a misunderstanding. I didn't want to chase you two off."

"Because you were desperate to get out of town."

"I was. That's a story that would have you on the phone longer than you'd like. But things have changed."

Gabriel paused. "I heard back about that property I mentioned to you earlier. Give me a second to talk to my wife. I'll call you right back."

The line went dead. Brandon hopped out of the car and began to gather things from the back seat. Other than the meeting at his attorney's office, Babs and Inez had sent him on a seemingly never-ending series of errands to buy things for Halloween night.

Or as they called it, the night he'd make things right with Sabrina. He peeked into a bag bursting with fall flowers. A feeling of dread settled over him.

Maybe she wouldn't forgive him. Perhaps the wounds of the past were too big to heal But he had to try. Even if Sabrina didn't want him, it was time to start over.

He was halfway to the door, his arms laden down with bags when Gabriel called back. Brandon didn't get a chance to say hello before Gabriel spoke.

"Your speech about the Pumpkin being a family business really spoke to me. I talked it over with Merit, and well…we're going to move to Falling Leaves. This seems like the right decision to make."

The bags dropped from his arms and he exhaled. He felt a hundred pounds of weight releasing from his shoulders. He'd kept his promise to his mother.

The Pumpkin would live on.

"I'm sure Babs will like you better as a boss than me. She'd do anything as long as you talked to her in that posh accent of yours."

Gabriel snorted at that. "We'll come back into town before the holidays to finalize everything and talk things over with the staff. We're thrilled to be taking this step, Brandon. I hope you are too."

"I couldn't be happier. Now, about that property. Do you have a pen handy?"

He ended the call with Gabriel and bent over to gather his bags. He hadn't been quite honest with Gabriel. He *could* be happier.

He just had to prove to Sabrina that history wasn't repeating itself.

Chapter Thirty-Five

"It's a money pit, but lucky for you, that's our specialty."

Sabrina walked side-by side on the sidewalk with her older brother. Gretchen and the boys scurried ahead. They were already half-dressed for trick-or-treating.

They'd been changing in and out of costumes all day, not that anyone minded. Lainey was beyond thrilled to have all her grandchildren in one place. Sabrina was grateful for it, since it took the heat off her.

"As long as you don't mind us living with you a little longer, I think a money pit will be fun."

Sabrina snorted. "You gonna wield a hammer, big bro? Or are you going to go after that baking dream once and for all?"

His gaze became wistful. "Maybe occasionally, but I'm not the professional on the job. I think we might chase after the bakery dream I've been talking things over with Inez. She's trying to phase out the bakery side of her business. Says she's going part-time in the new year. She seems serious this time."

"That would work nicely, then. You went to look at that vacant space, right?"

"It's a bit rough, but workable. How about you, then? The space you warned me to stay away from, the one near the Weird Sisters?"

She shrugged. "Dad started cleaning out his office at Loose Screw. I don't want to push him too fast. It's not like anyone's in a rush to rent it. It's been vacant for a time. The space is really great, though. We could make it a real showpiece."

"Sounds like the Ellises are moving up, huh?" Sebastian said.

Sabrina managed a small smile. "It looks that way."

Caleb came up at the rear, having tagged along for the last part of the tour. "Do you think there's another house on the market for me?"

Sabrina's mouth dropped open. "Now you're staying, too? What about your job?"

He shrugged. "I accepted a job as an adjunct faculty at Virginia Tech. It's just temporary, filling in for the winter semester. But we'll see where it goes."

The college was less than an hour away from Falling Leaves.

Lainey whirled around. "When were you going to tell us that?"

"Well, I just got back. Olivia had the kids."

Lainey stopped dead on the sidewalk. "*She's* here?"

"Mom, don't make me rethink the idea of moving already."

Lainey pursed her lips and turned around. Once she'd fallen far enough ahead of them, Sebastian turned to Caleb.

"So? Is she going to be moving here, too?"

Caleb laughed. "Oh, hell no. We're getting divorced. But she will be moving to Virginia at some point. With her new girlfriend."

An alert chimed on Caleb's smartwatch, and he cursed under his breath. "Gotta go. I'll see you back at Mom and Dad's for trick-or-treating."

He took off and Sabrina fell into silence. Well, for as long as someone like Sebastian would allow since he couldn't bear to be alone with his own thoughts.

"You doing okay? Really?"

"Oh, no. We're not talking about me. I had enough of that with Mom and Dad this morning. We're not the type of siblings to talk about our feelings, Sebastian."

They came to Sabrina's house and paused at the mailbox while she pulled out the day's mail.

"Maybe we could be? People can change, Sabrina."

The mailbox creaked as she closed it. "They can, but they usually fight it tooth and nail."

She flipped through the mail and ignored her brother's attempt to start conversation as they stepped inside.

A thick, cream envelope stood apart from the bills. There was no return address or stamp on it, meaning someone had hand-delivered it.

"What is this?"

Sebastian peered over her shoulder. "Looks fancy."

Her stomach turned over. "It looks like the kind of notes Brandon was getting." She thrust it at Sebastian. "I don't want to open it."

Lainey stepped out onto the porch. "What's all the fuss about?"

"I got one of those creepy notes. Look at how they scrawled my name. Only serial killers write like that."

Lainey huffed as she took the envelope. "To me, it looks like they used a fountain pen of some sort."

"It doesn't matter the instrument they used. Maybe Eleanor should dust it for prints."

"Oh, I doubt it needs all that." Lainey walked inside and quickly produced a butter knife. She sliced through the envelope and tugged out a card in the same shade of cream.

Lainey held the card away from her. "I think I need my reading glasses."

"Because of the serial killer handwriting?" Sebastian plucked the card from their mother's fingertips. Sabrina peered around her brother's shoulder to read the note.

All will be revealed 8:00 PM. Saint Paul Square.

"Oh, hell to the no," Sabrina said. "That *definitely* sounds like the beginning of a horror movie."

"We *are* in Virginia's most haunted town," Sebastian added.

She elbowed him. "Thanks for the reassurance."

"Are you going to go?" Lainey asked.

"Who else got one of these notes? I'm not going there by myself," Sabrina said.

"I'll go with you," Lainey said.

Sabrina cocked an eyebrow. "Since when are you down for adventures on Halloween night? You're normally in bed by that time."

"I'm up for the occasional adventure. Now, come on. We need to get the kids ready to trick-or-treat."

* * * *

Brandon's phone buzzed with a text.

She got the note. But Inez's crazy handwriting has made her think that Michael Myers will be waiting for her. So maybe ditch the mask? Ha, ha.

He tucked his phone in his back pocket.

"Well?" Inez looked up from trying to untangle a ball of twinkle lights.

"Your handwriting scared the bejesus out of her, according to Lainey, that is."

"She knows my handwriting! I had to try and disguise it!"

Caleb ran to the gazebo. "Here's the flowers. I've gotta get back." He carefully set down several bundles of flowers before taking off.

Brandon looked at the bouquets—an explosion of oranges, yellows and reds. He plucked a handful and began setting them in mason jars.

"Do you think this is too much? Do you think she'll forgive me?"

"I doubt her family would be pitching in to help if they thought you had no chance." Inez stood and began stringing the lights around the gazebo.

"I'm just eager for the night to get here, already. At least then, I'll know."

"Here, plug this end in," Inez said.

He pivoted, took the end of the lights and plugged it in. The lights lit up against the quickly fading autumn sky.

"It'll be pretty by the time we're done, I think," Inez said.

"And you promise they'll keep her away from this part of town until it's time?"

Inez huffed out a breath. "Why don't you go home and get changed, Brandon? Let me handle the finishing touches. And the biddies and I will handle all the trick-or-treaters coming to the inn, too. That way all you've got to do is get your nerves settled."

He asked her twice more if she was sure before he insisted she leave.

On the way home, he went over his words. He had one chance to get this right.

Chapter Thirty-Six

Sabrina should've known better than to let her mother pick her costume. For a brief period in college, she'd worked weekends as a party princess. She'd worked with a whole group of girls and they'd been short one Snow White.

Even though Sabrina wasn't really the type to play dress up, she'd made bank. Her mother had found her old costume in the closet at her house and when it'd fit, she'd insisted that she relive her "princess days".

Complete with one somewhat unkempt dark wig.

"Mom, you have granddaughters you can dress up now," Sabrina groused as Lainey began pulling her blonde hair up to fit under the dark Snow White bob wig.

"Hey, we don't assign gender roles to our kids," Caleb called from the other room.

Lainey rolled her eyes. "Of course, you don't."

"Don't you say a word," Sabrina hissed. "Caleb raises his kids as he sees fit. You're gonna have to get used to that when they move here for good."

Lainey huffed. "At this point, I'll take anyone who wants to dress up."

"Wasn't me embarrassing myself at the pageant enough for you?"

Lainey finished tucking Sabrina's hair. "No. I want to see you get married one day."

Sabrina groaned and reached for her cape. "Don't start, Mom. Especially not now."

The wound had yet to scab over.

"Come on, the porch lights are coming on. Let's get this show on the road," Sebastian called.

There had to be a mini fashion show and photo call for the grandkids in their costumes. After that, Sabrina headed out with Emerson on her hip.

It was easier to trick-or-treat in her parents' neighborhood, especially with little kids. They lived in a subdivision at the edge of town, where lots of young families had taken root. The kids were all little and would likely tire out after the initial rush wore off.

They made it to the end of the street before Sabrina was mobbed by a group of little girls, all bedecked in their own princess costumes.

Her old training came back to her, as she entertained the children.

"Are you a princess?" one of the little girls asked.

"For tonight, I am," Sabrina said.

Lainey overheard her and chuckled. "Maybe the spell will last a little longer, dear."

As they finished taking the kids around the neighborhood, Sabrina checked the time.

"I should head to meet my fate at Saint Paul Square. Anyone want to come with as back-up?"

Caleb yawned. "I thought Eleanor was going to meet you over there?"

Eleanor had promised that she wouldn't leave her to meet her fate alone. But hey, the more the merrier. She told her brother that.

"This is just one of those town pranks. Likely you and a bunch of other people got invitations," Lainey said.

"Well, fine. But if I go missing, don't go on TV saying I didn't run off to meet my fate alone. Y'all refused to go with me."

Lainey laughed. "We did not refuse. Our plans changed. Besides, you're not going to end up on a true crime podcast. You should leave now, or you'll be late."

Sabrina didn't argue as she climbed into her truck. It took a moment to get her cape and costume inside the seat. After that, she took off.

She hadn't thought too much of the invitation, what with her family keeping her evening jam-packed. She hoped it was just some sort of prank.

Would Brandon be there? It was too soon, yet some part of her missed him.

"It's the last day of the month," she murmured to herself. "Perfect for starting over."

Sabrina wrestled with her nerves the rest of the short drive to Saint Paul Square. Downtown was filled with families and she had to park on the far side of the square. On the short walk there, her gaze carried to the gazebo, lit up with a million twinkle lights.

It wasn't uncommon to see the gazebo decorated for the holiday, so she didn't pay much attention to it. She was grateful for all the people milling around. If the note writer had nefarious intentions, they wouldn't get very far.

As she approached the gazebo, she noticed someone in costume sitting on the steps. Was this the mysterious letter writer?

She quickened her pace, her footsteps smacking against the cobblestones until she was at the front of the gazebo. Her eyes were drawn to floral bouquets tucked into mason jars. Was this a party she'd been invited to?

"Sabrina."

Her gaze followed the voice like a dart hitting a bullseye. Brandon stood from his spot on the steps. He was dressed like the Huntsman to her Snow White. He stood with his arms open, gesturing around the space.

It seemed too tidy. As if their argument had never happened. This was a grand gesture, with a neat little bow on top to make her forget what had happened.

"Did you write the note?" Sabrina managed.

"No." He fussed with the strap on his quiver full of arrows. Clearly, he was unnerved that she hadn't swooned into his open arms. "That was Inez. The biddies...well, they were behind all of the notes."

A group of children gave a shout at the other end of the square. She turned to look—finding them fleeing away from a group of boys dressed up like Michael Myers, Freddy and Jason. Dutch and his friends, most likely.

She turned back to Brandon. "What? Even my mom?"

The wind blew and he tugged his hood up. "It was a last-ditch effort from my mom, from beyond the grave. Well, that's what it started as. It morphed into something more."

Sabrina didn't need to ask what that meant. They'd interfered with their relationship, of course. She was too tired to be angry. Her feelings were all over the place.

"Did you do this?" She nodded to the gazebo.

He turned toward it. "Yeah. Come up."

He extended a hand to her. They both knew the gazebo steps were wobbly at best. She gazed at it. What was the point of this if he was just leaving?

He helped her inside to where a small table sat in the center of the gazebo. Flowers were everywhere, surrounding a pile of papers, held down with a crystal paperweight.

"What's that?"

He nervously tapped his boot against the table. "It's the rough draft of the contract to sell the Pumpkin to the Westmores."

"Oh." She drew her cape around herself.

"Shit. This isn't going like I planned. I'm not leaving, Sabrina." He stepped around the table and removed the paper weight. The wind immediately snatched up the sheets.

Brandon rushed off to catch the papers. Sabrina grabbed the rest before they could escape the gazebo.

She couldn't help herself—she looked it over. Obviously, he wanted her to see it. Why else would he have brought them here?

"You're going after your dream? The mountain retreat?"

"I hope so. I put an offer in. The Westmores helped me find the location and are going to invest, until my inheritance comes in."

"Wow," Sabrina said. "They've turned out to be powerful allies."

"Spoken like someone who reads a lot of fantasy novels," Brandon teased.

Sabrina didn't smile at the joke. Brandon looked away and coughed. "They have. Although nothing is final yet. We're still haggling out details. Gabriel is a stickler for going over every contract with a fine-toothed comb."

She handed him the papers back. He grabbed them and shoved them into a folder.

"Where is it?"

"About an hour south of here."

Tears prickled at the corners of her eyes. He was staying. So why wasn't she jumping into his arms?

"Show me, then."

He whipped around, face full of surprise.

"Seriously? I had other things planned—"

"I appreciate the effort you went through." She reached forward and snapped up one of the mason jars. "But I need to see this for myself. That would mean more than any romantic gesture. If you're not willing to do that, then I don't see a point in discussing this further."

The time for toeing around the truth was over. If they were going to do this—the time was now.

Brandon nodded. "I understand. You have every right to doubt me. So, let's go. We'll need to leave now if we want to get home before midnight."

Brandon kept looking over at Sabrina. They were both still in their costumes, although she'd discarded the dark wig. She was the most beautiful princess he'd ever seen. If he told her that, it would earn him an eye roll.

She was silent as they left downtown—which took longer than usual as they had to avoid all the trick-or-treaters. Once they got on the interstate, she looked over at him.

"What about Paris? Or DC?"

"Cassandra took care of Paris. I fumbled the ball there, but luckily enough they didn't want anyone to start until next year, so she can still find them a new candidate." He flicked on his high beams. "I need to go to DC to hand in my notice and sell my condo. I'm done with that life."

Sabrina fell quiet again, which only made him nervous. This night felt like he was proving something to her. Which was fair, given their history and how he'd bungled things. He hadn't expected instant forgiveness. But she wasn't going to make it easy for him.

He was pretty sure he deserved that.

"Are you sure? You always hated this place."

He switched lanes. "I did, when I was a kid. Then, when I came back, I hated it, because well, you hated me."

"Can you blame me?"

"No. But it still made me want to get out of here. To know that you'd always be here and I'd done you wrong. I know how you can hold a grudge."

"It was never a grudge, Brandon. It was...." She peered out of the window. "It was awful, knowing you'd only come back in matters of life and death."

"I was wrong, Sabrina. A million times over, I was wrong. I know I can't make up for what I did when we were kids. Or hell, even how I screwed things up two days ago. But I'm staying. If you want nothing to do with me, I'll have to make do with that. But I know what I want now. And that's you."

Her expression was hard to read in the dim light. "I always wanted you, Brandon. So much that no other man lived up. It's why I avoided you. It hurt too much. Even knowing this thing between us had an end date, I was willing to hurt myself for you again."

"Well, you don't have to do that, Sabrina. I'm here for good, no matter what happens. If that means I have to watch you move on with someone else, so be it. I'm not leaving."

They fell into silence again for the remainder of the drive.

Brandon nearly missed the exit for the resort. The road had seen better days, dirt and gravel in some parts. He slowed down as they took their turns.

Sabrina leaned forward in her seat, eager to see anything beyond the trees. Finally, he came to a stop in front of a group of abandoned buildings.

"We're here."

Chapter Thirty-Seven

Cool, autumn air whipped Sabrina in the face as they stepped out into the night. Brandon fumbled around in the truck and returned with a lantern.

"Let me lead the way."

She gathered her cape around her with one hand. The light only cast so far, so she found herself grabbing onto Brandon's arm for support.

"You don't seem so afraid of the dark anymore," she observed. "Especially considering we've quite literally just walked into the plot of a horror movie. Old, abandoned mountain lodge? On Halloween, no less?"

"There's no one here, save some raccoons I'll need to rehome if I buy the place. Come on." He turned to her as he helped her down the step. "I'm never going to like the dark. But it's better when you're not alone."

Sabrina turned away from him. She couldn't let him see his charm campaign was winning.

Her grip on his hand was tight as they stepped down. A lone security light illuminated what appeared to be the main lodge. It was a large A-framed building. If it'd been sitting vacant, she could only imagine the state of the roof.

"There's still power in the main building, if you want to see it."

"How do you have a key?"

Brandon chuckled. "The owners told me where they hide it. They're thrilled someone is interested in this old place."

"Well, yeah, I can see why. It's pitch dark and I can tell this place is going to be one hell of a project."

"Which is why I wanted you to see it before I made any decisions. Being my contractor, and all."

"Who says I'm even that?" The words came out more harshly than she'd intended. "Sorry, I'm not trying to pick a fight. Show me the lodge."

She didn't mean to be cold to him. He'd obviously gone through an effort to prove to her that he was sure about staying. She'd expected it to be like the movies — a switch instantly turning her heart over.

Real life was something different.

They approached the lodge. Brandon swung the lantern around until he located a small groove, nearly hidden in the battered wooden siding. It popped open and Brandon pried out a key. He fumbled for the lock in one of the two arching wooden front doors. Several of the intricate glass panes were boarded up, several more looked as though they could shatter with the slightest pressure.

"No one else has been interested in this place for years. That's why they took it off the market."

The door creaked open. Brandon stepped inside and flicked on a row of switches. Sabrina winced as the building lit up against the night.

Her expression didn't change as she took in the building. Carpet in a cornea-burning shade of green, brown and orange. The walls were stenciled into a pattern of trees. The more she looked at it, the wilder it was.

Her gaze carried up to the ceiling. She didn't see any obvious leaks, which was a good thing.

"You're quiet," Brandon said.

She was momentarily startled when she glanced over at him, forgetting he was in costume.

"I have to adjust to the time difference." She paused. "Since we've gone back in time to the seventies."

His laugh echoed around the cavernous, empty space. "It's been closed for a long time now. The decor appealed to the guests for a long time after it was in fashion."

"Then they all died?"

He walked over to the front desk and brushed thick dust off the guest book. "Well, yeah."

"It's not haunted, though? Promise?"

Brandon chuckled. "They didn't die *here*, Sabrina."

She tried not to give in to his attempt at a joke. But she found herself smiling, anyway.

She wrapped her arms around herself. "Good for you, for not showing your skepticism right away."

"Hey, I'm just happy ghost tours will be a thing of the past."

Sabrina's smile dipped. Despite him finding this place, nothing was set in stone. He could still leave.

"Well, the space itself is amazing." She gestured to the grand staircase on either side of the lobby, leading up to the second floor. "What's up there?"

"Private event space. And the walkway to the first block of rooms. There's even a tree house room. It's in rough shape now, but it'll be a beauty once it's renovated. I was thinking of making it the honeymoon suite."

She thought back to the two of them spending time in the old treehouse. How Brandon buying this property seemed like the past meeting up with their future, somehow.

Or maybe she was getting ahead of herself again.

She cleared her throat. "They're all private cabins, right?"

"They're in particularly rough shape. More so than the rooms in the main building."

Sabrina sat on the bottom step and motioned for Brandon to sit next to her. He squeezed into the space.

"It's dark as the inside of a cow, and I can see this place needs a lot of work. Are you sure you're up for it?"

He dropped his elbows onto his knees and turned to look at her. "This is what I've always wanted, Sabrina. And I know that if I sell the Pumpkin, my mom would be happy with me doing something like this. Instead of going back to my job in DC and hoarding the money from the sale. Well, once it comes in, that is. You know I have to wait for a year until it's mine."

"Are they going to give you a fair price, then?"

He nodded. "Yeah. Like I said, they closed over a decade ago. Buyers have been scared off by the amount of work, among other things. With the Westmores as potential partners, we should be able to make it work."

Sabrina looked around the place. "You could make this something amazing. There isn't anything like what you have planned in this part of Virginia."

He tapped his fingers against her knee. "Do you see, now? I know I messed up not once, but twice. But I won't leave again. Not without you." Their eyes met. "If you'll have me."

The coldness in her heart melted. He was staying. There was no doubt about it. Well, there was one.

"Nothing is final yet. I mean, everything's happened so quickly. The lawyers haven't had a chance to review the contract for the sale of the Pumpkin. And you're just looking at...whatever this place is."

She looked around—her mind bursting full of ideas that she didn't want to grow attached to.

"It could all fall apart, is what I'm saying."

"Or maybe it's coming together quickly because it's meant to be."

"Sky House Mountain Resort and Villas is what I was going to call it. I've had that Sky House name in mind for ages. I didn't even know for what, until I found this place."

She shook her head. "You didn't have to do all this to prove to me you were going to stay." She extended her hand to him. "Since, technically, you're not. This isn't in Falling Leaves."

"Not so far away we can't make it work, though." He took her hand and brought it to his mouth to kiss it. "I had to do this for me, too. To prove to myself that Falling Leaves wasn't just a place to escape from. That this could be my home. With you."

"Well, if you're going to buy this place, you'd probably want to live closer, huh?"

"There's a caretaker's cottage in the back. Do you want to see it?" He stood with a start and took off through the building.

"Hey, wait up!" She gathered up her skirt and ran after him.

Their laughter echoed through the empty space. As she ran, she looked around. Visions of a new space came to her. Modern, bright and filled with families and couples excited for a mountain escape.

This was their future. For real. There was no more running — for either of them.

She caught up with him at the back door. He flicked on another light switch and attempted to open it. It stuck so much they both had to push on it to get it to open.

"The punch list on this place is gonna be a mile long."

Sabrina gave a non-committal shrug.

Brandon cut her a glance. "I assumed that Ellis & Daughter would take the job. I guess that was wrong of me."

"Let's keep looking. Before I make any commitments."

He took her hand and led her onto the leaf-covered path. "Say you decided to take the job. What would be your first step?"

"Well, work at the Pumpkin won't wrap up until after Christmas. In the meantime, planning could begin on this project. We'd have weekly planning meetings to address what needs to be done. Work could begin in earnest in the spring."

She didn't have a chance to continue before they came upon a charming little two-story house. It had a small front porch, with decorative detailing on the posts and roof. An impressive garden took up the front path in front of the house.

"The family who owns the lodge still come up here to maintain the house. It's nearly a hundred years old. It was the start of their lives here. They still spend the holidays here. Well, they will until we buy it, of course."

Sabrina motioned for him to unlock the door. He quickly did, and they stepped into a space that appeared larger than the simple A-framed building let on. They'd kept up with this space, as it had a modern kitchen, flooring and paint. Up the stairs was a loft and what looked like a couple of bedrooms.

"It's beautiful, Brandon."

This was the cottage in the woods she'd always dreamed about as a child. No fairies would visit her here, but this was as close as she could get to a fantasy world and still be in Virginia.

"You like it, then?"

She met his gaze. "I do."

He came around her and took both of her hands in his. "It's ours if you want to come on this crazy journey with me. We can keep the house in Falling Leaves, too. We'll likely be splitting our time between there and here." He took her hands. "Your business is important, too. We'd be working on this venture together. But maybe it's time that Ellis & Daughter expands, too."

She squeezed his hands. "No more secrets and half-truths, then. If you're staying, we're a partnership. In life and business."

He gave her a gentle tug, pulling her in until his head rested against hers. "I promise, Sabrina. I know my place now, and it's here. With you. I will never leave again."

She gave a half-hearted laugh. "Good, because I don't think I'd survive a third time."

He brought a hand to her chin, tilting it upward. "Technically, I never left a second time. So we're just talking about the one time I left."

She laughed. "I mean, I guess you're right, there."

"I've never felt more settled, Sabrina. I want to stay here with you. Forever."

Gazing into his eyes, she saw nothing but sincerity. "I'll have to discuss that with Dad. I want to hire more people. Having another significant job lined up could make that a reality."

"Then we'll talk to him." He kissed her cheek.

It seemed so easy. But maybe it was meant to. That they'd had their struggles, and it was time to move on. Tears formed in the corners of her eyes.

"Yes," she said to a question he hadn't asked. "*We* would."

"Yes?" He nudged his glasses up his nose. "Does that mean you forgive a careless old lout?"

She gazed up through the skylight as a shaft of moonlight cast a perfect square around them.

"I forgive you, Brandon." She arched up onto her tiptoes and pushed his hood down from his face. "You, me, and a house up in the sky. Like we're kids again in my treehouse."

He laughed. "Stop putting ideas into my head, or I'll drag you up to the ramshackle treehouse. I don't think that'll end well for either of us."

She laughed. "The other bit can wait until we get home."

He brought her face into his hands. "Done."

She closed her eyes as he kissed her. This felt like the beginning of the rest of her life. It felt like they were finally on the same page.

He brought her close as he deepened the kiss. They wove their arms around each other—kissing as if they would die if they stopped.

She arched against him, her arms coming around his waist to pull him close.

Eventually, he pulled away from her, eyes wild. "Let's get back. To celebrate." He leaned close. "I don't think it's good form to christen the place until it's officially ours, don't you think?"

She rested her head against his chest. "Yes. Celebrate."

They went through the building, locking up and turning off the lights. They paused every so often to kiss. Now that the path in front of them was clear, there was no stopping them.

Chapter Thirty-Eight

Spring

"You're a disaster." Brandon palmed his face.

"Only the best kind," Sabrina called from the roof. She was latched into a safety harness on the A-frame roof, inspecting the shape of the shingles.

After a very long winter, and renovations carrying on at the Pumpkin longer than hoped, they were finally starting work on making Sky House a reality.

Work that would take place in three stages and take nearly two years. Sometimes, he thought he was crazy. Then he remembered he had an in-house general contractor to oversee the work, and his frantic mind eased some.

"I'm coming down!" She called something in Spanish to Carlos, who was on the other side of the roof.

Brandon held his breath as Sabrina cascaded down the roof until she landed on the ladder. She scaled down it like an overeager kid. He walked over to her.

"I don't think OSHA would approve of that little maneuver."

She brushed her hair out of her face. "Are you going to report me?"

He wiped at a smudge on her face. "Hmm. I might be willing to accept bribes to stop me from making that call."

He drew her in for a kiss, not caring that she was sweaty and covered in roof tar.

"Ugh, will you stop?" Caleb covered his eyes.

Sabrina's brother had come onto the Ellis & Daughter crew after his divorce. He was working for them part time while he waited for a full-time teaching opportunity to open up.

They'd also hired two new employees. One that worked in their—still in progress—office as a project coordinator, and another general contractor to oversee smaller jobs.

They were busier than ever, with Sebastian and Gretchen's house undergoing work, as well as the opening of Sebastian's bakery, Loaved Up. They even had a few smaller jobs booked in, too. The business was secure. Which was good, considering she was also going to help Brandon run Sky House.

Their lives were busy, but he didn't mind.

Carlos hopped off the roof and came behind Caleb.

"Just because you two snuck away to get married doesn't mean we need to see the honeymoon."

Sabrina and Brandon exchanged a look before laughing. They'd decided on Thursday to make it official at the courthouse. It just made sense. Given that they were in business together, it just seemed easier. Well, that they were head over heels in love.

Lainey had lost her ever-loving mind when she'd found out her only daughter had eloped. She'd briefly taken it out on Brandon. As if he could tell Sabrina no once her mind was set on something.

Her ire decreased about fifty percent when they promised she could plan a wedding once Sky House opened in phase one, later in the summer. They'd have it here, in their woodland chapel. It'd be the fantasy wedding Sabrina had always dreamed of. They'd be first of many couples to wed there if everything went to plan.

Brandon and Sabrina's phones chimed with texts at the same time.

"Ah, that must be Lainey," he said.

Sabrina groaned. "Wasn't letting her plan the wedding enough? Why do we have to go to some brunch?"

"So she can show you two off. You better go, or you'll be late. I will stay and work. When I finish up here, I'll go to the office and hit some of the items off the punch list," Caleb said.

They'd finally moved Ellis & Daughter next to the Weird Sisters shop. The work was almost done, so Caleb's excuse was flimsy, at best.

"You just don't want to go," Sabrina said.

"Mom knows I'm staying. She'll get over it."

Seeing as Caleb's divorce was fresh, he had an easy out of the marriage related events. Neither Brandon nor Sabrina took offense. Especially as their wedding had come as much surprise to them as to anyone else.

"Oh fine," Brandon said. "Guess we should stop off at home before we go to your parents' house. Lainey won't want us showing up so...fragrant after a morning's work."

Sabrina elbowed him. "Speak for yourself!"

They were full of plans on the way back into town. They'd been married less than forty-eight hours, but the partnership had been solidified Halloween night. He'd moved into Sabrina's house shortly after the Pumpkin had sold to the Westmores.

Eleanor and Dutch had moved out to an old farmhouse on the edge of town, but there was still a full house with Sebastian, Gretchen and the kids living there while their house was under construction. Yet another project for Ellis & Daughter. Business was booming.

Now that work had fully begun on Sky House, Sabrina was based out of the cottage at the lodge. She tried to get into town at least once during the week, in addition to spending the weekends in Falling Leaves.

At first, the noise of so many souls living under one roof had been a lot for Brandon. He'd lived alone since he'd left college. Now, he worried the big old house would be too quiet once they'd left.

They'd have to start a family of their own, then. But one thing at a time.

"What are you over there smiling about?" Sabrina looked up from her phone.

"Thinking about you, me and the future."

She laughed. "What specifically about the future?"

He grinned. "I don't know, kids?"

Sabrina shook her head. "One thing at a time, mister. I'm not ready for kids." She paused. "We'll talk after phase two of the renovation."

"Deal."

* * * *

They'd barely made it back from Sky House to their house on time. Lainey had insisted on a dress for Sabrina to wear to lunch. Apparently one she'd had in her closet for a while, given that her mother had tailored it to fit. Sleeveless, floral and tight, it clung to her like a glove.

He backed her into a corner and kissed her. When his hands began to wander, she pushed them away.

"Stop. Mom had the dress pressed. She'll know what we were getting up to. I don't want to give her a reason to judgmentally stare at me from across the dinner table. Or worse, start inquiring about grandchildren."

He pushed her hair back from her face. "Oh, fine. We'll make up for lost time after."

"You, me and little house in the sky."

After a few more kisses, Sabrina urged him out of the door. This time she drove, her high heel pressed down on the gas as they were already five minutes late.

"You better hope Eleanor doesn't catch you," Brandon said. "She's been setting up speed traps around town."

"Best friend privileges should get me a pass." She took a speed bump a little too fast, causing him to grimace. "Okay, I'll slow it down."

Brandon looked over at her hands gripping the steering wheel. She wore his mother's wedding ring on her right hand. He'd known that Sabrina had always admired the ring. His father had bought it for his mother in Paris, on a trip to some hotel conference.

Now the two of them would be spending their honeymoon there, when time allowed. He'd been surprised when Sabrina had suggested it, since he'd almost accepted a job there. To her, it'd been an obvious choice. The city of love, with the man she loved.

"You'd think they would've saved a spot for the guests of honor in the driveway," Sabrina grumbled.

Cars were lined up and down the Ellises' street. Knowing Lainey and Greg, they'd invited the whole town, in addition to their family.

"We'll have to check in on the Pumpkin on our way out of town," Brandon said. "Merit and Gabriel were asking about some key they found. They'll want a construction update too, since they missed out on the last meeting."

The Westmores had quickly become fast friends with Brandon and Sabrina, in addition to being business partners. Once Brandon's full inheritance came in, he'd pay them back. Sky House would stay under the Westmore Group brand.

Sabrina pulled onto the street behind her parents. "Look at you, being all sentimental about the Pumpkin."

"I'm not! Gabriel and Merit asked me to check in when I had a chance, that's all. Babs is here with the rest of the biddies, and it's their first time running the place on their own. I think they're a little scared."

"We'll be there to help them. Now c'mon. We'll have to hoof it."

They hopped out of the truck and walked hand-in-hand to her parents' house. Brandon looked around, a smile on his face. Funny, how he'd once hated Falling Leaves. Now, he couldn't see himself anywhere else.

"You look handsome today, I have to say. The beard looks good on you." She reached up to touch his cheek.

"My wife"—he leaned down to touch her face—"likes a man with a beard. I had to try my best to accommodate her." He reached forward to touch the locket he'd given her all those years ago. Now shined up and with a new photo inside, of their courthouse wedding.

They paused for a kiss on the porch and had just enough time to break apart before the door swung open. A harried Lainey stood on the other side.

"There you two are, finally! Come around back, already. Everyone's here," she said. "Oh, wait a damn minute." She ducked inside momentarily before returning with a box. She threw the lid to the side and pulled out an intricate floral crown.

"I had Midge at Falling Leaves Florist make it special for you."

Brandon watched as his wife's face lit up as the crown was placed on her head.

"Thank you, Mom."

Lainey smiled as she pulled a tendril of Sabrina's blonde hair through the crown. "Now, scoot around back. We're already running late."

The door closed again, and they took to the stone path leading to the back yard. Music and laughter filtered through the air as they approached. Sabrina pushed open the gate and they stepped inside.

A large banner proclaiming *Congratulations, Mr. & Mrs. Blake!* Hung across the porch. He quickly looked around at everyone assembled before his eyes came to rest on the biddies in the corner.

"Looks like we did it, huh, gals?" Babs said.

Tiffany dabbed at her eyes. "It's just what your mom would've wanted, Brandon."

As much as he wanted to tell the biddies they were being oversentimental, they were right. His mother would've loved every second of this.

"Oh, stop your crying. We have some partying to do!" Inez grabbed both of their hands.

"First stop, photos!"

"No, that's the second stop." Eleanor ducked in front of Sabrina and Brandon with her hand out. The two of them exchanged a glance before Sabrina reached into her purse and passed over a hundred-dollar bill.

"There. You were right. We really are meant to be, huh?"

"Damned straight." Eleanor snapped the bill from Sabrina before disappearing into the crowd.

Brandon and Sabrina exchanged a glance before bursting into laughter. "Oh, I love you." He threw an arm around her shoulders and kissed the side of her head.

She grinned. "Not more than I love you."

Want to see more like this?
Here's a taster for you to enjoy!

Logan County Love: Rekindled
Roxanne Blackhall

Excerpt

Flames leaped and crackled, tearing up the side of the makeshift building inside the Fire Research Lab, casting shifting orange-and-yellow light on the walls of the warehouse. Drea swallowed against the lump in her throat. Even through her respirator, the ashy air was sickly sweet from starter fuel mixed with the scent of burning pine. She clenched her fists and forced herself to watch as the ATF fire crew hauled out hoses. When the first hiss of water produced a cloud of steam, a tendril of panic coiled in her chest. She sucked in a sharp breath, refusing to give in to the rising tide of fear.

"Hey, Hidalgo!" The shout came from her side, and she tore her gaze away from the flames to Gabe Mattix, who had her mask pushed back, eyebrows knitted together. "I called your name three times. You okay, kid?"

Drea flipped her off — she'd known Mattix for years, their communication ranging from high fives to the bird — and shoved her mask back.

"I'm good." She steeled herself and turned to the group of trainees. "The purpose of this little exercise, aside from giving those hose jockeys an excuse to impress us all, is to encourage observation. You'll see things during the active phase of a fire that are clues."

She ignored the scoffing laugh of one trainee. Peter Adams was an incurable smart-ass, but Drea thought he had the makings of a good investigator if his ego would stop getting in the way. She cleared her throat and addressed the group.

"What color were the flames? How about the smoke? These things can tell you a lot about the fire. What suppression methods were used? How long did it take?"

"I know all this shit. When are we gonna get in there and do something?"

Drea turned to face the trainee, and he had the sense to shut up.

"Well, Mr. Adams. Since you know it all, perhaps you would be so kind as to turn your back."

He blew out an exaggerated sigh, but she waved her hand at him and waited until he turned around.

"Good. Think about the perimeter. Anything combustible?"

She didn't have to see his face to know he had no clue. The uncomfortable shifting of his shoulders told the story.

"No, ma'am." His response came out sounding confident.

"Turn around and look again," Drea replied.

Adams turned and glared at her, then at the building. Drea pulled out her stopwatch, punched the button and waited for the ah-ha moment. It came nearly a minute and a half later when his eyebrows rose, and a muttered, "Shit," escaped his lips.

"There's a gas grill on the northeast side." He mumbled the words, barely audible in the noisy warehouse.

"Thank you." She turned the stopwatch, showing him the numbers, and Adams cringed.

"I'll repeat myself." Drea addressed the class again. "The purpose of this little exercise is to encourage observation. If you rely on what you know, or think you know, you will fail to truly observe, and you will miss things. That's true whether you're fighting a fire or investigating it. We're going to break for lunch and let this thing cool down, then we're going to get messy. Adams, c'mere."

She expected attitude. Instead, he looked down at his shoes as he shuffled over to her. She waited until all the other trainees were well out of earshot before she turned to him.

"I'm sorry, ma'am," he said before she could say anything. "I mouthed off."

Drea blinked in surprise. She'd been ready to give him a piece of her mind, but here he was apologizing.

"Did you learn something?" She waited for his nod. "Good. That's the point of all this. I'll be blunt. Questions are fine, attitude is not. You got a problem, you come to me one-on-one, like I'm doing with you now."

When he didn't smart back at that statement, or give her any other grief, she cracked a wide smile. "Instead of telling me how much you know, show me how smart you are. You wouldn't be here if you weren't, and I believe you've got the potential to go somewhere with this. See you back here in an hour."

Adams ambled off. Steam billowed off the burn, and the shouts of the fire crew faded, replaced with the roar of uncontrolled flames. *It's in my head. This is a controlled burn, not the house fire.* Drea forced herself to look at the fire crew — hoses spewing water, the flames nearly out. The concrete floors of the warehouse were so wet they looked like glass. She breathed, in for five, out for five, then shoved her gear into her bag and hustled to the door, desperate for fresh air.

"I hear you're headed back into the field soon." Mattix leaned her nearly six-foot-tall frame against the big roll-up door, arms crossed over her chest. Her dark eyes drilled into Drea.

"Yep. Final eval with the psych is next week." Drea did a little happy dance. "You gonna miss me when I'm gone?"

Mattix chuckled. "Shit no, Hidalgo. You've been a pain in my ass since your first day as a student in my fire science class. Seriously, you should switch to teaching. You're good with these guys."

"Oh, hell no," Drea said. She adored Mattix. The older woman had quickly gone from teacher to mentor, and finally, friend. But after months of being in the classroom, Drea was itching to get back in the field. "I'm not staying. I got into this job to chase bad guys, not teach the good guys how to do it. As soon as I get my walking papers, I'm outta here. Love ya, but not that much."

"No bullshit." Mattix fixed her with a pointed stare. "How are you holding up?"

Drea waggled her hand so-so. Class time was easy. She could stand in front of a group of students and talk fire theory and investigative techniques all day. Being here, next to a burn, with soot and ash and smoke billowing was a different story. She swallowed hard and forced a smile. She'd be fine. She had to be if she was going back into the field.

"The occasional nightmare still," Drea said, and blew out a breath. The flashbacks still happened sometimes, too, but they were getting easier to control, at least. "Even I'll admit I wasn't ready to get back in the field so soon the first time."

Mattix shook her head, sending her short braids bouncing. "I don't know why the doc cleared you."

Drea shrugged. "I seemed good. Everything seemed good. Then the ceiling caved in and landed on me, and yeah, I had a flashback, on a cold scene, with only my partner around. Not a huge deal. I got lucky. It could have been worse."

Mattix gave a sharp laugh and leaned back against the wall again. "And you're good now?"

Drea flashed a bright smile. "Hey, I held it together today, didn't I? At a live burn. I'm coping."

"Tell that to someone who doesn't know you so well." Mattix grinned. "Promise me you'll be honest with the psych, okay? If you're not ready, then you're not ready. There's no shame in that."

Drea wanted to be ready. Needed to be ready. Fire investigation was her career. Not teaching.

Her cell buzzed. Unknown number. West Virginia area code. All thoughts of fires and investigations and her upcoming psychiatric evaluation disappeared. Drea had only one thought… *Gramps*. She drew in a trembling breath and tapped the screen to take the call.

"Hello." Her voice was far steadier than she felt.

"Ms. Hidalgo?" The unmistakable lilt of Appalachia came through in that short greeting. The caller waited until Drea identified herself, then continued. "Your grandfather requested we call. He was hurt while helping clean up after a fire…"

Drea sagged against the wall, and her fingers clenched around her phone. Mattix shifted, her tall frame shielding Drea from any curious looks. The rest of the conversation passed in a haze of half-heard information as Drea's mind whirled on what she had to do next. She hung up the phone and stuffed it into her pocket.

"You're gonna eat before you go tearing off to West Virginia," Mattix said. "No arguing. Gimme your keys, I'm driving."

Mindless, Drea dug her keys out and tossed them to her friend. She didn't care about food. She wanted to get on the road.

Mattix drove, ordered burgers, and pulled into an isolated parking space at the back of the lot. Drea's hands shook as she unwrapped the burger. She tried to hide it, but Mattix didn't miss things.

"It's a six-and-a-half-hour drive to West Virginia, kid," Mattix said. "You could fly." Her eyes narrowed as she peered at Drea. Always assessing.

Drea swallowed and shook her head. "Still an hour from the airport. If I hurry, I can get to the Regional Medical Center before visiting hours end."

"What did the doctor say?"

Drea took in a shaky breath. "Gramps had a heart attack. The doctor wouldn't say much, only that he's stable, but they're keeping him for more tests."

They finished their burgers in silence. Mattix had never been one for filling every moment with idle chatter. When she spoke, it meant something.

"I need to pack," Drea blurted as she tossed her wrapper into the bag. "It's the end of this session, I've got a couple days. The Deputy Director will understand."

Mattix's hand closed over Drea's. "Don't worry about Wilkes."

At her apartment, Mattix helped her pack, then pulled Drea into a tight hug before she headed out the door. "Call me if you need anything." Mattix glared at her. "I mean that."

"Yeah, yeah." Drea waved her off and shouldered her bag. She didn't allow herself to think until she was past the sprawl of Manassas, on her way back to Orchard Creek and the home she hadn't seen since her grandmother's funeral.

About the Author

Claudia Ambrose has been in love with words her whole life. She's been writing for nearly as long. *Build You Up* is her debut novel. She lives in a small house in Virginia with her husband and far too many cats.

Claudia loves to hear from readers. You can find her contact information, website details and author profile page at https://www.firstforromance.com

Home of Erotic Romance

Sign up for our newsletter and find out about all our romance book releases, eBook sales and promotions, sneak peeks and FREE romance books!